INSPECTOR FRENCH:
FEAR COMES TO CHALFONT

Freeman Wills Crofts (1879–1957), the son of an army doctor who died before he was born, was raised in Northern Ireland and became a civil engineer on the railways. His first book, *The Cask*, written in 1919 during a long illness, was published in the summer of 1920, immediately establishing him as a new master of detective fiction. Regularly outselling Agatha Christie, it was with his fifth book that Crofts introduced his iconic Scotland Yard detective, Inspector Joseph French, who would feature in no less than thirty books over the next three decades. He was a founder member of the Detection Club and was elected a Fellow of the Royal Society of Arts in 1939. Continually praised for his ingenious plotting and meticulous attention to detail—including the intricacies of railway time-tables—Crofts was once dubbed 'The King of Detective Story Writers' and described by Raymond Chandler as 'the soundest builder of them all'.

FREEMAN WILLS CROFTS

Inspector French: Fear Comes to Chalfont

COLLINS
CRIME
CLUB

COLLINS CRIME CLUB

An imprint of HarperCollins*Publishers*
1 London Bridge Street
London SE1 9GF
www.harpercollins.co.uk

HarperCollins*Publishers*
Macken House, 39/40 Mayor Street Upper,
Dublin 1, Ireland D01 C9W8

This paperback edition 2022
1

First published in Great Britain by Hodder & Stoughton Ltd 1942

This novel is entirely a work of fiction. It is presented in its original
form and may depict ethnic, racial and sexual prejudices that were
commonplace at the time it was written.

A catalogue record for this book is
available from the British Library

ISBN 978-0-00-855421-7

Set in Sabon Lt Std by Palimpsest Book Production Ltd, Falkirk, Stirlingshire

Printed and bound in the UK using 100% Renewable Energy at CPI Group (UK) Ltd

MIX
Paper | Supporting
responsible forestry
FSC™ C007454

This book is produced from independently certified FSC™
paper to ensure responsible forest management.

Find out more about HarperCollins and the environment at
www.harpercollins.co.uk/green

Contents

1

The Dutiful Wife

Julia Elton paused and looked about her with a critical eye. She was engaged in the work which of all others she loved: gardening. She was in fact a gardener. Not a professional gardener, which after all is only the external accident of following a trade. But a gardener by nature and spirit. She kept the flower garden at Chalfont almost single-handed, being jealous of the interference of the man employed for the purpose. She loved her plants, and the plants seemed to appreciate her feelings, for they throve at her touch. From their vigorous thrusting life she derived inspiration and strength, and when anxiety filled her mind, as at present it did, she found that to get down to the earth was an unfailing tonic and relief.

Today was the 25th of March, Lady Day, and on Lady Day when the weather and other circumstances permitted, Julia invariably began the pruning of her roses. This afternoon was warm and spring-like and she had no engagements, so she took advantage of it to follow her custom. She found relief in her work as she bent over the bushes, snipping and trimming and paring. Though she did it in the hope that the season's bloom might—if possible—surpass her triumph of the previous year, yet she had a subconscious feeling that she was helping her friends the trees by leaving them just that growth which would enable them to put forward their best efforts.

She was lucky, as she often told herself, to be mistress of Chalfont and to have such a garden to work in. The house stood on the lower slopes of the North Downs, not far from Dorkford, that attractive Surrey town lying little more than twenty miles south-west of London. Sheltered by the Downs from north-east winds, it looked south across the valley to the Green Sand ridge of pine-clad hills which stretched eastward from Leith Hill. The road ran above and behind the house, and in front there was first a terrace and then a tennis court. The terrace had been made at the best vantage point, and very charming was the view. In the lower right-hand corner of the little estate was the garden. It was not formally separated from the terrace, but beginning with clumps of small shrubs, grew more intensively flower garden as it proceeded westward towards its holy of holies—the greenhouse just inside the boundary fence.

But though the lines for Julia Elton had thus fallen in what most women would call outstandingly pleasant places, she had not always enjoyed a sheltered life. Indeed, she had known both poverty and hardship.

Her father had been a captain in His Majesty's Navy, and she had been brought up in a comfortable home in the Isle of Wight, knowing all the 'right' people, and with money for all reasonable requirements. When she was twenty she had married Captain Langley, a retired army officer with private means, who lived the rather idle life of a country squire not far from Dorkford. She had one child, Mollie, a sturdy urchin, who grew to be a good looking, competent and entirely estimable girl, with more character than either her father or mother. Then when Julia was thirty-six and Mollie fifteen, their first serious trouble descended upon them. Bertram Langley was killed while driving alone in his car.

Her misfortunes did not stop there. When Langley's affairs were gone into it was found that he had been living on his capital and had left little more than a crop of debts. Indeed it was whispered—though never proved—that this situation had been the cause of his accident.

It was then that hard times had descended on Julia and Mollie. Julia had a little money, just enough to keep a very thin roof over their heads. She looked for work, and because she had no training, without success. She had admirable social gifts and could hold her own in any company, but she could find no way of turning these assets into money.

In the end she took rooms in Dorkford, where she tried to make a few shillings by organizing charitable and other functions, while Mollie studied shorthand and typing against the day when she could enter an office. For a year and more they existed in this way and then their horizon became slightly wider.

One morning Julia received a letter from the head of the principal firm of solicitors in Dorkford, saying that he would esteem it a favour if she could call at his office at any time suitable to herself to discuss a matter of business. Richard Elton at this time was a man of about fifty, wealthy and prosperous and the owner of this charming property of Chalfont. He was unmarried and lived alone except for a nephew, who was a junior partner in the firm. She had met him on different occasions during her husband's lifetime, but had never taken to him. His manners were dry, his small talk nonexistent, and though his reputation for professional competence stood high, he was too hard a bargain-driver and too close in money matters to be a favourite.

Later that day Julia called to see him. He received her with courtesy, apologizing for sending for her instead of going to see her, and explaining that he had done so because he believed it was what she would have preferred. Promptly he stated his business. He was, he said, giving a dinner and dance to some people from Town, and he wondered if she could see her way to be present and organize it for him. His aunt was coming down and would act as hostess, but she was too infirm to undertake the arrangements. Julia would have to be at Chalfont for twenty-four hours to cover early arrivals and late departures. The fee would be five guineas and she would have a free hand and undisputed authority. There was a polite invitation to Mollie to accompany her mother.

Julia was overwhelmed. The money would be a tremendous boon, while the function she believed she might enjoy. But she did not agree too quickly. She asked a number of questions spent some time in apparent consideration, and finally, said she would undertake it. Elton was obviously pleased declaring that he felt much indebted to her.

Under Julia's guidance the affair was a success. Not a hitch took place in the arrangements, and she managed to induce an easy informality which people enjoyed. Richard Elton was most appreciative, and Mollie brought her pleasing tales of complimentary remarks she had overheard.

A few weeks later the proceedings were repeated, again with satisfaction to all concerned, and then came an invitation to Julia and Mollie to dine, a small family affair, 'just Jeff and myself', as Richard put it. Jeff was the nephew who lived with him.

As this was obviously a purely social event and carried no fee, Julia hesitated. She was not, she felt, in a position to accept hospitality. Then she thought that Richard had been very nice to her and that it would be churlish to refuse. She had little idea of what was in his mind as she wrote her pleasantly worded reply.

During the meal she felt a slight constraint in the atmosphere. Richard was attentive and polite, but the austerity of his manners was always against him and tonight he seemed particularly absent, as if immersed in matters extraneous to the occasion. Jeff also seemed reserved, though he obviously did his best and kept up a running fire of fairly adequate conversation. The dinner was good, if a little too elaborate.

When they had finished, whether by accident or design Julia never knew, Jeff took Mollie off to the billiard room, leaving Julia alone with Richard. Immediately Richard's manner grew positively distrait. He did not answer a number of Julia's remarks—indeed, he did not appear to have heard them. Then he suddenly cleared his throat portentously and came to the business for which the meeting had apparently been arranged.

It was, in brief, a proposal of marriage. 'I do most earnestly hope,' he declared in his stilted way, 'that you will not take offence at the somewhat unusual suggestion I am about to make. It is for a marriage of convenience. At my age I do not pretend to have fallen in love like an ardent young man, and I am well aware that I can hope for no more from you than toleration. I don't know whether I can even get that. But apart from love, I think we have a great deal to offer each other. I am lonely and I cannot single-handed run my house and invite my friends to it. You could, if you would, solve these problems for me. On my part I could offer you and your daughter security, money, affection and a real respect. What do you say? Would you be willing to think it over?'

Julia was amazed. It was the last thing she had expected. Immediately she felt herself drawn in opposite directions. From one point of view here was the solution of all her difficulties. The nightmare problem of how she was to carry on, which would grow more pressing as the years passed, would vanish and be no more. Mollie's future would be assured. Richard was an influential man, and her position as his wife would be unassailable. Chalfont was a gem of a house in an ideal setting, and there was a gorgeous garden. The advantages were enormous, and the more she considered them the greater they appeared.

The proposal indeed had only one drawback: Richard himself. She did not and never could love him, and then he had only asked for toleration. Her heart softened towards him as she thought of his humility, though she wondered if she could give him even this negative regard. Then she thought she could. His proposal after all was for a business contract, and there she should be secure.

The scheme of course carried its obvious danger. Suppose she married him and then fell in love with someone else? Well, if that happened she would have to suffer. There could be no accepting what he offered and failing to pay the price. But it was unlikely that she should fall in love again. For her that experience was past.

In the end it was the advantage to Mollie which decided the issue. Julia had told Richard that she would take a week to think the matter over, and at the end of the time she had decided to accept. She would be absolutely honest with him; she would tell him exactly what her feelings towards him were, and if he still wished to marry her she would agree, giving him a straight deal as far as in her lay. He did still wish to carry on and a few months later they were married.

She soon found that her forebodings had been justified. She did indeed receive the benefits she had been promised, but the price was heavy. Before long, she disliked Richard more even than she had feared. Though upright and honourable according to his lights, he was narrow in outlook, censorious in expression, and terribly hard. He had indeed something of the Puritan in his composition, though without the strength and genuine goodness of the Puritans' religion.

What irked Julia more than anything else was his suspicion. She had never given him the slightest cause for it, and yet it was there. He watched her unceasingly. She even imagined, though she could not prove it, that he employed the butler to watch her. She kept on reminding herself that the arrangement was a business one, and so long as the contract was fulfilled, she could not complain.

She now saw more clearly his object in the marriage. Gradually indeed she learned his entire history. He was ambitious, was Richard Elton. His first goals had been professional success and money. These he had obtained. He was not merely the head of his firm, Elton, Ridgeway and Elton. Rather he was the firm itself, for Ridgeway was dead, and Jeff Elton, the other partner, besides being his nephew, was too junior to do anything except what he was told.

Having achieved all that was possible in his business life, Richard's desires turned to social advancement. For this he laid his plans with his accustomed thoroughness. His first move was to buy Chalfont and his second to engage a butler. He had selected a man named Croome, who had been for years with a titled family and had lost his job through the death of his employer. Croome was tall and thin with a dark hatchetty face, in whose manner imperturbable dignity and a persistent grievance seemed to be waging a continual struggle for the mastery. But even Chalfont and Croome got Richard little further. He needed a wife before he could entertain as he thought necessary, and he began a careful search for the right woman. Twice he found the very person, and twice the lady had other views. Then Captain Langley's death turned his attention to Julia, and when he learnt of her reduced circumstances and that she was moving into Dorkford, he felt that his search was over.

For a year he waited, feeling firstly that too precipitate an approach would defeat his purpose, and secondly, that the more experience Julia had of poverty, the more desirable his proposal would appear. On both points, she told herself grimly, he had been right.

In spite of its drawbacks, the marriage had not been unsuccessful, though in one matter Julia felt she had failed her husband. Though she had run his weekends and his dinners admirably, she had not made him personally popular. It was of course his own fault. His hardness, his self-seeking, his unpleasant voice and his not too gracious manners were against him. People accepted his invitations because they liked Julia and were made comfortable, but with their host they never grew intimate.

But Richard's personality was not the only worry which preyed on Julia's mind. Another was Jeff, who lived with them permanently.

Jeffrey Elton was the son of Richard's only brother, now dead. He was an inoffensive young man, rather pleasant indeed in the house, though with one curious trait. He was extraordinarily secretive. A year after her marriage Julia felt that she knew him no better than on the first day. She did not suspect him of having guilty secrets: he was equally mysterious about everything. But this excessive reserve irritated her.

This in itself was of little importance. What troubled her was that he seemed more than a little attracted to Mollie and that Mollie apparently appreciated his devotion. Julia wanted no entanglement with such an unknown quantity.

At this time, a year or so after her marriage, Mollie herself had become rather a worry. Mollie, now eighteen, was Julia's greatest joy in life. She was affectionate and warm-hearted and gratifyingly fond of her mother. But though Julia had considered the changed outlook for Mollie one of the chief advantages of her marriage, Mollie was evidently not happy at Chalfont. She actively disliked her stepfather, and though she was always polite to him, her antagonism often made itself felt. Moreover her training for a job made her discontented with an existence in which games and parties were the chief items.

Julia at length had it out with her and found that what she wanted was to go in for journalism. They discussed the idea interminably, and it ended in Mollie's getting a position on a ladies' paper. She had to live in Town, though she was able to return home for weekends.

Time now began to pass uneventfully and it brought slow changes to the Chalfont household. The most obvious was in Richard Elton himself.

After a couple of years of effort to achieve popularity among the influential people of the district, Richard had tacitly acknowledged his defeat and given up striving. Julia was sorry for him, though she could do nothing about it. The fault was his own. He seemed to realize this, and to his credit he never attempted to blame her for his failure. But he did become bitter and sardonic in manner: often hurtful in the things he said, though Julia believed he did not mean it. It had the effect of throwing her even further in on herself and making her more and more lonely.

About this time Richard took a decision which drew them still further apart. It happened that his firm had been employed in an important case of infringement of patent rights in a newly discovered chemical process. The evidence was involved and highly technical, and Richard had to work up a good deal of the chemistry he had learnt at school and subsequently forgotten. He had always liked chemistry, and now he found it so interesting that when the case was over, he decided to carry on his studies as a hobby. Accordingly he built a small laboratory in the Chalfont grounds, and there he spent an increasing amount of his spare time. Julia at first hoped it might prove a bond between them. Though not particularly interested in the subject, she would have been glad to have helped in his work. Again she was disappointed. It merely meant that he spent less time in the lounge, and he never spoke of his experiments any more than of the details of his business.

Another three years passed and then a series of events took place which was to lead, though no one suspected it, to tragedy in the house of Chalfont.

The first of these was the episode of Mrs Pilkington's emerald.

Mrs Pilkington was a flamboyant lady of uncertain age, the wife of a professional friend of Richard's. The pair occasionally spent a weekend with the Eltons. She was a woman of strong views, downright of speech and impatient of opposition, though really good and kind at, heart. Julia liked her and was always glad when she came. Her husband was a small dried up, rather silent man, whose chief interest lay in old glass.

It happened that after dinner on Saturday the conversation turned to Richard's chemical experiments, and Pilkington, though not an expert, expressed a wish to see Richard's laboratory. Mrs Pilkington, who did not like to be left out of anything, seconded his request. Richard was obviously not too pleased, but he could scarcely refuse, and after some faintly deterrent remarks he led the way. Though he talked at length about what he was doing, Julia noticed that his customary lucidity was strangely absent. She could make neither head nor tail of his explanations, and she shrewdly suspected that his visitors were in no better case. However, they achieved an adequate show of interest, the party presently filed back to the house, and in due course everyone went to bed. They had not reached their rooms five minutes before Mr Pilkington called Richard.

'I'm terribly sorry to make trouble,' he said with a deprecating air, 'but the fact is that something unfortunate has happened. Margot has lost an emerald, a rather valuable stone. She has just missed it, and I thought I should tell you at once, so that if you will be so good, we might have a search.'

The loss of jewellery is traditionally an unpleasant matter between host and guest, though in this case they were saved from embarrassment, as the question of theft could scarcely arise. Further inquiry showed that the stone had fallen from a brooch worn that evening by Mrs Pilkington. She had pinned on the brooch when dressing for dinner, and the stone had then apparently been firm; moreover, after dinner Julia herself had noticed it still in its setting.

If it had dropped out inside the house or the laboratory,

they agreed that there should be no difficulty in finding it. But the path through the grounds connecting the two was a different proposition. Richard produced a powerful acetylene lamp and by its light they went over every inch of the way along which Mrs Pilkington had passed. They had no success.

Richard was very much upset and swore that he would find the stone if he looked for a month. Next morning the servants were taken into their confidence, a reward was offered, and the search was repeated: again without result.

It was not until that evening, nearly twenty-four hours after it was lost, that it turned up. Richard himself found it. It had slipped into one of his chemical vessels, and he had previously missed seeing it owing to its having rolled under one of the broken pieces of plastic with which the bottom of the vessel was covered. He appeared greatly relieved, though he never again referred to the matter.

It happened that just at this time events in the household and Richard's reactions to them were cast into the shade. They were neither noted nor thought of in the light of the great world tragedy which was then inexorably unfolding. A week after the Pilkingtons' visit Germany invaded Poland and Britain went to war.

This is not an account of the war, nor will any unnecessary reference be made to it, but its effect on the actors in the minor drama cannot be entirely disregarded. For a time the Elton household, like every other household in England, was overwhelmed by the disaster. Then as immediate hostilities did not follow, and as in these early days no one at Chalfont considered himself young enough to volunteer for the army, life returned gradually to something approaching normal.

Some four or five weeks after the declaration of war Richard had so far recovered his poise that he was able again to interest himself in his hobby. He now explained to Julia that he wanted an assistant to help in his experiments, and had engaged a man named Philip Harte. Harte was, he said, a man of good education and pleasant personality and had been recommended by a mutual friend, a Mr Pegram, the head of the chemical firm for which he had acted in the patent rights infringement case. Harte had been with the Pegram firm, but was leaving owing to a reduction of staff and so was looking for a job. Richard would like him to live in the house as one of the family, if Julia had no objection.

Julia had none. Her life at Chalfont was triste enough. Mollie was now away more than ever, and the addition to the household of a personable young man would be all to the good.

A fortnight later the newcomer appeared, and once again Julia's heart sank. He was all that Richard had said. He had easy polished manners, a good flow of interesting small talk, and was always obliging and willing to help. Undoubtedly he was an acquisition, and yet—Julia disliked him from the first moment she saw him. She could not tell why. He was deferential enough to her, and never attempted the slightest liberty. Yet somehow she felt that she could not trust him. Then she told herself that she should not judge him, and tried to make up for it by being particularly nice to him.

He made no trouble in the household, slipping easily into their ways. He got on better with Mollie than with Julia. He evidently liked her, and she accepted his mild attentions as a matter of course. The only person he did not get on with was the butler, Croome. This Julia discovered by accident, overhearing Croome addressing him with but thinly veiled insolence. The remark produced a considerably sharper reply than Julia would have expected from the pleasant mannered chemist.

Richard obviously thought a good deal of Harte. He was more friendly to him than to the others; indeed, at times he was almost deferential, at least in as far as Richard could be deferential to anyone. Richard was taking his chemical hobby more seriously since Harte came, and spent more of his free time in the laboratory. They talked at meals about chemical matters and even joked together, a development so unlike Richard that Julia could scarcely believe her ears.

Another result of Harte's appearance was that Jeff's interest in Mollie, which seemed to have died down, now obviously revived. He sought her out and paid court to her in every possible way. Mollie did not actually encourage him; she pretended to take his dancing attendance as her natural clue, but Julia saw that she liked it. Not unnatural of course for a young girl.

Julia herself, indeed, had gradually become reconciled to Jeff Elton, or at least she had become accustomed to him. He was there in the house just as were the tables and chairs. He was certainly more responsive than a table or a chair, though not much. Now, rightly or wrongly, Julia had come to believe his reserve was a mere natural characteristic. All the same she hoped Mollie would not get really fond of him.

As the weeks passed the various members of the household became absorbed in war work. Richard spent half his time in Town at some mysterious job in Whitehall, Jeff and Croome were in the Local Defence Volunteers, Harte had joined the fire fighting service and Julia was knitting with urgent constancy. Mollie had put her name down for some form of service, but had not yet been called on, and was still in her post.

It was when matters were in this stage that the third event occurred which heralded the approaching tragedy. This also was the entry into Julia's life of a man. This time his name was Frank Cox.

2

The Ingenious Lover

Frank Brownrigg Cox was one of those men whose careers start with scintillating brilliancy at school and college, and then when they come up against the rough and tumble of life, peter out into mediocrity. Usually such persons have intellect but not character, though in Cox's case the cause was rather to be looked for in the accident of birth. His father was well off, and when he died Frank found himself in possession of rather more than a competence. Work was unnecessary and he therefore did not do any. He settled down to enjoy life, but in his own way. He was too intelligent to join a set who lived for entertainment only. Instead he travelled, studying the life and thought of other countries, writing a few books which he had published but which did not sell, and discussing philosophies and isms with anyone who would spare him the necessary time. In 1914 a chance encounter brought him to the notice of one of the heads of the Intelligence Department, and there his particular twist of intellect came into its own and he did invaluable work in solving enemy ciphers and constructing codes for our own services.

When eventually he had knocked about enough, he decided to come home and take up a hobby which during his wanderings had grown more and more alluring. Seeing other countries had made him more content with his own, and his ambition now was to write a series of historical novels which should make known the past of his native county, Surrey. He therefore looked round for some congenial place which would prove a convenient centre and where he could work undisturbed.

He chose Dorkford, buying a cottage across the valley from Chalfont, and with almost as delightful a view. Though it was small and, his personal wants were modest, he made himself pretty comfortable. He redecorated the place from top to bottom, putting in costly and elaborate fittings. As household staff he engaged a discharged batman and his wife.

His life would have bored most people, but he found it thrilling. He spent a good deal of time in the British Museum obtaining data for his books and looking up references. Then he went to see the places where the events he read of had occurred. He walked over the routes his characters had trod and absorbed the scenery in which they had lived, in the hope of reproducing the atmosphere of their time.

Though retiring, Frank Cox was by no means a recluse. He was a member of a Pall Mall club, spent at least two afternoons a week on the golf links at Dorkford and frequently dined out. In appearance he was of medium height and build, with a good chin, blue eyes twinkling with intelligence, a high forehead and hair of a distinctly reddish tinge. He was upright and honourable in disposition, generous to those in need, and would take any trouble to help a friend. He was in his late forties and since the War had become A.R.P. Warden of his district.

One failing he had, though not indeed a very serious one. He was cursed with a fiery temper. At slight provocation it would flare up and for a moment he would rage like a thwarted tiger. But the storm passed quickly. He always regretted his outbursts, was quick to apologize if he thought himself in the wrong, and never harboured ill-feeling.

Richard's firm had carried through the purchase of his house, and Richard had put him up for the local golf club. He had indeed asked him to lunch one day to meet the secretary. When Cox was settled in he had asked Richard and Julia to dine, and they had accepted. Since then he had once or twice attended the dances at Chalfont which Richard insisted on giving.

Julia had thus early made his acquaintance. She had liked what she saw of him, but had never really given him much thought. They had met perhaps half a dozen times, and had never had any personal or intimate conversation. Then just about the time at which Philip Harte came to Chalfont, they became more friendly.

Julia had taken the small car to Town, and on the way back the power had suddenly failed. She knew but little about cars, and when she had looked at her petrol gauge and had buried her head with ostrich-like effectiveness in the bonnet, she found she had exhausted her resources of first aid. She was standing a little disconsolately on the road, hoping that some miracle would produce a scout, when another car stopped and a man got out and came over. It was Cox.

'In trouble, Mrs Elton?' he asked, glancing at the open bonnet.

'Oh, Mr Cox, I'm so glad to see you. You're a friend in need. It's stopped and I can't do anything with it.'

'I wonder if I can? I'm afraid I'm not much good about cars. May I look?'

He in turn buried his head in the bonnet. Then after some magic rites he said he believed it was the ignition, and that if so, it was beyond him.

'Suppose you lock it up,' he concluded, 'and let me drive you to a garage, where you can give instructions about it.'

This seemed good advice and she agreed thankfully. He drove her to the garage she patronized, arranged her business, and took her home. It was close on teatime and she asked him to stay.

He did so and she enjoyed it. She took him round the garden and his appreciation went straight to her heart. Then with some hesitation he told her about his literary work. She felt this a compliment and drew him out on the subject. He warmed to her sympathy as if he too were lonely.

'In connection with my work I've recently got hold of some rather interesting old engravings,' he said presently. 'Two or three go back to James the First's time. They're comical in a way, though I daresay the dresses? and all that are what were actually worn. But you can recognize all the backgrounds. This hill, for instance, behind your house appears in one of them, and there's another which must have been sketched from where this house stands.'

'I should like to see them.'

'I was going to ask if you would come up some time and have a look at them,' and again he spoke with a diffident hesitation which charmed her. 'I would bring them down here, but they're in biggish frames and it makes them a bit unwieldy.'

'I'd love to go.'

'That will be wonderful,' he said gravely, and presently took himself off.

It was Julia's loneliness which made this first confidential talk with Cox a notable event in her life. She found in him an understanding and a sympathy to which she had long been a stranger. And when in due course she went to see the prints, her feeling was strengthened.

It was only natural that before separating after this second meeting, they should arrange for a third. Julia meant nothing by it and in all probability neither did Cox. But their talk had been a pleasure to both and neither saw any reason why it should not be continued.

There was no reason of course—but the one. The third meeting was followed by others, and before either of them was aware of what was happening, the mischief was done. They had fallen in love.

Julia realized the truth with mixed feelings. One part of her was appalled and foresaw that nothing but misery could result; another was filled with an exulting happiness which far outweighed her forebodings. This was something she had never experienced before: something that neither of her marriages had given her. At her age—no less now than three and forty—she felt she was beginning to live. She told herself that it was absurd; but it was the truth.

For a time both of them tried to pretend that no fundamental change in their relations had taken place; then this grew impossible. Finally Cox put the matter into words, 'We may or may not like it, Julia,' he said with a whimsical smile, 'but there is no use in trying to blink the fact: we love each other and will never be happy as we are. And no matter what trouble it may bring, I for one am more delighted and thankful about it than about anything else that ever happened to me in my whole life: far more than I can ever put into words. I feel as if for the first time I am living.'

This was so exactly Julia's experience that she could only agree. Their discussion abruptly ceased to be introspective and became impassioned.

For Julia life now became more difficult than ever. She felt herself surrounded by inimical influences. Of the four men in the house, two were actual enemies and the other two potential. There was Richard, full of suspicion and constantly watching her. He would be merciless to such a break as she was making. There was Croome, now passively hostile, but awaiting, as she thought, only the opportunity to become actively so. Of the others she saw less. Philip Harte's work kept him pretty constantly in the laboratory, but she was unpleasantly conscious of his sharp eyes following her about, and felt that he missed little of what went on. Jeff Elton was another problem. She had never yet discovered what he knew and what he didn't know of the household affairs, but she had learnt that he also was anything but a fool.

Of course up to the present she and Frank had been discreet. From the beginning they had instinctively kept their meetings secret, except for occasional formal calls known to Richard and Croome, and during which they treated each other as the merest acquaintances. Their vital interviews took place in private rooms in obscure hotels in Town, and they were careful never to approach these together. But it was all terribly unsatisfactory. For a time they tried to live in the present, snatching such satisfaction they could out of these vital interviews. But both knew the situation could not last.

Then one afternoon an event took place which brought matters to a head. Their practice had been for Frank to arrive at the meeting place some quarter of an hour before Julia, and to remain for the same time after she had left. Today, a Wednesday, they had lunched at the Bellerophon Hotel, off Kingsway, and Frank had explained that he must leave a little early as he had an appointment with his dentist. To gain the maximum of time together, Julia had decided that on this occasion she would let him start first.

After duly waiting for the allotted period, she left the hotel to regain her car. A few yards from the door she noticed a man looking into a shop window. There was something vaguely familiar about him, though at first she could not place him. At that moment he glanced round, saw her, and immediately moved off in the opposite direction.

He had been quick, though just not quick enough. In that glance she had recognized him. It was her butler, Croome.

Had he not retreated so promptly, she would have assumed a chance meeting. But that almost guilty movement and the look of evil triumph on his dark, saturnine face gave him away. She felt certain he had been watching her. And if so, why? Surely there could be but one answer.

Cursing her stupidity in coming to Town on his free day, she turned into a telephone booth and rang up Frank at the dentist's, whose name by a lucky chance he had mentioned. She insisted that the matter was serious, but he tried to reassure her, pointing out that even if Croome had seen him also, he could prove nothing.

All the same, Julia found the incident perturbing. She had never given much thought to Croome, though she had never liked him. Now she wondered if she had not underestimated him. He was undoubtedly an able man. He was not only an efficient butler, but a highly skilled mechanic and electrician. At his own request he did all the Chalfont house and electrical repairs and had fitted up a really excellent system of plug-in speakers in the various rooms. He ran a motor bicycle, and Hawthorne, the chauffeur, was not above asking his help if the cars gave trouble. On many occasions Julia had noted his ingenuity and resource.

She was aware that he, as he probably would have put it, reciprocated her antagonism. Why, she could not imagine, because she had always tried to be pleasant to him. Instinct also told her that he was vindictive and would injure her if he could. She wondered if she had put herself in his power. If this meeting were not accidental, and she could not believe it was, he must know about Frank. Such knowledge would not be allowed to lie fallow. Probably it would mean either a report to Richard or blackmail. She grew increasingly worried, particularly as the one thing she wanted most, to discuss it with Frank, was the one thing she must at all costs avoid.

A couple of days later, while she was still puzzling over this problem of meeting Frank, she received an unexpected letter. It was typewritten on a quarto sheet of good quality paper and read:

> 76, Wiverton Crescent,
> St John's Wood, N.W.8
> 21st March.

Mrs Elton,
Chalfont,
Victoria Road,
Dorkford.

MADAM,

In reply to your advertisement asking for historical pictures of the Dorkford area of Surrey, I happen to have one for disposal which might meet your requirements. It is 13 ins. x 19 ins. and represents King James I surrounded by a hunting party on Box Hill, near Dorking. It shows him at the point where the modern belvedere stands on the Burford Crag, which, as you know, is a lower spur of Box Hill; in fact, had the belvedere then been built, his throne might have been actually inside it. The contour of the hills, which remains unaltered, shows the position with accuracy. The engraving is in a state of excellent preservation except for part of the bottom margin and title. The day of meeting, Monday, remains, but the date has been torn off.

Should you be interested, you could see the engraving here at any time and no doubt we could agree on terms.

Yours faithfully,

(Mrs) Hilda Glendinning.

For a moment Julia stared open-mouthed at this incomprehensible communication. She had never before heard of Mrs Hilda Glendinning, nor had she ever had anything to do with an advertisement about prints. Obviously, this was Frank's handiwork, but why had he approached the lady on her behalf?

Then her heart grew lighter. Why, of course! They were to meet at her house! Clever!

But when? Slowly she reread the somewhat stilted sentences. No; it could not be that. There was no indication of either date or hour. Unless Monday was meant. But still, that did not cover the hour.

Probably he had left a note there for her arranging a further rendezvous. At all events the first thing was to make inquiries. She would go to Town that very afternoon.

She looked up her map of London to locate Wiverton Crescent, for she knew that St John's Wood covered a considerable area. Then a cold breath of doubt assailed her. There was no Wiverton Crescent, neither in St John's Wood nor in any other part of London.

For an hour she puzzled over the affair, and then light flashed into her mind. The letter was from Frank: from Frank himself. He must have given it the false address to confound unauthorized readers. And why that elaborate description of the belvedere on Box Hill? Simply because that was to be their meeting place. She knew the Burford Crag and the little open-fronted building placed to include the best view. An admirable spot for a meeting, at this time of year certain to be deserted. And the time was clear enough after all. Monday! Monday next, of course. And since the time was not mentioned, it could only be at the London hour: half-past twelve.

How like Frank, she thought tenderly. So ingenious, and yet so like a small boy in his love of mystery and intrigue and subterfuge! She wondered if she could play up to him, answering his letter after his own pattern. Then an idea occurred to her. What were the essential words of her reply? Belvedere, Box Hill, 12.30, Monday next.

She tore a half sheet from the back of a letter and wrote in a disguised hand:

Glendinning House.
Monday.

Dear Major Cox,

What about the following additional solutions for your prize crossword?

4 across	....	Outlook
7 "	....	Chest
21 "	....	Mountain
3 down	....	Dozen
8 "	....	Demi
16 "	....	Moon
24 "	....	Proximo

Yours sincerely,
Joanna Burford.

25

As she looked at this effusion, she felt that she had kept her end up. If it was not so hideously serious, it would be an amusing enough game.

But Monday, when it came, was not amusing, though Julia found her expedition grew more exciting the nearer she approached her destination. She started early in the small car, and having made a round through Horsley and Leatherhead, turned south and took the hill road at the back of the Burford Bridge Hotel. At the top near the closed restaurant she parked, and walking along the hill crest, reached the rendezvous just before twelve-thirty.

It was a really charming position. The belvedere, a small structure in discoloured white stone, was built as a diminutive replica of what is usually though incorrectly called the Temple of Vesta. It stood on a projecting spur of the hill with its back to the woods and its open front looking down on Dorking, with the Weald to the left, the valley and Green Sand Ridge to the right and Leith Hill straight in front. It was a view which Julia loved, and she had often before come up to see it, as well as the similar one from the larger outlook with the panoramic chart beyond the restaurant. It was true that the weather was not pleasant. A thin rain was falling which a cold wind drove searchingly along the slopes of the hill. But this was all to the good. On such a day no better secret meeting place could have been found.

Cox was waiting and as she entered he took her in his arms. For a moment she clung to him, then pushed him away.

'No,' she said, 'we shouldn't. Oh, Frank, what are we going to do? I don't trust Croome. I'm sure he'll make mischief.'

'His being there might just have been an accident. You've no real reason to think he was following us?'

'I'm certain of it; his manner was unmistakable,' and she

told her story in greater detail, ending up: 'We were wrong to choose Wednesday. A day when he was engaged at Chalfont would have been safer.'

'Well, this is not Wednesday.'

'No, and we're all right here. But in any case he's gone up to Town today. He asked for and got special leave to meet a sister from South Africa, who was passing through on her way home to the North.'

'Well, don't let's talk about him. If this has brought our little matter to a head, Julia, I for one cannot pretend to be sorry. I have been going to say something to you for a considerable time, and now I can't put it off any longer. My dear, we can't go on like this, or at least I can't. After all I'm only flesh and blood, and I just can't live when I only see you at long intervals and with all this stealth and secrecy. Julia dear, let us face it. Let us go to your husband and tell him the truth and ask him to release you. If he has any decency he's bound to do it. Let's give him the technical evidence so that you can get your divorce. Then we can be married.'

She was deeply moved. 'Oh, Frank, it sounds heavenly. But you don't know Richard. He'd never agree. He has strange views, you know, and one of them is about divorce. He's got a complex about it.'

'Not religious surely? He's not a Catholic?'

'No, I don't think he's anything. All the same he hates divorce. I think he imagines it would injure his solicitor's practice.'

'That's nonsense.'

'I'm not so sure. However, it doesn't matter: he doesn't think it's nonsense, and if you knew anything about him you'd know that nothing that you or I could say or do would move him.'

27

It was not till this idea had been fully discussed and finally rejected by Julia that Cox made his second proposal. 'Then if you won't do that,' he said, 'there is an alternative. It's one I hate to suggest, and if you don't like it you've only to say so, and I'll never mention it again. Would you—come away with me and—start a new life elsewhere? We could be very happy, Julia, even—without the divorce.'

She turned the proposal down, though not so decisively as he had expected. In fact, she seemed so undecided that presently he referred to it again. This time she discussed it in detail.

'I don't think we need consider it,' she began, and again she spoke doubtfully. 'We wouldn't be happy. We might just at first, but the weight of the thing would be there on our minds and it would get us down. Besides, the need for this dreadful secrecy would be as great as ever, and we'd be at the mercy of any blackmailer.'

'If after the War we went to the right country we wouldn't have to keep out relations a secret.'

'Yes, and what sort of people should we meet? Besides, Frank, there's my bargain with Richard. I made it deliberately and with my eyes open. Richard has kept his part. How could I break mine?'

'It was an iniquitous bargain.'

'Oh no, it wasn't. It was perfectly fair. He wanted a hostess and I wanted security. We were both satisfied.'

'My dear, that's just like you. But we must settle something. What you saw outside the Bellerophon also altered the position. We are definitely in danger now, and whether we like it or not, we must act.'

She knew he was right, but she could not make up her mind. It was not so much the plunge, though she feared that too. It was her innate honesty, which urged her that a bargain which one party has kept should not be lightly broken by the other.

'Very well,' he said at last, evidently realizing that they could not reach a decision that day. 'I do understand your difficulty and that you must have more time to think it over. But it involves another meeting, and I for one won't quarrel with that. It must be secret of course and I thought of a scheme in case we might need it. You told me you were giving a dance next Friday. Why not slip out during the time you're supposed to be dressing and meet me for ten minutes in your summer-house?'

She considered this. 'I think I could manage it,' she said at last. 'The house will be pretty full, but they'll all be dressing. I could go down by the back stairs. Perkins will be on duty upstairs and Croome and the others will be busy about dinner. I shouldn't be seen.'

'That's fine. You'd never be suspected at that hour.'

'Suppose you were seen?'

'I shall not be. I'll be careful.'

Again Julia paused in thought. 'Wouldn't it be better if you were to come to the dance? And to dine, for that matter? I should ask Margaret Crawford to balance the numbers. I think it would tend to allay suspicion.'

'You're probably right.'

'I think it would be argued that you wouldn't have been asked, or have come, if we were—what we are.'

'Yes; it's an idea. Then what time do we meet?'

'Let's see. Dinner's at eight, and I should want, say, fifteen minutes after I came in. I suppose a quarter of an hour would be all we'd want?'

'I expect so.'

'Then say half-past seven. The dressing-bell rings at seven and I'll be dressed by half-past.'

He nodded. 'Then that's settled. I mustn't talk about it, but oh, my clear, how I hope it'll be favourable! Well, the sooner you're home, the better. I'll wait till you've got a good start. I walked up by the face and I'll go down the same way.'

'Oh, Frank, what am I to say on Friday?'

'Courage, my darling. Courage does it.'

Julia felt physically tired from the interview. The conversation, the secrecy, the acting a part, had taken it out of her. But more than all these was the problem with which she was faced. She loved this man, and though she would scarcely admit it to herself, she hated Richard. She had always tried to lead an upright life, and she knew that hatred was a corrosive, poisoning both hater and hated. Yet in spite of all her striving, her dislike of her husband had grown steadily during the years of her married life, and it required only the meeting with Frank to fan this dislike into something stronger. She felt that as long as she remained in Richard's house, she could never be happy.

But though this was true, it by no means solved her problem. There was, she felt, only one satisfactory solution. If Richard would give her her freedom and let her marry Frank, all three might yet be happy. Unfortunately she could not count on this. If he refused, what should be her next step?

To go away with Frank would be joy inexpressible. And yet, she told herself, the joy would not last. To remain in the society to which she was accustomed would be scarcely possible, and to change it for worse, as would be inevitable, would be to sow the seeds of disillusionment and misery. Besides, it would end Frank's literary work. Away from the British Museum and the fair county of Surrey, he could not carry on. She did not suppose this would matter very much to anyone but Frank; but to him it would be a bitter disappointment, and he would subconsciously blame her, and a feeling of irritation would rankle and grow.

The more Julia thought about it, the more evenly balanced the arguments on either side seemed to grow. She simply did not know what to do. Fortunately there was still five days in. which to make up her mind. Surely by then she should have seen her way clear?

3

The Disgruntled Clerk

If Julia's actions were unintentionally leading her towards tragedy, what about the other actors in the coming drama?

Richard Elton, the head of the house, had by this time grown into a lonely and embittered man, ten years older than his age, which was fifty-four. His powerful frame was stooped and his face with its strongly marked features was grey and lined, though his eyes behind their glasses remained clear and shrewd and the narrow line of his lips expressed an unyielding determination. Of his professional competence no question had ever been raised and he bore that indefinable stamp which the law so often imprints on its votaries. His expression was unpleasant and he looked a man difficult of approach.

His efforts to achieve the various goals he had set himself had had disappointing results, principally due to the fact that never in his life had he been able to make friends. He could not make advances himself, and without meaning to, he repulsed the advances of others. He felt driven more and more in on himself. At first the fight for money and position had been a thrilling adventure, but when these had been obtained he had discovered that he could not enjoy them alone and that no one cared enough for him to enjoy them with him. Even Julia, though he agreed that she had technically carried out her bargain, was only an acquaintance. He believed she had honestly tried to conceal her dislike for him, but she had failed. She could not deceive him. He knew what she felt.

And he also knew what practically everyone else felt. Mollie made but little attempt to hide her feelings, and though Jeff was more circumspect, his reaction was equally clear. In Dorkford Richard had many acquaintances, but none sought his society. Though the personnel of the office was obsequious, he appreciated how much that was worth. Only Croome, his butler, seemed friendly beneath the veneer of his calling. But Croome, though he valued him as a butler, Richard definitely did not trust. Beneath all this weight of animosity, real or imagined, Richard's hardness and suspicion grew steadily greater.

And yet he was far from being evilly disposed. He was abstemious and self-controlled. He was honest and straightforward and considered that his word was his bond. He did not deliberately harbour resentments. He gave money in charity. He tried to be fair in his dealings with others. He could not understand why his efforts for popularity had so little result.

Until recently his marriage had been successful to just the extent that he had had a right to expect, but latterly he had noticed a change in Julia which had given him furiously to think. She had become absentminded, as if living an inner life which she did not share with those around her. Her looks had improved. At times, particularly when she was more than ever lost in her thoughts, she grew almost beautiful, her face becoming lit up with a sort of internal glow.

There were days when this was specially apparent, and from casual conversations, mostly with Croome, he discovered that on most of these occasions she had been to Town. Richard guessed what had happened to his wife, and though so far he could not prove his suspicions, he watched with increasing bitterness for further developments.

To Richard Elton, Mollie Langley was a complete contrast in disposition. Impulsive and warm hearted, she found life an increasing thrill. While she had been bored at Chalfont, her incursion into literature had proved entirely delightful. The paper she was working on was a rag, though she thought it a national asset. Its press day was the high spot of her week. It was run by a decent enough crowd and she was soon a favourite. She had begun by covering minor social events, weddings, balls, funerals: second-rate stuff, notice of which was good for circulation. Soon she had been promoted in addition to a weekly feature under the title of 'How I Do It', which discussed life from the viewpoint of women who ran tea-shops and hat-shops and suchlike. This she considered a Prelude to Interviewing and she had made it quite a success. Then a few months earlier the high light in her career to date had come into view. One of her hat shop fraternity had taken a fancy to her enthusiastic young visitor and a friendship had sprung up between them. This woman decided to take a holiday in Canada and asked Mollie to go with her as companion. When Mollie tentatively sounded her editor as to the possibilities of leave, he put his head on one side and looked at her shrewdly.

'How about a series "How Canadians Do It"?' he asked.

At her expression a slow smile disintegrated the rocky mask of his features, and it was presently decided that she was to go on her full salary and with a strictly controlled expense account. The war of course had put a stop to the trip, but her editor's offer remained a warm and comforting memory.

The next member of the family belonged to still another type. While Jeffrey Elton had something of Richard in his make-up, he was less self-centred than his uncle. But like him he was sober and restrained in manner, somewhat heavy in society and in fact also old for his age. As Julia had found, he was reserved to the extent of secretiveness, not necessarily because he had anything to hide, but as an unconscious protective mechanism.

His life would have been the envy of countless young men. His position in the firm was good and his prospects better. He lived comfortably in a luxurious house. He had enough money for all his reasonable wants and expectations of wealth. He had sufficient amusements and a circle of pleasant friends. And yet he was not satisfied. His uncle's manners and methods were to him a source of continual irritation. At the office he felt that he was not given his proper place as junior partner. In Richard's presence he was always made to feel like a small and rather naughty boy and more than once he had caught the insufficiently discreet grins of the typists at his discomfiture. At Chalfont too, he felt anything but free: not that Richard actively interfered with his comings and goings, merely that his presence and disapproval were always there. Often Jeff had considered breaking away from the home circle and going into rooms in Dorkford, but he knew this would arouse Richard's active hostility. What he would have liked would be a transfer to another firm, but this he had so far been unable to arrange.

Julia he admired. She was always friendly and pleasant and she certainly made life easier in the house. Often he was sorry for her, believing she had a thin time with Richard. Though he didn't know the terms of their marriage, he at least knew that it was not all it should be.

But if he admired Julia, he adored Mollie. In her character she represented everything that he lacked himself. He had loved her from the first day he had seen her, though he had not at first realized the fact. He had greatly resented her going to London, but even this had not opened his eyes. It was not till he found Philip Harte, the newly imported chemist, carrying on a mild flirtation with her that he became alive to the truth. With the discovery his love became a torment as well as a joy, for now he was no longer sure of her favour. He did not mind her taking his adoration as a matter of course. What worried him was that she seemed willing to treat Harte in the same way. Indeed, Jeff grew frightened about the strength of his feelings towards Harte. At times he felt that to kill him would be a relief.

Recently Jeff had been more troubled than ever. He had evolved a suspicion which, if well founded, might prove a disaster, not only for himself, but Mollie. He, like Richard, had noticed the change in Julia, and like him, had diagnosed the cause. Knowing his uncle's ideas, he realized that if he discovered aberrations on Julia's part, he would be absolutely implacable. Julia would not be granted a divorce; she would be asked to leave the house and cut out of Richard's will. Mollie, of course, would go too. In which case, if Mollie accepted him, he himself would follow.

But if he were to follow, it would mean a complete breach with his uncle. Richard, he knew, intended to make him his heir, with the exception of a life interest in certain sums for Julia. And Richard according to moderate standards was wealthy. Jeff believed that his share would be not less than £50,000. If he married Mollie against his uncle's wishes, he would never see a penny. Certainly also he would lose his job.

Had he only himself to think of, Jeff knew what he would do. He would marry Mollie and let the money go hang. Unfortunately he could not consider himself alone. Mollie certainly would receive many proposals, and unless he had reasonably good prospects he dared not ask her to marry him. It was therefore with intense misgiving that he watched the situation develop.

Of this rivalry and jealousy, Harte, to do him justice, was unaware. He also was worried, though about something totally different. While he appreciated Mollie's charms, the idea of a flirtation with her had never entered his head. Harte, to give him a name which he had not always borne, was engaged in the perilous task of living down a past, or rather of keeping an episode of the past shrouded in the oblivion which he felt was desirable. Harte had unhappily been indiscreet in certain financial matters and had seen the inside of a Canadian prison. On release he had come home, had changed his name, and had applied for help to his uncle, Mr Pegram, the managing director of the chemical firm for which Richard had acted in the patent rights case. Pegram for his mother's sake had given him a start on condition that their relationship was kept a secret. At the same time he had decided that at the first opportunity he would get rid of his unwanted nephew. He therefore recommended him to Richard. He did so in good faith. Harte was not only a skilful chemist and in the matter of other people's property had learnt his lesson, but while with his uncle he had tried hard to make good.

It was on that same Monday afternoon of her meeting with Frank Cox at the belvedere on Box Hill—Lady Day, the 25th of March—that Julia began the pruning of her roses. While she was working an event took place which added still further to her perplexities. She had not been long in the garden when Ada, who acted in Croome's place when he was off duty, appeared.

'A Mrs Underwood has called to see you, madam. She's in the morning room.'

'Oh,' said Julia, looking regretfully at a half pruned bush. 'Who is she, do you know?'

'I think she is the wife of one of Mr Elton's clerks.'

'Oh, of course. I'll go in. No, I won't. Bring her out, will you please?'

'Certainly, madam.'

Ada moved off while Julia tried to recall what she knew of her visitor. She had met her at the previous Christmas at a fête given to the inhabitants of a local charitable institution. Julia as a hostess had poured out tea and Mrs Underwood had been one of the waitresses. She had liked what she saw of the kindly and rather handsome middle-aged woman who, as they were chatting, had told her who she was. Richard never spoke of his staff, so that though Underwood had been in the firm for over twenty years, Julia had not even known his name. In virtue of their indirect connection, she had intended asking Mrs Underwood out to tea, but for one reason or another the invitation had never been given and she had not seen her since.

'How do you do?' she said a moment later. 'I hope you'll forgive my not going in, but I'm just in the middle of some pruning, and as it's so warm I thought we could talk out here.'

'I'm afraid I'm disturbing you, Mrs Elton. It's so good of you to see me.'

Mrs Underwood was evidently acutely nervous. Julia tried to put her at her ease.

'I'm very glad to see you and you're not disturbing me in the least,' she said kindly. 'In fact I just wanted a breather and you've given me the excuse. One gets tired stooping over the bushes.'

'Thank you so much, but I'm afraid you won't be so pleased when you hear what I've come about. In fact if you simply send me home again you'll be perfectly justified.'

Julia smiled. 'I shall not do that at all events. You look worried. I hope there's nothing wrong?'

'I'm afraid there is: for me at least.'

'Well, let's sit down and be comfortable and then you can tell me all about it.'

'I'm very grateful. But if you change your mind when you hear my story, I shall understand. What a perfect situation,' she went on as they walked to a seat from which spread out a charming vista of the valley.

'Yes, it's a lovely part of the world, isn't it? Now, Mrs Underwood, let me hear your trouble, and if there's anything I can do to help, I shall only be delighted.'

Mrs Underwood shook her head. 'It's more than good of you, but don't promise too soon. It's to speak to Mr Elton on my husband's behalf.'

Now Julia regretted Richard Elton's reticence about his business. She didn't even know Underwood's position.

'What about your husband?' she asked cautiously, hoping the information would be forthcoming.

'He's been dismissed,' Mrs Underwood spoke with difficulty. 'I'm not complaining, you understand. William did wrong and Mr Elton was justified. But in a way it was an accident. William didn't mean any harm, and he can put everything right if, only—'

'If only?'

'If only he was allowed a little more time.'

Julia thought over this. She would greatly dislike to interfere in Richard's business, but her instinct was to help people
who were in trouble, irrespective of her own desires.

'I'm afraid,' she said, 'that before I could undertake anything,
you'd have to tell me the whole circumstances. As it is, I know
nothing about them.'

'I couldn't wish for anything more. Thank you very much.
Then I'll have to begin with a little about our history. But
first I want to explain that this is entirely my own idea. William
doesn't know I've come, and he'll be mad when he hears. I
thought I would take the risk because, if I may say so, you
were so kind when we met at that fête.'

Julia murmured politely and Mrs Underwood went on:
'William entered Mr Elton's firm as a junior clerk after he left
school. When the last war broke out, he joined up when he
was old enough: in 1917. He was shell-shocked and rather
ill for a time, then he got well enough to work, and Mr Elton
gave him back his job. We've always remembered that with
gratitude, for many employers weren't so honourable. Then
we were married and William got promotion till he became
the second clerk, which position he retained until—this
happened. We have two children, a girl of fifteen and a boy
of seventeen, and in our small way we were contented and
happy. Some time ago Bee, that's my daughter, had a fall and
hurt her spine. They were willing to give her ordinary treatment in the local hospital for a small fee, but they didn't offer
much hope of a permanent cure. Then we learnt that there
was a Scotch doctor living in Aberdeen who had developed
an operation for just that sort of thing, and whose results
were marvellous. Well, we wanted if possible to give Bee the
chance but of course it was terribly costly for us. We found

when we scraped together our available cash we were short by about forty pounds. It was just unlucky that our rent and certain other expenses became due at the same time.'

In her time of poverty Julia had learnt something of the world, and as this hard luck story began to develop she instinctively grew critical. Then glancing again at Mrs Underwood's steady, straightforward eyes and dependable face, she felt that the tale would at least be true.

'Then one evening William brought me forty pounds. With my approval he had lent fifty to a friend some time before, and he said he had been to the friend and had been repaid. I can't tell you my relief. I took Bee to Aberdeen and the doctor said there was every chance of a cure. I left her in his nursing home and came back full of hope.'

Mrs Underwood suddenly seemed to find it harder to go on. 'Then I had a dreadful shock. When I got home I found William in a terrible state. At first he would say nothing, but at last I got the truth out of him. Mrs Elton,' Julia could see her hands clenched behind her bag, 'I simply don't know how to go on. William admitted that his friend had not paid the debt. William—was in charge of some money in the office and—well, I needn't try to hedge—he had taken the forty pounds.'

She looked beseechingly at Julia, who murmured vaguely, finding she could not make a suitable comment. With an air of disappointment Mrs Underwood went on.

'I'm not trying to make excuses for him: he did wrong and there is no excuse. But in fairness I don't want you to think worse of him than the facts warrant. He did go to see his friend and the friend promised to pay him within a month. It was not a mere vague promise; he showed William papers to prove that he himself would be paid some outstanding debts. He was an honest man and William had no doubt that he would keep his word. William knew that the office money would not be missed until the half-yearly audit in June, so that he felt he was merely borrowing and would be able to pay it back in ample time. He also knew that the longer the operation was put off, the less likely it was to be successful. So it was for Bee's sake and mine that he did wrong.'

Again she paused and again hurried on. 'At the end of the month William went to his friend, only to learn that he was just about to declare his bankruptcy. The forty pounds William had been counting on was gone. Our misfortune didn't stop there. We probably could have paid before June, but it happened that there was an unexpected call for the money in the office and the whole thing came out. Mr Elton heard William's story and was not satisfied with it. He dismissed William. He said that owing to his long connection with the firm he would be lenient and that if William paid up the money by the first of next month he would drop the matter, otherwise he would prosecute for theft.'

Julia felt taken aback and some indignation against her husband rose in her mind. Of course he was justified in dismissing Underwood; she supposed that nine out of ten employers would have done the same. But it did seem a little hard to threaten the man with prosecution—after all those years and with such extenuating circumstances. But perhaps Richard hadn't believed the tale.

She didn't know what to say, and while she was considering Mrs Underwood went on: 'You can see now why I decided to make an appeal to you to intercede with Mr Elton for William. I can't think it's so bad, because all the office staff are on William's side. But of course I will understand if you turn me down. It isn't that we can't repay the money; we can, but not before the first: that's this day week, you know. All we ask is a little more time. Do you think, Mrs Elton, you could see your way to ask Mr Elton to grant us, say, another two months?'

'Could you do it in another two months?' Julia asked, and her voice was very gentle.

'I think so. I don't suppose William will ever get a job like his old one, but he'd make a good jobbing gardener. We'll give up our house of course and move to rooms. We're not grumbling and given time we could pay off the debt. But prosecution would be complete ruin for us all, particularly for Bee and Tom.'

Julia quickly made up her mind. 'I'll certainly speak to my husband,' she said, 'but it's only fair to tell you that I don't think he'll change his mind. He never by any chance discusses office affairs with me. You'll think it strange, but I didn't know till we met at Christmas that your husband was with the firm.'

Mrs Underwood looked at the same time grateful and disappointed. 'I can't thank you enough,' she said, 'for I feel that you'll do your best for us. To be candid I'm really frightened for William. He gets so excited. It's his shell-shock, you know. During the last week I've been terrified that he'll do himself an injury, and when he goes out I count the minutes till he comes back.'

'I'll do what I can,' Julia declared. What about your daughter? Is she still in Aberdeen?'

Mrs Underwood's glance was of warm gratitude. 'Yes, and the operation is over and the doctor thinks there's every prospect of a cure. You may wonder why under the circumstances we went on with it. It was because I had paid the fee for everything when I was there: operation, treatment and all. I couldn't have got it back even if I had wanted to.'

Julia kept her chatting for a few minutes, trying in her kindly way to help her by a show of quiet sympathy. And indeed this was not assumed. The more she saw of the woman, the more she felt she could like and trust her, and the more convinced that every word of her story was true.

When she had gone Julia sat on in the pleasant sunshine. The matter had now come to affect herself. She would have to make a request to Richard which her relations with Frank Cox would make hateful. Moreover in all probability Richard would not grant it, which would be unpleasant. Richard was just, but he was terribly hard. He made no allowance for the frailty of human nature: he forgave no mistakes. It was the way, she supposed, he had made his money, but if he had had less money and more heart their lives might have been very different.

Richard normally came home about six and until dinner was usually to be found in his library. That evening Julia decided to get her unpleasant job over as soon as possible, and shortly after she heard the car, she went to look for him.

He was reading the evening paper before the fire, but he got up when Julia entered and drew forward another armchair.

'This is an unexpected pleasure,' he remarked sardonically, and his voice was unexpectedly harsh and unpleasing. 'To what happy chance am I indebted for it?'

'I want to talk to you' Julia returned, sitting down, 'about something I would much rather not mention.'

'Then why mention it?'

'Because I've been asked to and because I think I ought. It's about Mr Underwood.' She paused uncertainly for a moment, then went on. 'You know, Richard. I have never interfered with your office or your business. I have recognized that it was yours and yours alone and that my comments on it would not have been welcomed.'

'A very proper sentiment: though I don't know how you could have acted otherwise, even had you wished to.'

'Well, this is an exceptional case. I want to make a request on this occasion, but I don't want you to think I'll repeat it.'

'Not a precedent, in fact?'

'No. It's this. Mrs Underwood called on me today, without the knowledge of her husband, and told me about his dismissal. She said they both recognized that you had had a perfect right to do what you did, and that they had no grievance against you. But—'

'Satisfactory to know that, I'm sure,' he broke in ironically.

'Neither is questioning the fairness of his treatment,' Julia repeated doggedly. 'They also can pay back what Mr Underwood took. But they can't do it in the time. They beg for an extension.'

'No doubt. And they show an admirable spirit by approaching my wife behind my back.'

'Mrs Underwood approached me because we met and liked each other at the charity fête last Christmas. Her husband knew nothing about it.'

'So she told you.'

Julia felt her temper rising, but she knew that if she failed to control it, she would defeat her own aim.

'Yes,' she said quietly, 'and if I hadn't believed her I wouldn't have mentioned it to you.'

He shrugged. 'When you've lived as long and learnt as much about human nature as I have, you'll be less confiding.'

'Apart from that, Richard, what do you propose to do about it?'

'Do? Why, what I said. What else is possible?'

'You might give them more time to pay.'

'But why should I? I've been most lenient. I put the man into a position of trust and he abuses my confidence. When my back is turned, so to speak, he robs me: steals the firm's money. Then when he's discovered he whines about it and wants to get off paying the price. Nine out of ten employers would have sent for the police then and there. I didn't do that. Against my better judgment I gave him an excellent chance.'

'I admit all that. I admit that you were just. I ask you to go further and be merciful.'

'But, Julia, you mustn't allow sentimentality to overthrow your common sense. If every employer did what you suggest, it would be the end of our civilization. Every employee would steal if he knew that by telling a hard luck story he could avoid the consequences. In any case it's not what one would or would not like, it's a question of one's duty. And one's duty to the community in a case like this is to prosecute.'

That was always the way with Richard,' she never could defeat him in argument, even when she felt satisfied that he was in the wrong. As always, there was a lot in what he said and even now she was doubtful if he were not right.

'Don't you ever believe in showing mercy?'

'I believe in cause and effect. If I stole myself and was caught, I should take my medicine without whining. Besides, he's not in the desperate position that you make out. You say he could pay if he were given more time?'

'Yes, that's what his wife said.'

'Then all he has to do is to pawn some of his belongings, and redeem them when his money comes in. No hardship in that.'

'They seem to be hard up; as if they hadn't much that was superfluous.'

'Then why is that? It's not my business, but a man in Underwood's position and with his salary should have been able to save.'

Julia felt that she had been a fool to open the question, as she had known what her husband's reaction would be. All the same she did not regret her action. She was convinced that the clerk had been innocent of any intention to defraud and she thought that this should have been taken into account. She wondered how she could help that nice woman.

As she went up to change for, dinner Julia felt a little bitter. It was no new thing to be slighted by her husband, but this had been a humiliation. No matter about the abstract justice of the case, he ought to have given in to her request. Despondently her thoughts dwelt on the incident.

4

The Clandestine Meeting

Julia had avoided all mention of Cox while discussing the affairs of Underwood with Richard before dinner, but at the meal she mentioned casually that she had met him in the Dorkford High Street and on the spur of the moment had asked him to dine. Richard made little comment, but his manner was so dry and sardonic that for a moment panic filled her mind. Then Jeff sailed in with a remark about the coming dance and the tension eased. Though the subject quickly dropped and Richard did not again refer to it, she remained a little shaken. Richard *could* not himself have suspected anything. Croome, however, was a different proposition. Croome knew something—unless his presence outside the Bellerophon was a pure accident—and if he were Richard's spy, presumably Richard knew it too.

As that night Julia lay thinking over the situation, she grew more and more anxious to do what Frank had suggested: to have done with secrecy and subterfuge, to put their case before Richard and to go away with Frank, with a divorce if possible, without it if Richard refused to co-operate.

The next day, Tuesday the 26th of March, passed without incident, but on Wednesday an event was to happen to which Julia had been looking forward with eagerness. Mollie had at last been called up and was coming home for a short holiday before joining her unit.

Mollie at this time was twenty-two and old for her years. She and Julia had always been good pals, and her absence from home had not, as might have been expected, forced them apart. Both looked forward to periods when they could be together, and Julia's loneliness had made her strain every nerve to maintain this sympathy and companionship.

Mollie's arrival on this occasion seemed to bring a breath of fresh life into the strained atmosphere of Chalfont. She was so natural and healthy-minded, so direct and uncompromising, so crystal clear in her attitude to life. Had Julia been told that she would come to lean on her daughter as on a stronger woman she would naturally have scouted the idea, but so it was.

Mollie arrived in time for tea, then to Julia's delight they settled down over the fire for a long chat. They discussed Mollie's work, her London life, her Canadian offer, and her start in the W.A.A.F. Presently the conversation turned to the coming dance.

'Richard's rather incomprehensible, isn't he?' Mollie remarked. 'If he wants to be conventional, one would have thought he'd have avoided a dance at present. First there's the war and next it's Lent.'

'I think this is really a business affair: there's a clientish flavour among the guests. Of course we're having a few locals, but most are from Town.'

'How many are coming?'

'Only a few: between thirty and forty, and of course it's to be very simply run.'

'Who are coming that I know?'

'The three Alinghams, the Pegrams, Margaret Crawford and Mr Cox to dinner: that'll make us twelve. Half a dozen local people are coming in afterwards: the Holts and the Martins and so on, but most are Richard's friends from Town.'

They discussed the guests and then Mollie made a remark which had unexpected consequences. 'I'm glad Mr Cox is coming,' she said with unaffected warmth. 'Now that's a man I like. He writes historical novels.'

Julia stared. 'How do you know that?'

'Jessie Milner met him in the British Museum: one of our staff, you know. She was looking up stuff for an article and they got talking. She asked me if I knew him because we both came from Dorkford. Didn't you know?'

'Know what?'

'That he wrote historical stuff.'

'Oh, yes,' Julia answered slowly. 'I knew.'

It was absurd to feel embarrassed before her own daughter, yet try as she would, Julia could not entirely hide the excitement the topic provoked. She longed to talk of Frank, but it would be dangerous. As it was, Mollie was glancing at her with disconcerting shrewdness.

Mollie lit a fresh cigarette, then said a little too casually, 'Do you know him well?'

For a moment Julia did not answer. She was suddenly seized by an overwhelming desire to unburden her mind to this young woman of the world. She turned away, fumbled with a cigarette, and murmured in a low voice, 'Yes. Very well.'

Mollie did not answer and Julia swung round to her again.

'I didn't intend to tell you, Mollie, but now I want to. Perhaps it would be better if you knew. Frank and I are— we've—we've fallen in love.'

Mollie gripped her hand. 'Oh, Mummie,' she cried, and it was not often she called her 'Mummie', usually she said 'Julia'; 'that's good news! I'm glad to hear it! When did it happen?'

'A little time ago. But is it good news, my dear? I can't make up my mind. At one time I'm just overwhelmed with delight, and at another I fear that it'll only bring suffering. I can't explain it.'

'There's nothing to explain: it's natural. And it is good news. You've had an awful time with Richard. You've been brave and you've never said anything, but I knew. It's just splendid that you've met someone that you can be fond of.'

'Richard never offered me love. He offered me security. He's given me everything he said he would. He has kept his bargain.'

'So have you kept yours. He wanted popularity and you did all you could to give it to him. It was his fault that you failed, not yours.'

Julia knew it was the truth. 'I did my best,' she agreed.

'Of course you did, and in any case you couldn't carry out a bargain of that kind indefinitely. No one could.'

These views were tremendously comforting. 'I thought I could do it,' Julia answered, 'but I found I wasn't so strong as I believed. I didn't mean to—get fond of Frank. It just happened.'

'And a good thing too. What are you going to do? Will Richard divorce you?'

'That's the whole point, Mollie,' and Julia went on to tell her story in detail. Mollie looked grave when she heard about Croome at the Bellerophon and laughed with glee about the Box Hill rendezvous.

'I think Frank Cox is dead right to want it settled one way or another,' she declared emphatically. 'But I'm not keen on

51

your meeting him secretly. I think he should come here openly and both of you beard Richard in his library.'

'We would do that if I finally decided to go away with Frank, divorce or no divorce.'

'You have, haven't you?'

'No, I can't make up my mind to that.'

'Well, you will. As I say, I don't see the need for a secret meeting, but since you're going to have it, I think your Friday evening idea excellent. Except perhaps for Perkins. Mightn't she see you leaving your room?'

'I thought I could avoid her.'

'A bit risky, I fancy. Look here. I can get her out of the way. I'll ring and want something done at their critical moment.'

'Oh, my dear, that would be splendid. I was rather afraid of Perkins.'

'Right, then we'll synchronize our watches and do it by time. It'll be a sort of game for me. I'll keep her engaged from seven-twenty-eight to seven-thirty-two, and from seven-forty-three to seven-forty-seven, and you slip out at seven-thirty and come back at seven-forty-five.'

They grinned like a pair of children, though to Julia the affair was no game. She felt immensely relieved by the arrangement. Presently Mollie changed the subject.

'How do you get on with Philip Harte?' she asked. 'Rather a queer fish, isn't he?'

'I don't take to him much, if you really ask me.'

'Nor I particularly. Always seems to have something on his mind.'

'He certainly is queer in some ways,' Julia smiled. 'He took an obvious fancy to you.'

'Did he? I'm afraid it won't get him very far.'

'And Jeff also: queer and unbalanced in the same way.'

'Ah, Jeff's different. Jeff's a good sort really, though you mightn't think it from his manner. I'm fond of Jeff.'

There was something in her tone which startled Julia.

'You don't mean—really?' she asked with a sudden tenseness.

'Yes, of course. If Jeff asked me to marry him, I'd probably do it.'

Here was another problem for Julia. Jeff was by no means the son-in-law she would have selected. Moreover, if she herself obtained a divorce, such a marriage would be an unfortunate complication. But she did not want to seem unsympathetic, particularly after Mollie's reaction to her own news.

'My dear,' she said, 'I had no idea. If you're fond of him and would like to marry him, then I'll hope you'll do so and be happy.'

Dinner that night was a pleasanter and less formal function than for a considerable time. Mollie's presence brightened everyone up. She chaffed Jeff and Harte, and was even smilingly pleasant to Richard. Afterwards for a wonder Richard remained in the lounge and there was bridge, Mollie and Jeff taking on Richard and Harte. Julia sat out on the plea of wanting to write letters.

During her talk with Mollie Julia thought she had settled her major problem. But as Wednesday night and Thursday dragged slowly away she realized that she had done nothing of the kind. Indeed she found herself more sharply divided than ever between duty and desire. She had made a bargain; could she break it and retain her self-respect?

Now she recognized a further complication: if she broke off the affair she would let Frank down. She should not have encouraged him if she had not intended to stick to him. Whichever course she took, she would wrong someone.

Through the long hours of that Thursday night she lay awake grappling with the problem, but on Friday morning, the morning of the fateful day, she realized that she had at last reached her decision.

Her first duty was to Richard. She could not let him down. A bargain was a bargain. He had kept his part: she would keep hers too. This idea of going off with Frank was infinitely alluring, but it would not be right. And because it would not be right, it would not give lasting happiness.

It would lead eventually to the misery of all three.

During the morning she told Mollie of her decision. As she had before obtained sympathy, she now feared opposition. To her surprise Mollie agreed with her.

'I would have urged you to do whatever you thought best yourself,' she declared, 'but since you feel like that, I believe you're doing the right thing. I'm afraid though that Frank will be hit pretty hard.'

'That's where I've been wrong,' Julia said sadly; 'letting things run on instead of making up my mind at once. Both Frank and I will have to suffer for that now.'

In the afternoon the guests began to arrive. The Pegrams came to tea and the Alinghams a couple of hours later. Both families had lived in Dorkford before moving up to Town, and both were staying the night. Mr Pegram was short and stout and dogmatic. His daughter—his wife had been dead for many years—was a quiet, colourless young woman with no apparent opinions of her own.

Sir John Alingham also expressed his views with force. He was tall and heavily built, with a massive head, large strongly marked features, a hooked nose like a vulture's beak, and an air of polished aggressiveness. In fact, he was a rising K.C. and looked it. His wife was a complete contrast in appearance, with a small trim figure, tiny features and a tight mouth. She did not say much, but to what she did say her husband listened with deference. Patricia Alingham, their daughter, concealed her thoughts, if she had any, by a smooth and effortless stream of self-evident clichés.

As the time approached for Julia to put Frank's scheme into operation, she grew increasingly nervous. She was not accustomed to carrying out secret enterprises, and what from a distance had seemed easy, became terrifying now that it was upon her. It was an effort to keep the conversational ball rolling, while time dragged interminably on. Fortunately Sir John and Mr Pegram had gone to the billiard room with Richard and Harte. That left only the three women, and Mollie was lending more than a hand. The two younger were easy to deal with, but Lady Alingham's eyes were sharp as needles and more than once Julia was aware of being the object of some extremely searching glances.

But everything comes to an end, and at last the clock in the hall began with appalling deliberation, first to chime, and then to deliver seven measured strokes. Julia listened for the gong. There was an interminable silence. What was Croome about? Didn't he recognize seven when he heard it? Then at last came the first sombre waves of sound, rising slowly to a crescendo that almost shook the house. Julia glanced at the clock. It was only one minute past the hour. She was suddenly in a panic lest her nerves should betray her.

Now how soon could she get away? It did not do to hurry in these matters. Some hanging about with more idiotic conversation was necessary before a move could be made. She bore it for four more minutes, then began tentative suggestions about dressing.

There! At last she was in her room, and with credit! She

had not hurried nor seemed impatient, though once again she had been conscious of Lady Alingham's scarcely veiled scrutiny.

She wished now she had never agreed to see Frank under these fantastic conditions. They could easily have met in the daytime—in Town or in half a hundred other places. Provided they had not chosen Croome's off day, they would have been perfectly safe, and it would have saved this nerve-racking ordeal. Once again it reflected Frank's extraordinary love of mystery and intrigue.

The plan had been foolish from every point of view. Now that she had decided to break with Frank, the interview would be distressing, and it would leave them both in a poor frame of mind for the evening's festivities. However, it was too late for regrets. Though she might let Frank down on the larger issue, she could not fail him at the rendezvous.

She quickly dressed, then put on a dark cloak and rubber boots, and very carefully, so as not to disarrange her hair, a dark felt hat. She had during the afternoon deliberately opened a frame of rare and valuable plants, so that if by some unlucky chance she were seen on her way out, she could say she was going to close it.

Waiting with her eye on her watch, her senses were keyed up, and through the heavy door of her room she heard a good deal of what went on without. The guests had gone to their rooms at the same time as she had, then Mollie had come up, then Harte and lastly Richard. Perkins on several occasions had passed along the corridor. She recognized their various steps.

At precisely twenty-eight minutes past, she heard a bell. Then came Perkins' steps again and a knock at a door. Silently Julia opened hers a fraction. She heard Mollie's voice: 'Oh Perkins, I'm in trouble. I've—' It died down into a murmur.

There was a higher-pitched reply from Perkins and the shutting of a door. Momentarily silence reigned.

Zero hour! Julia pulled her door open, slipped through and closed it softly behind her. The door to the back stairs and servants' quarters was close beside hers, and in a couple of seconds she had cut off all sight of the corridor and was silently descending. At the bottom of the stairs was the side entrance off the passage to the cellars, where at this hour no one was likely to be. Without making a sound she reached the outer door, and in another couple of seconds was out of the house. She breathed more freely. So far it had been easier than she could have hoped.

It was not absolutely dark. The sky was clear and some faint traces of daylight still remained. The light, indeed, was just right for Julia's purpose. She could see enough to avoid obstacles, but the chances of her being observed were negligible. She walked quickly across the grass of the terrace towards the summer-house. It stood in a separate area of the grounds, approached through an opening in a yew hedge.

At this opening Frank was standing. Instantly she sensed something wrong. He was bent crooked and she heard him gasping as if in pain.

'Frank!' she exclaimed softly, 'what is it? What's the matter?'

He held up his hand as if to stop her passing through. 'So sorry, Julia,' he answered, and his voice came unevenly, 'but I'm not well. A tropical disease. Had it for years, but thought I was cured. It's not really serious: only unpleasant for the moment.'

'Oh, Frank, I'm so sorry. Can I do anything? Will you come in and lie down?'

'My dear, it's just like you, but that would never do. No, all I want is my medicine; puts me right at once. But I'll have to go home for it immediately and I'm afraid we must postpone our talk.'

In spite of this new anxiety, a surge of relief swept over Julia. 'Of course,' she answered. 'But can you get home? Will you be all right?'

'Perfectly. The car's parked in the trees farther down. I'll be home in five minutes.'

'Then we shan't see you at dinner?'

'Oh yes, I expect I'll be back in time. If not, I'll phone. Relief when I get my medicine is almost instantaneous.'

'Then I mustn't keep you. Oh, Frank, I'm sorry, and I hope you'll be better.'

As she spoke they were moving slowly back across the grass. She wondered if she should give him a hint of her decision, then he was so obviously in pain that she felt she could not do so.

'You weren't seen coming out?' he asked, and his voice was almost like a groan.

'No. But it wouldn't matter so much if I had been. I left a valuable frame open so that I could come out to close it.'

'Good idea! Where is it?'

'Just there, near the hedge.'

He turned towards it. 'Better close it now,' he said. 'You'll have to do it yourself. I'm afraid I can't help you.'

'Of course I'll do it. But don't wait. Go quickly and get your medicine.'

'Five seconds more or less won't make any difference to me. I'd be happier if I knew you had got back to the house unseen.'

'My dear man,' she returned, 'who could see me?'

They reached the frame and he stood back while she softly closed it. Then he turned with her towards the house.

58

'This is out of your way,' she objected. 'You can get out quickest by that side gate.'

'Right,' he returned, 'but I'll see you in first.'

'What nonsense!' But in the dark her smile was very tender. All the same her protests were of no avail. Though bent and limping as if crippled with his pain, he insisted on accompanying her to the side door.

She closed the door and regained the back stairs unheard. Then just as she was about to emerge at the top, she remembered that she was too soon. At seven-forty-five the coast was to be clear, and it was now only seven-forty.

For a moment she was tempted to take the risk and return to her room. Then she thought the staircase was a safe hiding place and decided to remain where she was.

The next three minutes seemed an hour; then again she heard the bell, Perkins' answering steps, and very faintly the intonation of Mollie's voice. A door closed in the distance. Five seconds later Julia was in her room.

She was profoundly thankful that her little ordeal was over, and over so successfully. No one on earth save Frank and Mollie had any idea that she had been out. Quickly she obliterated the only possible trace of her adventure by washing and drying her boots, which had picked up a little clay from round the frame. Equally quickly she completed her dressing, so as to be down in the lounge before the second gong.

She was very much worried about Frank and his illness, not only on his own account, but because the evening's happenings were not going to make it any easier for her to carry out her decision. She felt that her silence was a tacit admission that her break was going to be with Richard, not Frank.

Another point also troubled her. When at last she did reveal her decision, would Frank imagine that his illness had weighed with her? Not for worlds would she have him think such a thing. But of course he wouldn't. He would know her better.

At five minutes to eight she swept into the lounge. Only Philip Harte was there. He got up as she entered.

'Some excitement tonight, Mrs Elton,' he said, with his crooked smile.

For a moment her heart leaped, then she saw that he was speaking of the dance. A mere idle greeting, and yet a prophetic utterance.

5

The Tragic Absence

Julia had scarcely achieved an adequate reply to Harte, when Sir John and Lady Alingham entered. Sir John, moving as if the house belonged to him, took up a dominant position on the hearthrug and glared round him preparatory to laying down the law on whatever subject should chance to be mentioned. His wife's manner laid no claim to the house, but did manage to suggest that had it been hers, it would be a vastly improved place.

'I was so glad to see Mollie looking so well,' she began sweetly, taking a chair close to Julia, and by a turn of the shoulder cutting off her husband's entry into the conversation as effectively as if she had closed a watertight door. 'And to hear she is going into the W.A.A.F.s. She'll enjoy it.'

'I hope she will,' Julia answered, while Sir John, shrugging slightly, engaged Harte with a leading question about his chemical work. He liked to consider himself as being all things to all men, and therefore made the mistake of tackling experts on their own ground.

As a source of information Harte proved disappointing. He

was not communicative as to his experiments, and more regrettable still, exhibited no sense of the honour done him by notice from so great a man.

'Mr Elton's doing a paper on ion exchanges, he answered casually, but with an indefinable suggestion that his tongue was not far from his cheek. 'He wants some figures got out for it.'

But Sir John was not going to be beaten. 'That surely is a very advanced branch of chemistry for a layman like Mr Elton to take up? I should have thought it was an expert's job?'

'Well, he's got the expert,' Harte grinned. 'But actually there's no chance of reading a paper unless it's about something that sounds advanced to the outsider.'

As he spoke Mollie entered, and Sir John seized the opportunity to make a dignified retreat. 'Ah, my dear young lady,' he greeted her, turning away from Harte, 'I hear you're joining the W.A.A.F.s in a few days? Splendid!'

'Yes,' put in Jeff, who had followed her, 'do her good, won't it? Nothing like a bit of discipline for a girl like Mollie, is there, Sir John?'

Jeff had come home later than the others and he now paid his respects to Lady Alingham.

They discussed Mollie's future until the entry of the Pegrams and Miss Alingham created another diversion. Regrouping had just taken place when Julia heard what she had been listening for so intently: a ring at the door. A little delay and Croome announced: 'Miss Crawford.' Choking down her sharp disappointment, Julia advanced to meet her.

'So glad you were able to come, Margaret,' she murmured. 'I think we're all old friends? You know Sir John and Lady Alingham, don't you?'

Miss Crawford knew everyone. Various greetings followed.

Julia glanced at the clock. It was now three minutes past eight. As she listened to a dreary account of domestic inefficiencies from Miss Pegram, her mind was occupied with Frank Cox. Had his medicine proved effective? Would he be able to come? She hoped her replies were intelligible. Fortunately Miss Pegram was not an exacting conversationalist.

Then at four minutes past there was another ring. Frank at last, thank heaven! In a moment Croome showed him in. Greetings gave her the opportunity for a searching glance at his face. He was looking better, was holding himself upright and seemed free from pain. But normal? No, he was certainly not normal. He was pale and though he was obviously trying to appear at ease, acute anxiety showed on his features.

'I'm afraid I'm late, Mrs, Elton,' he apologized, 'but through some oversight I had let my petrol down and I had to get some more. So sorry.'

'You're in heaps of time,' she assured him. 'Now let's see: I think you know everyone, don't you?'

It appeared that he knew Mr and Miss Pegram, but the Alinghams had left Dorkford before he had arrived. Introductions followed.

Again Julia glanced at the clock. It was now six minutes past eight. There was no need to hold up dinner any longer.

At that moment the door opened and Croome appeared. But instead of his usual measured 'Dinner is served, sir,' he glanced round the room, hesitated, and then mysteriously withdrew.

At the same moment Julia realized that Richard had not yet joined them. She wondered how she could have missed the fact and chid herself for too complete immersion in her own affairs.

At ten minutes past Croome again entered. He moved across the room to Julia.

'I can't find Mr Elton, madam,' he said in a low tone. 'Do you wish to wait for him or proceed with dinner?'

Julia thought rapidly. 'We'll go on with dinner.' She turned to the others and raised her voice.

'I'm so sorry, but Richard has been detained. He'll turn up as soon as he can, but we won't wait for him.'

As she spoke Croome had retreated to the door. This he now threw open and stood before it like a priest before his altar. His 'Dinner is served, madam,' reminded Julia of the striking of Big Ben.

They filed into the dining-room. Soon all were seated and the meal began.

When quarter-past eight showed on the clock on the chimney-piece, the first little flicker of alarm entered Julia's mind. Richard was a man of meticulous accuracy in most things, and time was no exception. He was punctual and he was reliable. If he were absent now, it was because he was unable to be present. What could have happened to him?

While keeping the ball of conversation going between Sir John and Mr Pegram, seated respectively on her right and left, her mind remained occupied with the problem. Presently a distressing thought occurred to her.

Could it be that Richard had discovered about Frank, and wishing to humiliate her, had selected this occasion to leave her? For a moment it seemed likely, but on further thought she became sure she was mistaken. He would not insult his guests if he intended to remain in the district, and his practice was too profitable to give up. No, whatever the cause, it was not that.

Twenty minutes past! Croome had been round with the

wine and was just removing the soup plates. Julia beckoned to him.

'Ask Mr Harte to speak to me for a moment.'

Harte looked surprised, but excused himself to his neighbour and came round the table.

'Mr Harte, I wonder if you'd do me a favour?' Julia said in a low voice.

'Of course, Mrs Elton.'

Pegram had paused in a remark to Sir John, but now he tactfully resumed the conversation.

'It has occurred to me,' Julia continued, 'that perhaps Mr Elton may have gone to the lab and been overcome with some fumes. I'd be grateful if you'd see. If he's not there, perhaps you'd ring up Hawthorne and tell him to look for him.'

'A pleasure.' Harte disappeared quietly and Julia tried to interest herself in the latest by-election, which her two neighbours were discussing.

In spite of her efforts, nobly supported by all present, dinner dragged. Jeff made a surprisingly good host, courteous and deferential to the ladies on his right and left, and when the conversation showed signs of collapse, throwing in a remark which galvanized it again into some sort of life, Mollie also was indefatigable. Only Frank was failing to pull his weight. He was absent, almost moody, and seemed to be fighting some distressing worry. He was opposite Lady Alingham and Julia felt grimly that his every movement and hesitation was being recorded in that lady's acute brain. Over all Croome presided, grave and portentous, yet looking to Julia as if he also was burdened with some secret fear.

Half-past eight. Quarter to nine. No sign came from without. Harte had disappeared as completely as Richard. His absence made Julia almost sick with apprehension. Something terrible must have happened. She found it more and more difficult to carry on.

At last the meal was finished, and the blessed moment came when the ladies could retire to the lounge. Croome was waiting in the hall as they streamed across it. He moved up to Julia.

'Mr Harte would like to see you and Mr Jeff in the library, madam.'

After a glance at his face, no longer professionally composed, but working with emotion, Julia nodded.

'Pour out coffee, Mollie,' she said casually. 'I'll follow you in a moment.'

'What is it?' she breathed tensely as the lounge door swung to behind the others.

Croome looked starkly terrified. His cheeks were grey and his lips quivered. He shook his head.

'It's Mr Elton, madam. I'm afraid he's—he's—' His voice trailed off.

'Tell me,' she said in low but sharp tones, 'has he met with an accident?'

Croome nodded. He seemed unable to speak. Then at last he whispered, 'He's—he's—*dead*!' He pointed to the library. 'Mr Harte knows. I must tell Mr Jeff.'

Julia felt stunned. Mechanically she turned and blindly walked on to the library.

Harte was standing in the middle of the room. He also seemed very much upset. His face was pale and she noticed that his hands were tightly clasped. But he had not lost his self-control.

'I see you know,' he said after a glance at her face.

She stood facing him, striving for composure. 'Croome told me. But no details.'

Harte did not seem to find it easy to give them. He hesitated, made two false starts, and then answered.

'We found him, Hawthorne and I. I had searched the lab and Croome the house. He wasn't in either. I rang up Hawthorne and we went out through the grounds. We've just found him.' Again he paused. 'Nothing can be done.'

'What had happened?' Julia's mouth was dry. She had a curious feeling that she was not taking part in the scene, but was merely watching it from a distance.

'He had hurt his head. We couldn't see exactly how it had been caused.'

'What did you do?'

'Nothing yet. I've only just got back to the house. Croome was going for you when you left the dining-room.'

The door opened again and Jeff entered. He also looked white and shaken.

'Croome has told me,' he said. 'Are you sure, Harte, we can't do anything?'

'Absolutely, I'm sorry to say.'

'Have you sent for the doctor?'

'Yes, I rang up for Dr Winn first thing.'

Jeff nodded, then turned to Julia. 'I think you ought to go up to your room, Julia,' he said with a note of authority in his voice which she had not heard before. 'I'll send Mollie up to you, and then Harte and I will do what is necessary.'

'I want to know details.'

'So you will directly we find them out. Do go. Staying here will only be unnecessarily painful for you and you can do no good.'

67

'No, not till I hear.' She looked at Harte. 'Tell me—all you know.'

For a moment he seemed too much moved to speak. Then he overcame his weakness.

'It's better that she should know now,' he said, glancing at Jeff; 'she must hear it before long in any case. You must prepare yourself for a shock, Mrs Elton. Mr Elton's head was injured. It couldn't have been an accident and—he couldn't— have done it himself.'

Julia scarcely heard Jeff's exclamation as the full implications of this beat upon her brain. She stood as if transformed to stone. Murder! Richard murdered! Oh no, it was not possible!

With all her will-power she fought for composure. 'And where,' she went on presently in a low, hesitating voice, 'did you find him?'

'Just beside the summer-house.'

Her heart suddenly stood still. She sat down in the nearest chair.

'I feel a little faint,' she muttered.

Jeff sprang to a side table. In five seconds he was holding a stiff brandy and soda to her lips. She gulped it down thankfully.

Beside the summer-house! No, she must not think of that. She *must not* think of it: not at present.

'Sorry for being so stupid,' she said a little tremulously, 'but it's been a shock. I'll do what you say, Jeff. I'll go upstairs.'

'Let me see you to your room.' Jeff was kind but pertinacious. He gave her an arm upstairs and sent Perkins hurrying for Mollie.

'I'll come up and tell you everything just as soon as possible,' he assured her, and with a friendly pressure on her arm he was gone.

Left alone, panic such as she had never known in all her experience surged up in Julia's mind. Beside the summer-house! She seemed to see Frank, upset, breathless and utterly unlike himself, standing at the opening in the yew hedge. He was barring her way in: subconsciously she had noticed it. Not that she had tried to push past him. But he *was* there, blocking up the opening. Why?

And then his refusal to leave till she was inside the house! Why had he insisted on that? So unnecessary; so inconvenient to him when he had so little time in which to go home for his medicine.

Oh no! She must not think these evil, wicked thoughts! Dear Frank, so kind and good! Frank, who wouldn't willingly hurt a fly! What madness had overtaken her? Not willingly hurt anyone: no. But his temper! His sudden bursts of furious rage, over in a moment no doubt, but terrible while they lasted. What might not happen during a burst of temper?

She shivered, fighting against the dreadful thought. In spite of her efforts, other facts came crowding into her mind. At dinner he had been so unlike himself. She had supposed it was the illness, but now she saw that it was mental worry, not physical weakness, that had ailed him. To what was this worry due?

And the illness! How was it that she had never heard of it before? And what sort of illness would affect him as he had been affected, and would be instantly cured by taking medicine?

For a moment Julia felt that all she wanted was to be dead like Richard, then a warm feeling of comfort took possession of her mind. Frank was the soul of honour. Whatever he might be betrayed into by his ungovernable temper, he would not lie. Above all, he would not lie to her. He would not make statements about illness unless they were true.

What a relief this thought was! She hugged it to her and tried to make the most of it. Yet the tiny cloud of poisonous doubt remained.

So sunk was she in these thoughts, that she scarcely noticed the opening of the door and Mollie's entrance. Then she felt her daughter's arms about her, and her voice vibrant with sympathy, saying, 'Mummie, dear.'

'Oh, my dear,' Julia answered, 'I've been so weak: letting it knock me out like this. Give me a few moments and I'll be all right. I must go back and speak to everyone.'

'You'll do nothing of the kind,' Mollie answered. 'Jeff has told them and is making all the arrangements. You're going to stay here. We can talk or you can lie down: whatever you like.'

'Dear child, you're so good. I would give anything not to have to see them again.'

Julia indeed longed to be alone. Mollie was the clearest of daughters and her sympathy was like balm, but at the moment Julia was desperately afraid of her. If they talked, as of course they would, she might reveal some hint of her fears. Not even Mollie must suspect those: and Mollie was terribly sharp.

'Go down, darling,' she urged. 'Go and talk to those wretched people. Probably under the circumstances they'll want to go home tonight. Get them away if you can. And Jeff will want your help in putting off the others. Do go. I'm perfectly all right. I'll just lie down for a little and then I'll come down.'

Mollie was unwilling, but presently went. Julia mechanically stirred her fire, and throwing a dressing-gown round her, lay down on a couch. From below nothing could be heard: a deep silence reigned in the house.

She remained sunk in a stupor, unconscious of the passage

of time till sounds below recalled her to the present. There was a ring at the door, the rattle of its being opened, then heavy steps and the muttering of deep voices in the hall.

For a moment she wondered what was happening, then suddenly she knew. Police! Those heavy steps and deep voices were not the doctor. Police were in the house: in charge. She ought to have foreseen it, but she had not. Of course the police would come. And what would that mean? She caught her breath sharply. For a time they would examine things outside, but presently they would begin to ask questions. They would ask her questions. What was she to answer?

Julia was again near to panic as she considered the prospect. What about the meeting with Frank: was she to tell about that? Was she to admit that he, and she herself, were close to the summer-house at about—she shuddered as she realized the point—at about the tragic time? She had heard Richard going to his room at about ten minutes past seven, and he failed to appear in the lounge at eight. Therefore it must have happened between these hours. But it was between these hours, at seven-thirty, that she and Frank had met. A clandestine interview with her lover, to be kept at all costs from her husband! How would that look to the police?

First it seemed to her that their meeting must be kept secret, then she saw that this was not necessarily true. It depended on what Frank said. One thing at least was clear. At all costs, her statement must coincide with Frank's. It would be better if the police knew nothing of what had happened, but it would be infinitely better that they should be told the truth, than that her testimony and his should differ. That would mean disaster, complete and unrelieved. What construction could be put on it—but the one?

It therefore became urgently necessary to find out from

Frank what he was going to do. And Mollie! Mollie must also know what to say. Bitterly Julia now regretted her confidence to Mollie. Oh, if she had only kept her own council!

However, now she must act, and at once. She got up, and with a glance in the glass, went downstairs.

The whole party, with the exception of Jeff, was in the lounge. She glanced round, forcing herself to look at Frank in the same casual way as at the others. Sir John, on the hearthrug with his back to the fire, was evidently declaiming on some point. He stopped like a shot on seeing Julia and looked slightly confused, in as far as Sir John could look confused. Then he rallied himself and bowed.

'It is good and brave of you to come down, Mrs Elton,' he said, and there was both kindness and respect in his tones. 'We were just discussing how we could give you the minimum of annoyance. Seeing that you have Jeffrey to look after things for you, we should all have gone home, but unfortunately the police have asked us to wait until they can take our statements.'

'Of course I understand, Sir John,' Julia answered. 'It's kind of you all. But you mustn't think of going: though I'm afraid that staying under the circumstances won't be very pleasant for you.'

'Thank you, Mrs Elton,' said Mr Pegram. 'We appreciate your action, but we have no option. The question of what you would like us to do, or what we would like to do ourselves, unfortunately does not arise. We all have to obey an order.'

'Does that order apply to those living in Dorkford? What about you, Margaret, and you, Mr Cox?'

'I'm afraid it applies to us also,' Frank answered. 'They said no one was to go. But they also said that they wouldn't keep us long.'

'They're within their rights,' Sir John pronounced. 'And

indeed my experience of the police is that they do try not to give more inconvenience than they need.'

'I think probably we'd like some drinks,' said Julia. 'Mollie, perhaps you wouldn't mind getting them? Croome's probably busy.'

'Let me help.' Harte sprang up and opened the door. He was still looking pale and anxious. They both went out, obviously glad of something to do.

As the desultory chatting continued, something like despair was growing up in Julia's heart. How in this gathering, with the eyes of all on her every movement, could she speak privately to Frank? She could not call him aside. Any suggestion of intimacy or of secrets between them would be another form of the disaster she feared. Nor could she think of any veiled way in which to put her question, which he alone would understand. Then despair sharpened her wits. Harte's lucky desire to help Mollie had made a rather poor scheme possible. She glanced at the small table near the fire.

'I think we'll have this other table over for the drinks,' she said, moving to a corner; 'that one is not very secure. Perhaps, Mr Cox, you'd carry it across?'

Frank, murmuring a polite 'With pleasure', followed her across the room.

'Thank you.' As she stooped to lift off a vase of flowers she added in a low, clear whisper, 'Do we tell?'

He stooped in his turn to lift the table. 'It's quite light,' he remarked in normal tones, then added, also in the faintest whisper, 'No. Say nothing.'

She waited till Mollie had ushered in Harte, carrying a tray, then went on: 'I think I'll ask you to excuse me. I want to go and lie down. Mollie, would you mind telling Croome about the morning?'

There was no one in the hall and Julia instantly seized the opportunity. 'Not a word about my meeting Frank,' she breathed. 'Not a word to *anyone.*'

Mollie nodded. 'Of course not. I understood that,' she whispered in reply and squeezed Julia's hand. 'I'm coming up to see you presently.'

Julia had done what was necessary, but when she reached her room her knees were trembling so that she could just totter to a chair.

6

The Disquieting Sequel

For a time Julia's brain seemed to have gone numb. She sat motionless before her fire, conscious only of horror at what had taken place and fear of what was yet to come. It was only when Mollie came in a little later that she recalled herself to the present. Mollie threw her arms round her.

'You poor dear,' she said softly. 'How ghastly for you! From every point of view!'

Julia rallied herself. 'It won't be so bad,' she declared, thinking of the one thing only. 'It's not like having to invent a story and build up its detail. I simply tell the truth. I went to my room a few minutes after seven, dressed, and came down just before eight. Every word of that is true.'

'Ye-es.'

'There's nothing to suggest that it's not the whole truth, nothing to raise the slightest suspicion.'

'No. That's right, of course there isn't. But it's desperately worrying for you all the same.'

'That's a small part of it. Tell me, Mollie, what's going on. That really is worrying: to be in the dark.'

'I'm afraid I don't know. They're all in the library, I think, but I've no idea what they're doing.'

'I must find out. It's unbearable to feel that things which may affect my whole life are happening in my own house, and I don't know anything about them.'

'Jeff's been arranging everything.'

'Then go and ask Jeff if he'd come up and speak to me. Do, like a dear.'

'Of course I will.'

Mollie vanished and presently there was a knock at the door and Jeff's voice.

'I'm sorry to bother you,' Julia explained when he was seated at the other side of the fire, 'but I feel I must know what's going on. You realize that I've heard *nothing*, except just that word in the library.'

He was still pale and anxious-looking. 'I'm terribly sorry, Julia; I should have come up to see you. But there have been a good many things to see to, and I just went ahead with them. Of course you must know everything. But I'm afraid you'll find it rather distressing.'

'Never mind that; I'd rather know. Just tell me the facts.'

'I'll do so as fully as I can. And may I say,' he hesitated, 'how tremendously we all sympathize with you.'

'Thank you, Jeff, you're very good.'

He shook his head in silent protest, then went on, speaking in a low, troubled tone. 'I went out with Harte to see—him, and I realized we must have the police as well as the doctor. They came and Dr Winn said that—it was what we had feared. They all discussed it, and here's something that I'm afraid will hurt you, they've decided that there must be a post-mortem.'

'Oh, Jeff, is that really necessary?'

'I'm afraid it is. It's always carried out under these circumstances. But it's not so bad. It doesn't—disfigure in any way.'

'I know. We can't help it. Go on, please.'

'There'll also have to be an inquest: I expect you've guessed that. The law requires it and we can do nothing about it.'

She nodded. 'I guessed.'

'Dr Winn wants to see you before he goes home. Inspector Dagg and a couple of men are in the library. They're taking statements. They've taken mine and they're taking Croome's now. They asked me to find out when you could let them have yours.'

'Any time—I don't mind. But, Jeff, I'd like to—see him. Where is he?'

'They brought him in to the couch in the morning room. It's a matter for yourself, of course, but, Julia, I do very strongly urge you to wait till after the post-mortem.'

'You, mean,' Julia's voice had sunk to a whisper, 'that he's—disfigured?'

'I'm afraid a little. But that will all be put right in a short time. Do wait.'

She considered. 'Very well, if you think so. Then I'll go down to the library when the police want me.'

'You wouldn't rather the inspector came up here?'

'I'd rather go down.'

Jeff rose. 'Then I'll tell them. And when they're ready I'll come up for you.'

As he left the room Julia felt she had done well. She had shown just the right amount of concern: not too much, for he must have known of her relations with Richard; not too little, for he was ignorant of Frank. She was not callous as she thought of this. It was just that if she were not careful, Frank might be in danger.

Suddenly an idea flashed into her mind. Underwood! She

had completely forgotten about the assistant clerk with his grievance against Richard; a grievance which would normally have come to a head on the following Monday.

A rising excitement took possession of her mind as this new vista opened to her thoughts. Underwood, expecting prosecution if by Monday he had not paid his debt. Underwood, his self-control weakened from shell-shock, and believing that Richard, and Richard alone, wished to take proceedings. Could it be?

Then doubt once more asserted itself. If this were so, what about Frank's manner? Why should he have been so upset?

The illness? It was with a shock that she found herself thinking that perhaps the illness was genuine after all. So far had she come to doubt Frank.

Presently she saw another and a more likely solution, and once again she grew happier. Suppose Underwood really had done it, and suppose Frank had found the body? Would not this account for everything?

She thought it would except for one point. Why in this case had he not told her what he had found? Why deny the fact which must so soon become known?

As she was pondering this point, another struck her. Should she tell the police about Underwood?

Here was another ghastly question; and *urgent*. She might be called at any moment to the study, and before she reached it she must have made up her mind. There must be no hesitations during that interview.

Once again she was not far from panic. This problem was almost as pressing as her own. She did not want to tell. She loathed the idea of suggesting suspicion against the clerk. She hated to think of his possible arrest and the dreadful trouble it would be for that nice woman.

But if suspicion should fall on Frank? How could she bear that? For in spite of herself, hideous doubt was still in her mind.

Choking down her fear, she forced herself to think. What did she know about Underwood at first hand? Nothing. She only knew what his wife and what Richard had said. And she had more than once heard Richard say that the report of a conversation was not evidence. Even granting that all they had told her were true, what did that prove? Nothing! What right had she to suggest that Underwood might be a murderer? She had no evidence for it whatever. Indeed, she now saw that if she were to mention such a thing, it might look as if it was to direct attention away from someone else.

Then she remembered another precept of Richard's. Witnesses, he had said, should answer what they are asked, and not volunteer information. Surely this should be her policy. If the police asked had Mrs Underwood called, she must admit it, otherwise the matter need not be mentioned. And should she afterwards be accused of keeping back essential evidence, she would plead Richard's dictum.

Just in time did she reach this decision. There was a knock and Jeff put in his head.

'Dr Winn would like to see you now, if you can receive him.'

Winn was elderly, with a sympathetic manner which seemed to come from something more than mere professional technique. Julia knew him slightly, and liked what she knew. He advanced slowly, peering before him as if his eyes were not strong enough for the light.

'I'm sorry to intrude on you like this, Mrs Elton,' he said in a surprisingly deep, full voice. 'I wondered if you were all right; if there was anything I could do for you? I needn't say how terribly sorry I am for what has happened.'

'That *is* kind of you, Dr Winn,' Julia answered gratefully. 'I feel all right. It's been a shock of course, but I'm afraid you can't help that.'

'Unhappily, no. But I was thinking of the night. What I had in mind was a mild draught in case you don't sleep.'

'Well, I should be grateful for that. Of course, I shouldn't take it unless it was necessary.'

'Then I'll let you have it as soon as possible. Is that all I can do?'

'All,' she said, 'except to tell me—about Richard. I know nothing in detail.'

He seemed to stiffen slightly. 'I'm afraid I can't tell you very much,' he answered slowly, 'except one thing: Mr Elton did not suffer at all. He received a blow on the head, and he—er—died instantaneously.'

'I suppose it's true—that it couldn't have been an accident?'

'Unhappily it is.' His voice was now sympathetic in the extreme.

'It's—incredible! Who could have done such a thing?'

He shook his head. 'I should have said it was incredible too. By the way, you'll find Dagg, that's the police inspector, a very decent fellow. He'll not trouble you more than he can help.'

'Everyone is being so kind.'

He got up. 'Well, I must run. I have several things to attend to. Then I'll send the sleeping draught, and if there's anything else I can do, don't hesitate to let me know. Now Inspector Dagg's waiting to ask you a few purely formal questions.'

Julia followed him downstairs, reassured partly by those words 'purely formal', but principally because her mind was now clear on every point as to her evidence. Winn opened the library door and she passed in. The door closed behind her.

The Inspector and a sergeant were seated at Richard's large, flat-topped desk, the inspector in Richard's chair, the sergeant at the end. Both had notebooks before them. As Julia entered both stood up.

'I'm sorry, Mrs Elton,' Dagg began, 'to have to trouble you in this way. You'll understand it's not my wish, but my duty. I'll promise to be as quick as I can. Will you please sit down?' He indicated an armchair drawn up to the fire.

He was a decent-looking man, Julia thought. Elderly, clean shaven and with grizzled hair, his eyes were straightforward if shrewd, and his expression kindly if not absolutely sympathetic; The sergeant was more of the regulation type: a big man with a rather stern expression and an official air.

'Thank you,' said Julia as she sat down. 'I quite understand. Naturally I'll help you in every way I can.'

Inspector Dagg bowed. 'Then the sooner I start, the sooner I'll be done.' He asked her full name, how long she had been married, and very briefly a few of the outstanding events of her life, while the sergeant noted her replies. Then he came to the immediate past. 'When, madam, did you last see Mr Elton?'

She did not answer too quickly. She wanted a moment to think over an awkward question, should such be asked, and it occurred to her that an invariable short delay would screen this. Besides, she wished to consider every answer.

'I last saw him to speak to in the lounge a little after six this evening,' she said. 'He went out of the lounge then with Sir John Alingham and Mr Pegram. I understood they were going to the billiard room. But I heard him after that, though I didn't see him.'

'When was that, madam?'

'Just after I had gone up to my room to dress. He passed along the corridor outside my door and went into his room.'

'How did you know it was he?'

'By his step: I could not be mistaken.'

'About what time was that?'

'About eight or ten minutes past seven. The dressing-gong goes at seven, and our guests and I went up about five minutes later. It was just after that that I heard him.'

'Thank you. In what frame of mind was Mr Elton? I mean, was he depressed or excited or absent-minded, or in any way other than normal?'

'He was normal; at least, I noticed nothing unusual.'

Inspector Dagg lowered his voice. 'Now, Mrs Elton, you are aware of what happened. Do you know of any enemies Mr Elton may have had?'

She shook her head. 'None.'

'No one who had a grievance against him; or thought he had? No one who had any reason to dislike him?'

It was sailing rather near the wind, but after due reflection she answered, 'No one,' without change of tone.

'What do you think Mr Elton went out to the garden at that hour for?'

This question came as a shock. She had been thinking so exclusively of her own part in the affair that she had missed the point. What *could* have brought him out? Surely he could not have known?

This would not do. She must answer at once. The inspector was already looking at her more keenly.

'I've no idea,' she replied; then in the hope of explaining her pause added, 'I never thought of it till now, but of course there must have been some reason.'

He seemed satisfied. 'Was he in the habit of going out into the grounds at night?'

'No, I don't think I've ever known him to do it. He would

go sometimes to his laboratory, which is in the shrubbery, but never to the garden: at least not to my knowledge.'

'Quite so. Was Mr Elton in the habit of discussing his business affairs with you?'

'No. He was very careful about that. He considered his clients' affairs were professional secrets and he never spoke of them even to me.'

'Thank you, Mrs Elton. I'm obliged for all that. I shall probably want to ask some further questions later on, but that's all at present.' He got up to indicate that the interview was over.

But Julia did not move. 'There are a couple of questions I should like to ask you while I'm here,' she declared. 'The first is,' and she made a suitable hesitation, 'when can I see—my husband?'

'Any time that you wish to, of course, madam. It's not my business of course, but I suggest that you would be well advised to wait till after the inquest.'

'But why?'

Dagg hesitated. 'Well, you see, madam, traces of the injury are still to be seen. The doctor's going to remove them, and you would perhaps have a happier remembrance if you waited till it was done.'

She appreciated his kindness and said so. 'When will the inquest be held?' she went on.

'Tomorrow, but the exact time is not yet settled. The body will be taken now to the mortuary, and after the inquest it was our intention to bring it back until the funeral. But that's only if you prefer it. It can wait at the mortuary and you can see it there if you'd rather.'

'No; what you suggested is better. Bring him back here after the inquest. Mr Jeff Elton advised me just as you have done. I'll take your advice and wait. Just one other question: When may my guests go home?'

'Just as soon as I can get their statements. I should like Miss—Miss Mollie's—Miss Langley's, isn't it?—and then I'll take the others' at once.'

It was with a vastly easier mind that, after hearing the statement read and signing it, Julia returned to her room. It had not been so bad, in fact, it had not been bad at all. She had been asked no awkward questions, and it was obvious that the inspector had no suspicion that she had done more during the evening than she had told him. Of course the danger was not over, but it had certainly receded.

Only one point brought up worried her: Richard's motive for going to the summer-house. At first sight it certainly did look as if he must have known of the meeting. What else would account for it?

Then she saw that this was utterly impossible. No one knew, except Frank and herself.

Suppose, she thought, Underwood were guilty. Could he have inveigled Richard out to meet him there?

It was obviously possible. But was it not too remarkable a coincidence that he should have chosen the very place and time of her meeting with Frank? She did not know what to think. The whole affair was dreadfully unsettling.

She longed beyond anything to see Frank in private. A word or two with him would, she felt, dispel all her doubts. He was sure to have a solution for all these distressing conundrums. Unhappily this was the one thing of all others which she must avoid. She had read that everyone connected with a murder case was watched by the police. Such a meeting might arouse disastrous suspicions.

After a few minutes Mollie appeared.

'I've just made my statement,' she explained. 'It was nothing of an ordeal. I always thought police enquiries were dreadful.'

'They haven't finished with us.'

'Had you any difficulty?'

'None.'

'They've sent for Margaret Crawford. Then they're going to take Frank Cox, so that those two may go home. It's so late the others have decided to stay the night.'

'I ought to say good night to them.'

'Nothing of the kind. They won't expect it. Jeff's doing all that. You get to bed. Better have some hot milk, or something to make you sleep.'

'We'll both have some. Bring it up, Mollie, and heat it here.'

They had their milk and Mollie went off to bed. Julia did not require her draught. She slept like a log, awaking only when Perkins arrived next morning with her tea.

She breakfasted with Mollie in her room, remaining there till the Alinghams and Pegrams had gone. Then she saw Jeff. It appeared that the inquest was to be in a hall in Dorkford at three that day. He had to go, but she need not unless she wished to. He understood that the proceedings would be only formal and that there would be an adjournment.

Julia said she thought she ought to go. Really she felt that she must know at first hand what was going on.

This morning the first shock of the affair had passed, and she was able to look at things more calmly. She felt deeply for Richard, and yet she could not pretend to herself that his death did not solve her personal problem. Now she was free: free after a suitable interval to marry Frank. No need to leave Dorkford; no loss of their friends; no reason for Frank to give up his writing; no grinding poverty to kill their love. Thinking

85

of all this, she could not keep back a growing feeling of relief and joy.

Or rather this feeling would have grown, had it not been for the distressing matters of her meeting with Frank and his strange illness: Here was something dangerous; something that might easily wreck all their happiness; something that might turn out inconceivably ghastly.

Once again she felt that at all costs she must see Frank and have her doubts laid to rest. But how could she do it with safety?

Distractedly she puzzled over the problem, and then she thought of Mollie. Mollie knew part of their secret: was there any reason why she should not know it all? If she received Frank in Mollie's presence, no suspicion would be aroused.

But would this be fair to Mollie? Just that bit of extra knowledge might make a vast difference to her if police inquiries grew embarrassing.

She had reached this point in her cogitations when Mollie came in.

'Thank goodness those people have gone,' she remarked. 'They did their best to be helpful and all that, but really they were ghastly! Well, Mummie, all this will solve your problem for you. I suppose you've thought of that?'

'My dear, I've thought of little else. But it's not so simple as it looks. Suppose they discover that I met Frank last night.'

'What if they do?'

'At the very place Richard was found, and about the time— it must have happened.'

'But it hadn't happened when you met.'

'But that's just what I'm so worried about. I don't know.'

Mollie stared. 'Don't know! But weren't you at the summer-house?'

86

The reply appalled Julia. She had not intended to convey any information, but unconsciously she had done so. Mollie's curiosity had been aroused: what if it had been Dagg's? It showed how terribly easy it was to make a slip. One incautious word and the entire affair might be given away.

For a moment Julia did not know what to say. Then she saw that to retain Mollie's sympathy she must tell her everything. She turned to her and instinctively lowered her voice.

'I've not told you what happened, but I will now. When I got out to the gap in the hedge, Frank was there,' and she recounted the story in detail, though of course without mentioning the doubts which had so worried her.

Mollie looked grave. 'Frank had found him,' she said slowly, 'that's surely clear. He didn't want you to have the shock of seeing him. That illness was just to prevent you asking questions.'

Her assurance was a relief to Julia. 'That's what I thought,' she said eagerly, 'then I wondered why, if so, he didn't say so instead of making all that pretence.'

'I don't know, but I'll bet he had a good reason. You've had no chance to ask him since, of course?'

'No, but I must manage it somehow.' For a moment she paused, then thinking she would never have a better opportunity, she plunged. 'I could do it with your help, Mollie, but I hesitated to ask you in case I might involve you in something unpleasant.'

'Why, Mummie, what nonsense! How can I help?'

'Just that I daren't see Frank alone. It would be too dangerous. But if you were present and were known to be present, it would make all the difference.'

'But of course, darling. Only it won't be very pleasant for you and Frank.'

'It might mean our safety.'

'Oh, all right. Then what do I do? Ring up Frank and ask him to call?'

'I think so. But not from here. Croome might be listening. You'd have to go out to a call box.'

'I'll do that. There's no difficulty about his reason for coming. It's to enquire for you—natural under the circumstances. He could say to Croome that he presumes you are not seeing anyone, and ask for me. I could then tell Croome that we're both together and to bring Frank in.'

'Yes, I think that would do. When would be the best time?'

'The sooner the better. Suppose I slip out now and ask him to call this morning, say about twelve: simply a formal inquiry, not to see either of us. But I'll be on the watch and invite him in. How about that?'

Julia thought it was an idea. Ten minutes later Mollie was speaking to Frank, who luckily had answered the telephone in person. He willingly agreed to carry out the plan.

7

The Threatened Exposure

From one of the bathroom windows Mollie could see the drive and a little before twelve she went up and began her watch. Already the household was falling back into its normal routine. The office was officially closed, but Jeff had gone in to see if there were any urgent letters. Harte was in the laboratory, where, he had explained, some tidying up was desirable. Croome and the maids were going about their usual tasks.

Presently Frank's car appeared, and circling to the door, stopped. Frank got out and the bell sounded. Stealthily Mollie opened the bathroom door and listened to Croome's feline tread crossing the hall. As the hall door opened she was going downstairs. She heard the voices and went over.

'Good morning, Miss Langley,' Frank said when he saw her. 'I just called to enquire for you and Mrs Elton. I hope she's not too exhausted.'

'How kind of you! She's wonderfully well, but naturally rather overwrought. She had a reasonably good night.'

'I'm glad to hear that. Will you give her my sincere condolences.'

He was turning away when Mollie stopped him.

'I wonder if you'd come in and see my mother for a moment, Mr Cox. I think it would do her good: take her out of herself.'

He hesitated. 'Well, I hadn't intended to, but of course I will if you wish it.'

'If you don't mind, I think it would help her.' So this fence was taken, and satisfactorily. As soon as the lounge door had closed Julia came forward and took both his hands.

'Frank,' she said in a low but urgent tone, 'you mustn't stay long and we've a lot to settle. Let's begin at once. I must tell you that Mollie knows—*everything.*'

'I gathered so when she rang me up,' he answered equally softly. 'How are you, Julia? Keeping up all right?'

'Yes, but don't worry about that now. If we're asked questions at the inquest, what are we to say? That's what's so urgent.'

'I don't think it is, my dear,' I'm told the inquest will be adjourned after evidence of identity is taken. But of course it'll be resumed later and of course the police may raise the points you have in mind.'

'Then what are we to say?'

He glanced round. 'You're sure we can't be overheard?'

'Certain. It's quite safe here.'

'All the same, let us sit in the middle of the room and keep our voices low. I have been racking my brains to find a way to see you, with the same object. I congratulate you on your scheme.'

'Oh, Frank, never mind things like that! Get on to the point.'

'Dear heart, it's all right. A minute or two one way or another won't make any difference.' He looked at Mollie. 'Do I understand that Miss Langley knows—about my illness?'

'Mollie's my name, Frank.'

He smiled. 'That's very nice of you, Mollie. Then you know?'

'Yes, Julia told me.'

'I told her *everything*,' put in Julia impatiently.

Frank nodded thoughtfully. 'Well, that saves a lot of trouble. I agree that we should get at once to business and the first thing is to tell you what really happened last night. I'm afraid, Julia, that what I said wasn't true. He—was there—when I arrived. I found him—lying on the ground.'

'That's what I said,' interjected Mollie. 'I knew it.'

'I got there a little early; I naturally wanted to be before your mother. He was lying on his face. I thought of first aid and of giving the alarm. Then I examined him with my torch and I saw. I'm sorry, Julia, but I must tell you. The back of his head was crushed. I could do nothing. He was dead.' They did not reply and he went on, speaking principally to Julia. 'I was terribly upset by the discovery, then I grew worried as to what I should do. Obviously it was a case of murder and my duty was to give the alarm, but the objections to this were overwhelming. First, our meeting would come out, with your part in it. I was naturally anxious to prevent that. Then almost certainly I would be suspected. I had motive and opportunity, and my giving the alarm would be interpreted as a blind to put the police off the scent. Worse still, you would probably be suspected as an accomplice. I was horrified, for I felt that if the case went to court, it was exceedingly doubtful how it would end.'

'Poor Frank,' Julia murmured.

'No, dearest, I'm not asking for pity: only trying to explain. Then I saw that if on the other hand neither of us mentioned the affair, all these terrible results would be avoided. I felt the matter required careful thought, but I hadn't time for that.

You might arrive at any moment and I had to be sure of the line I was going to take. I decided on silence. I don't know even now if I was right or wrong.'

Again he paused, and again they did not reply.

'As we were then to keep our meeting secret, I saw that it was essential that you shouldn't know about the tragedy. Your manner must be natural. You must not show your horror and emotion at the wrong time. When you heard what had happened, your reaction must convince those present that it was news to you. At the same time I must account for my own distress and for cutting short the interview. I invented the illness.'

'Thank goodness, Frank, that it wasn't real,' Julia murmured, while Mollie repeated, 'I was sure of it, Frank.'

'It's an immense relief to hear it,' Julia added. 'All the same it doesn't settled our problem: are we to stick to our earlier statement?'

'It's very difficult to answer,' Frank declared, 'and I'd be glad to hear your views. My own is that we should stick to our story. It's unlikely that our meeting will be discovered.'

'I'm not so sure,' Mollie put in; 'it might come out easily enough. Your car might have been seen; you might have been seen yourself for that matter. Julia might even have been seen.'

'I'm sure I wasn't,' said Julia.

'I don't think I was either, but of course what Mollie says is undeniable.'

'Is it known what time you left your house?' went on Mollie.

'Well, yes, I suppose it is. My man, Jenkins, probably noticed it.'

'Then can you account for your time if the police ask you?'

'I should say that I made a mistake as to the hour, but on reaching this house and seeing no cars about, I realized what I had done, and as it wasn't worthwhile returning home, I drove about till eight o'clock.'

'Not terribly convincing, I'm afraid.'

'Then are you, Mollie, in favour of our telling?'

'I don't know. It's terribly difficult. Either course seems wrong.'

'That's true. As I look at it, there's a risk in not telling and the certainty of trouble if we do. And that trouble would be much more serious because of our not telling at the time.'

Julia nodded. 'Frank's right, Mollie. We'd be mad to say anything.'

'And remember,' Frank went on, 'our reason for not having told at the time remains good. I mean, if the police learn of the meeting, the explanation of our continued silence is that we were afraid we should be suspected.'

'Yes, and it's the truth. I'm sure, Mollie, Frank's right.'

Rather against her better judgment, Mollie agreed. The decision taken, Julia was urgent for Frank to leave. 'And no matter what we feel, we mustn't meet till this is over,' she insisted. 'I'm terrified, Frank, and we must run no unnecessary risks.'

Mollie tactfully withdrew to a bookshelf in the corner of the room while farewells were in progress, then they rang for Croome. Mollie accompanied Frank into the hall. She was satisfied that no suspicion could attach to the visit.

The inquest that afternoon proved formal and unenlightening. The coroner began by expressing a rather perfunctory sympathy with the relatives of the deceased, and then called Jeff. Jeff stated that he had seen the body upon which the inquest was being held and declared it was that of his uncle,

Richard Bertram Elton. He had been shown the body by Philip Harte and had at once rung up the police.

Philip Harte, having explained who he was, told of his finding the body and informing Jeff.

Inspector Dagg deposed that on receiving the telephone message he had proceeded to Chalfont and found the deceased as described. He had been making enquiries into the affair, but these were not yet complete.

Dr Winn followed. He said that he had examined the remains and found that death had resulted from a fracture of the back of the skull, caused by a heavy blow with some blunt weapon. In his opinion this could neither have been self-inflicted nor due to accident.

Upon this the coroner said that in view of the nature of the evidence they had just received, he would not complete the proceedings on that occasion, but would adjourn until that day three weeks, in order to give time for the police to complete their inquiries.

Julia found all this reassuring so far as it went. Everyone was kind and deferential to her and it seemed obvious that no suspicion as to the nature of her relations with Frank had been aroused. Of course the real danger would not come till later, but it was at least something that up to the present things had gone well.

Late that afternoon the body was brought home, and when the men had gone, Julia went to see it. The head was bandaged and the face looked calm and peaceful. Rather noble indeed, as if suggesting what Richard might have been, rather than what he was. Its appearance made Julia regret bitterly that their relations had not been happier.

On the following Monday an incident broke the leaden passage of the hours and gave Julia a moment of sharp panic.

She was pottering in her greenhouse when a card was brought to her. 'Chief Inspector French, Criminal Investigation Department, New Scotland Yard.'

She took a firm hold on herself. 'All right, Croome,' she answered coolly. 'Take him to the lounge and tell him I'll be in directly.'

Now it was coming! She recalled her precepts: Keep a stiff upper lip; answer what she was asked and volunteer nothing. If challenged about meeting Frank, admit it and say she had not mentioned it before, lest she or he or both might be suspected. Yes, it was all quite clear and cut and dried.

She was agreeably surprised to find that her fears were uncalled for. French was by no means a terrifying individual. Indeed his kindly expression and quiet manner inspired confidence. He was accompanied by a young sergeant and began by apologizing for intruding on her at such a time and explaining that having been called in by the local police, he was bound to interview everyone who figured in the case. He said he had wondered whether she might wish to discuss the affair with him, and if so, he would be glad to consider carefully anything which she cared to put forward. Then he went on to ask all the questions which she had already answered. Only in one direction did he go further than Dagg.

'Now your personal relations with the late Mr Elton, madam. I'm sorry to ask this question, but I must. How did you and he get on?'

She had thought of this and knew what to say.

'As well as any two people in our rather peculiar position,' she answered unhesitatingly, 'and that after living together for ten years.' She paused now for a moment. 'I should like to add to that, Mr French, for I'm anxious not to seem to mislead you in any way. Our marriage was not a love match. It was one of convenience only. When my first husband died I was left badly off and I wanted security. Mr Elton wanted a comfortable home and a good hostess. We made a bargain, and I think I may say that we both kept it and that the arrangement worked smoothly and well.'

He seemed to find this satisfactory. He thanked her, said he hoped he would not have to trouble her again, and took a courteous leave.

That same afternoon an event occurred which brought back in a flood all Julia's anxiety, leaving her once more in a stupor of fear and misery. After lunch she was again in the garden when Croome came to say that Mrs Underwood had called and would be grateful if she could spare her a few minutes. With a premonition of evil she told him to bring her out.

The visitor looked even more worried than on her previous call, though she had herself under complete control. She greeted Julia quietly and while Croome was within earshot apologized for calling at such a time. Then when he had gone she showed that this was a mask by dropping it.

'Oh, Mrs Elton, I'm again in great trouble and it may concern you. I felt I must come and consult you about it.'

'I'm sorry to hear that,' Julia said feelingly, leading the way to the seat they had previously occupied. 'Come and sit down and tell me about it.'

'You're so good that it makes it harder for me,' and she seemed as if she was not far from tears, 'but I do want you to understand that I'm only coming to consult you about the best thing to be done, not for me only, but for both of us.'

Julia's apprehensions grew. 'Tell me,' she repeated.

Mrs Underwood seemed to find it hard to begin. 'It's about this—this awful thing that happened on Friday, and William— my husband, I mean. I don't like even to put it into words, but I'm terribly afraid that the police—suspect him.'

Julia looked at her with shocked eyes. 'Oh, Mrs Underwood, I'm so sorry!'

'They've been questioning him and I'm afraid there's no doubt. I imagine they've found out about his debt: they could from the office of course. But I feel sure from what I know of them that the office staff would minimize the trouble. And I'm sure Mr Jeff would too. I happen to know that they all, including Mr Jeff, sympathized with William and were against his dismissal.'

'So you said and of course I agree with them.'

'Thank you, Mrs Elton.' She spoke with obvious gratitude. 'But I'm afraid there's more in it than that. It's important, in case the police act, that they should not be able to show that William and I took the matter too seriously. You can see that the more we dreaded it, the stronger the motive would be.'

Julia, her heart sinking, saw only too well.

'Perhaps,' Mrs Underwood went on, 'you can now guess what I'm going to ask? If the police knew that I had come to beg you to intercede for William, it would count terribly against him. To take such a drastic step—because it was a drastic and a costly step—would show how deeply I felt his position. Could you, Mrs Elton, see your way to avoid mentioning the affair?'

Julia did not reply. The request was natural, but extraordinarily embarrassing. Worse indeed than embarrassing. If Julia had had no secret of her own it would not have mattered so much, but this would mean more underhand dealing, more deceit, perhaps even direct falsehoods. If she did as Mrs Underwood asked and the police discovered it, her character as a truthful witness would be gone, and if suspicion about Frank were then to arise, her denials about their meeting would automatically become valueless. No, she could not possibly promise this. After all, Frank's safety was more to her than a stranger's. On the other hand, she could not bear to think of this woman's anguish if her husband were arrested. She did not know what to say.

But Mrs Underwood was speaking again. 'I'm afraid I haven't yet told you everything. This next part at all events you can keep to yourself, because you don't know it of your own knowledge.' She glanced at Julia and Julia nodded.

'Then I'll begin about Friday. All day on Friday William was particularly excited and upset. As you know, Monday was the last day of the month and he hadn't the money to pay his debt. He was fearing prosecution and wondering what would happen to me and the children if he was sent to prison. Then towards evening he decided he'd go to see Mr Elton and make a last appeal to him for a little more time. I advised him not to, saying that I didn't think that when it came to the point Mr Elton would be so hard as he had threatened. But he wouldn't listen to me and shortly before seven he shouted, "He'll be in by this time and I'll be able to see him before he has dinner." In spite of all I could say, he flung out of the house and disappeared.

'I don't deny that I was frightened. Not of course for Mr Elton. I knew William too well for that. He was good and he wouldn't hurt anybody; not even an enemy. I was afraid for William himself. I feared that if Mr Elton refused him, he might do himself an injury. But I didn't see what I could do about it.

'Then it occurred to me to follow him up here, so thatI might be on the drive to meet him when he came out. Perhaps I could help him to control himself if he was excited. I don't know whether I was right or not, but I couldn't wait to think. I must start at once or I might miss him. I threw on a cape and hurried up.

'I did not come up to the house, for I saw that I could not speak to him while the door was open. I therefore waited about half-way along the drive. I stood beside a big tree from which I could see him pass, but behind which I could hide if anyone else came along.

'I had been there perhaps five or six minutes when I heard a quick step. It wasn't William's and besides it was coming from the gate. I slipped behind the tree. It was a man and he passed close to me. But he didn't continue up to the house. Just beyond me he turned aside and went over the grass towards the garden: towards the summer-house.'

She paused, looking at Julia with a strange questioning intensity. Horror seemed also to be in it, as well as bewilderment. Julia felt her blood run cold.

Mrs Underwood dropped her eyes. 'Mrs Elton, it was Mr Cox.' She paused, then added almost in a whisper, 'And it was just before half-past seven!'

So that was it! That was how the blow was going to fall! It had been too easy. People did not escape things of this sort. The mills of God! She had done wrong. She had hoped to escape scot free. Vain hope!

Julia sat motionless, staring straight before her with sightless eyes. She did not even think of trying to put up a bluff before this woman, whom she had liked, but who she now saw was to be the instrument of vengeance. It seemed to her that if the police learnt this, Frank's fate would be sealed, and perhaps hers also. In the light of their own reticence, what hope could there be?

Once again Mrs Underwood's voice broke in on her thoughts. 'Let me finish my story,' she said gently, 'and then perhaps we might discuss it. I waited there on the drive, I don't know how long, but it seemed ages. No one else appeared. At last I decided that William could not have called or he would have been out by then. I went home.

'When two or three hours later he turned up, he—I hate to say it, but it's part of the story—I saw he had been drinking. It was the first time that I had ever seen him in such a condition, and even then he was not drunk, only a little affected. I asked him where he had been and he told me.

'He said he was on his way here, but half-way along the drive he had met Mr Croome. He had asked if he could see Mr Elton, and Mr Croome said he was afraid not that night; that there was a dance on and that Mr Elton had just then gone up to dress. William therefore turned back. Mr Croome asked him was he going towards Dorkford, and when William said yes, Mr Croome handed him a letter. "Just slip that in the pillar-box at the crossroads," he asked. William agreed and Mr Croome thanked him and turned back to the house. William posted the letter and then went for a long tramp, he said to walk off his despair. He ended up at the Green Pig, and there, thirsty and exhausted, he took too much drink.'

Mrs Underwood paused. She pressed her hands together and looked terribly distressed and embarrassed.

'I simply don't know how to go on, Mrs Elton. It's not my business and of course I know nothing about it; but the circumstances are very special and I think—perhaps—you ought to know—what he said.'

Once again Julia's spirit flinched. 'Tell me,' she whispered with dry lips.

'You'll forgive me, I hope. William was a little excited and a little abusive of Mr Elton; that was the drink, you know. "But there's something coming to him he won't like," he went on, and then he said—try to forgive me, Mrs Elton, for repeating it—he said that you and Mr Cox were—Well, you know what I mean.'

The whole bottom seemed to be dropping out of Julia's world. If her secret and Frank's, so carefully, and as they had believed, so successfully guarded, were known to an outsider like Underwood, from whom was it safe? Was it common property or had some perfectly amazing coincidence taken place in the case of this one man?

She felt so defeated, so overwhelmed, that she could no longer prevaricate. In any case, what would be the use? This woman would not have made such a statement unless she was sure of her ground. And yet Julia need not directly admit it.

'Why did he say that?' she asked tonelessly. 'He couldn't have known whether it was true or not?'

'I'm sure he knew nothing about it,' Mrs Underwood returned eagerly. 'He didn't say what gave him the idea.'

Then Julia amazed herself. Without conscious volition she heard herself say, 'Well, it's true, however he knew it. And Mr Cox did go to the summer-house. It was to meet me. He found the body. My husband was dead. We didn't report it for fear of being suspected.'

Mrs Underwood's reply was another surprise. She leant forward and squeezed Julia's hand. 'You poor dear,' she said with real sympathy; 'you're in the same trouble as I am. Now let's think what's the best thing to do for us both.'

It was not an easy problem, and the more they discussed it, the more difficult it seemed to grow. To each it seemed that the sacrifice of the other's dear one might be the only way to save her own. Both feared that the sacrifice, if made, might not achieve its object. Both shrank from a decision.

And yet action had to be taken. A policy of drift would defeat their purpose. Each felt instinctively that her wisest course would be to make a clean breast of everything to the police, but each also felt that this could not be done without the approval of her partner. When it came to the point also, each knew that she had not the nerve to take such a risk.

In the end they compromised, as Julia and Frank had already compromised about their own problem. They would answer truthfully any questions the police asked, but volunteer nothing. If the facts came out later, their explanation for withholding them would be the same: fear of suspicion.

Julia decided that she would not tell Mollie of the new development; Mollie knew more than enough for her peace of mind as it was. Julia would have given the world to be able to discuss it with Frank, but this would be too dangerous. She felt that she should not even see Mrs Underwood again, lest the police might obtain a clue as to where to look for information. She had therefore to carry her burden of worry and fear alone, and it was little help to her to know that at least three other people were doing the same.

Physically tired out, as soon as she was alone she stretched herself in a garden chair. How dreadful fear could be! And suspense! She found her ignorance of what was happening almost insupportable. She knew the police were acting, but whether their inquiries were drawing a net round Frank and perhaps herself, or whether happier times were in store for them, she had no idea. Always she had before her the horror of arrest: always the fear of losing Frank, with ruin for herself and Mollie.

But she was not allowed a long rest. Presently Croome reappeared. Chief Inspector French had come back and would be grateful if she could see him again.

As he had interrogated her only four hours earlier, it looked as if this could only mean disaster. With a feeling of sick horror she returned to the house.

8

The Ruined Weekend

When the murderer struck at Richard Elton he started a chain of events which profoundly affected the lives of a large number of persons, some of whom had never even heard of the dead man. Amongst these latter was Chief Inspector Joseph French of the Criminal Investigation Department of New Scotland Yard.

His entry into the case was primarily due to the illness of Superintendent Horniman of the Dorkford Constabulary. When Inspector Dagg had made his preliminary inquiry he reported to his Chief Constable. A conference was held during the night and the C.C. decided that owing to Horniman's absence, Dagg could not be spared to take on the whole time work of a murder investigation. Application to the Yard followed automatically.

Hence it happened that shortly after French's arrival on Saturday morning he was summoned to the room of the Assistant Commissioner, Sir Mortimer Ellison.

'Man,' said Sir Mortimer sententiously, 'is born to trouble as the sparks fly upward, and here,' he glanced quizzically at

French, 'are two sparks for you. You've been working in the City for some time, haven't you?'

'Yes, sir; that theft of secret plans left in an Air Ministry car. But as you know, that's finished now.'

'Then how about some more travelling for a change? Not to Washington or Athens, I admit, but all the way down to Dorkford in Surrey!'

French knew his superior. 'Matter of fact, sir,' he grinned, 'there's nothing I'd like better.'

'Fortunate, because that's your first spark and you may start right away. The leading solicitor and what not down there has been and gone and got himself murdered and a fine to-do they're making about it. Judging by the C.C.'s call they're all buzzing as if they were going to swarm. But you've got a chance this time: it only happened last night.'

'That's certainly not very usual, sir.'

'No, is it? Then remember me to Colonel Weldon; I knew him in India. Such courtesies count for more than they're worth, which is damn all. Well, that's your first spark of trouble as I said. But there's another, a much worse one. As you know, my conscience is fairly robust, yet it gives me twinges in unloading on you what may be a handicap.'

'I'll try and survive it, sir, whatever it is.'

'I think you'll survive it, though perhaps not much more. Briefly, it's Rollo.'

For the first time French felt a certain sinking in the direction of his heart.

'You mean—?'

'Yes, I do. I want you to take Rollo instead of Carter. Do you know him at all?'

'I've seen him, though I can't say I know much about him.'

'Well, he's not really a bad young tyke, though a mere

mewler and puker compared to the solid maturity of Carter. He's been recommended for promotion, so I want an unbiased opinion of him. Will you give him his chance and let me have your report.'

'I'll certainly do my best for him, sir.'

'He hasn't done too badly. Hendon and all that. To go with you he's getting the temporary rank of sergeant. If he makes good he'll hold it. Otherwise he'll return, so to speak, to the obscurity from which he is emerging.'

'I expect he'll be all right.'

'I'm all for optimism myself. One thing: don't let him get above himself.'

In spite of French's outward reaction, he was sunk in gloom as he returned to his room. Carter suited him well. True, he had neither brilliance nor initiative. But he was steady. Reliable. That was it. Tell him to do a thing and it would be done, and done properly. And he didn't talk. He could sit looking before him for hours together, not interrupting his superior's thoughts, but ready to help when needed. Yes, Carter would be a loss.

But the loss of a valuable assistant would be the least of it. The real snag would be the presence of the apprentice, French had come across some of these young men from Hendon with not too happy results. The A.C. had put his finger on the spot when he had warned him to keep the chap in his place. Well, French thought bitterly, he might fail in his case, but he certainly would not fail in that.

His forebodings were interrupted by a knock at his door. It opened and the subject of his speculations stood before him.

Arthur Rollo was a personable enough young fellow; indeed as French looked at him, he had to admit that his appearance was in his favour. He was tall and slight, clean built and athletic looking. He had a long, rather pale face with good features, a strong chin, a broad forehead and straightforward, honest eyes. He saluted smartly.

'Just got orders to report to you, sir,' he said and one fear of French's was shattered. He spoke ordinary English like other people, to wit, French himself, and without the affected drawl which for some unknown reason French called 'Oxford'. This he loathed, but had expected.

'It's Rollo, isn't it?' he said. 'Come in and sit down. Do you know what you're here for?'

'No, sir.'

This was not so bad; he was respectful and so far there was no appearance of side. French thawed.

'Like to come out as my assistant on a murder case?' he asked.

The young man stated as if he could not believe his ears. Then his face glowed. That he wasted no words, 'Love to, sir,' he returned shortly.

'Right. My regular assistant, Sergeant Carter, er—can't come. So you may take his place. I don't need to tell you that it won't be a game.'

'I'll do my level best, sir.'

'That's all I want. When did you leave Hendon?'

Rollo gave him particulars, detailed but condensed. French nodded and turned back to the present.

'You might collect these things and get a small car and load them up,' and he pointed to his 'murder bag' and certain other objects. 'We may have to stay the night, so you'll want things of your own. Where do you live?'

'Near Swiss Cottage. But that'll be all right. I'll ring up my mother and she'll send me on a suitcase. Where are we going, sir, if I may ask?'

'Dorkford.'

'Oh, that'll be easy. Do you wish to start now?'

'Yes. Get the car ready and I'll follow you down.'

Five minutes later they had passed out through the gates of the Yard and were turning south over Westminster Bridge.

Another five showed French that Rollo was a careful and skilful driver.

As his anxiety over his new assistant diminished, a quite different grievance took its place in his mind. The loss of his weekend—for he foresaw full days' work on both that day and the next—was, to say the least of it, disappointing. He had an exciting job on hand at home. He had bought the timber and glass for a small greenhouse and after weeks of preparation, the sides and ends had taken on independent shape. He had been looking forward to beginning the erection at the weekend. Now that was impossible. For at least seven more days he would not see those sides and ends go together. Annoying!

Of course there were compensations. He loved the country, particularly when it was country such as that around Dorkford. He gave but little thought to the case which was taking him there. One case after all was very like another. But there was no comparison between working among the Surrey hills and the dark alleys of the City.

He glanced surreptitiously at Rollo. Very correct: sitting upright, driving with care and holding his tongue. French thawed further.

'I'll not be sorry,' he said at last, experimenting on the make-up of this new importation into his life, 'to get my hands on the chap who has brought us out. A dirty trick to choose a weekend to commit his darned murder. Why couldn't he have waited till Monday? I had an interesting job on and now it's gone phut.'

Rollo, looking surprised and somewhat alarmed, glanced at him. French thought there was a lot of shrewdness in his eyes. Then the tension passed out of his face and he grinned.

'It was a bit inconsiderate and hard lines on you, sir,' he said, quite respectfully but without a trace of obsequiousness. 'But then look at the good turn he's done me.'

'Perhaps you won't think so, in another couple of days.'

'I'm sure I shall. Might I ask what your job was?'

French told him.

'It's a job I'd like too. Is it a big greenhouse?'

'Lord no. Ten by seven.'

'Not too bad. A chap I know has one that size and he gets a lot of stuff out of it. You should see his tomatoes. You wouldn't believe.'

French would believe. In fact, he hoped to do the same, if not better. Warming still further at this unexpected appreciation, he agreed that a tomato on the bush was worth two in the shop. The greenhouse motif proving fertile, they went into the question of brick versus timber foundations, on which Rollo seemed quite an authority. By the time they had discussed the niceties of glazing, their fate in the form of the Dorkford police station, was upon them.

'Do you know the men down here, sir?' Rollo asked as they pulled in to the kerb.

'I've met Old Horniman, the super,' returned French, 'but he's ill. That's where our trouble started: if he had stayed on duty we might have been at home today. I don't know the inspector, but I expect this is he. Looks a decent enough sort.'

Inspector Dagg, hearing the car stop, had come out.

'Good morning, sir,' he said. 'It's Chief Inspector French, isn't it? They rang up that you were coming. I'm Inspector Dagg.'

109

'Good morning, inspector. Yes, I'm French, and this is Sergeant Rollo.'

There were greetings.

'Won't you come in to the fire, sir? It's still a bit sharp in the mornings. As soon as I heard you were on your way I phoned Colonel Weldon, our C.C. He's coming over to see you and may be here any moment. He bid me ask you, sir, if you'd had breakfast.'

'Very kind of him, I'm sure, but we had it before we left.'

'We've been a bit handicapped here lately,' went on Dagg, politely trying to make conversation. 'Superintendent Horniman has just had an operation.'

'That's why you wanted us, isn't it?' said French with his ready tact. 'When you're Shorthanded isn't the best time for taking on extra work.'

As a matter of principle French was considerate of the feelings of those with whom he had dealings. But apart from his own desires, he found that a remark of this kind paid him well. The suggestion that the question of efficiency was not at issue obviously pleased Dagg. He had been polite in a coldly correct way. Now he became more human.

'I knew Mr Horniman slightly,' French continued. 'I hope he's going on well.'

His curiosity appeased, French turned to business. 'What about giving us an idea of the case before the C.C. comes,' he suggested.

Dagg looked doubtful. 'With pleasure, sir, if you wish it,' he responded, 'but I don't think I ought to say too much. The C.C. always likes to deal with such matters himself. But I can give you an outline. Last evening about—'

'If you think the C.C. would prefer to tell the story, perhaps we ought to wait,' French conceded. But before he could proceed there came an interruption. A car was heard pulling up and a moment later a heavily built man with strong rugged features and wide-awake grey eyes strode into the room. Dagg sprang to his feet.

'Colonel Weldon, gentlemen,' he said. 'This is Chief Inspector French, sir, and Sergeant Rollo.'

The newcomer shook hands with French and nodded to Rollo.

'Sorry to turn you both out on a Saturday morning,' he said in a voice surprisingly light and soft for his big bulk, 'but needs must and all that. I hope Sir Mortimer's well?'

French gave the necessary assurances.

'I knew him very well at one time: we were in India together.'

'So he told me, sir. He sent his kind regards to you.'

'He used to spend his time pulling our legs. Does he pull your leg, chief inspector?'

French grinned. This man was going to be easy to get on with. 'I'm afraid he does, sir. But even his jokes are pretty shrewd.'

'Shrewd? Shrewd's not the word. No one ever got round Mortimer Ellison.' He had divested himself of an enormously heavy coat and now took his seat at the table. 'Well, this won't find us the murderer of Richard Elton. Have you told the chief inspector the circumstances, Dagg?'

Dagg shook his head. 'No, sir. I was waiting for you.'

'There really wasn't time, sir,' put in French smoothly. 'We were only a minute or so before you.'

Weldon nodded. 'Then I'll just run over the story now and you, Dagg, pull me up if I get off the rails.' He settled himself more comfortably in his chair, glanced at each of his hearers in turn, and went on.

'The first thing was a telephone message received here at—when, Dagg?'

111

'Eight-fifty-five last night, sir,' said Dagg, looking at his notebook.

'Eight-fifty-five, yes. The message was from Chalfont, a house standing in its own grounds on the hills to the north-west of the town. Nice house and all that,' in reasonable moderation, plenty of money. The message said that the head of the household, Mr Richard Elton, had just been found dead in his garden and the circumstances pointed to murder. Elton, I should explain, is the senior partner of a local firm of solic-itors, Elton, Ridgeway and Elton.'

With promptings from the actor-in-chief, Weldon then recounted Dagg's activities. Having described the general circumstances, he told of his subordinate's examination of the ground and body and summarized the preliminary statements taken from those present.

'Dagg rang me up shortly after nine,' he went on, 'and again about midnight when he had finished his preliminary inquiry. I came over and we had a conference. From the information he had obtained we both thought there would be a good deal of work in the case, and we had to consider whether in view of Superintendent Horniman's absence we could undertake it without help. I needn't bore you with our discussion, but in the end we decided to apply to you people.'

French recalled with an internal chuckle Sir Mortimer's comment on a similar application.

'It's wonderful,' he had said, 'what efficient bodies these local forces are. They ask for our help because their C.I.D. men are on another job, or they have a wave of crime, or their big noise is ill, or something else that they've no control over. None of them have ever got tied up in knots and want to be unravelled, not even though they've mucked about with the case till all the scents are dead. You've noticed it?'

French thought it true, and when he played up by remarking that what Yard men were really wanted for was to provide scapegoats if things turned out badly, he thought this also true. However, it was unlikely to be Colonel Weldon's attitude. French remarked that he was grateful for such prompt action.

'We agreed that if we were going to call you in at all, it must be done at once,' the Colonel admitted. 'Better for both our sakes. So here you are, chief inspector, and now it only remains to settle what help we can give you. We've already made an extra copy of the evidence Dagg got for your personal file, and it goes without saying that we'll do everything we can in the normal way. But if you want anything special, it might be well to discuss it.'

'Thank you very much, sir,' answered French, though in his mind he added, 'for nothing'. All this was only his due. 'So far I only want normal help, but if anything unforeseen arises I'll apply to Inspector Dagg. I should like to talk with him in any case before I start. Perhaps, inspector, you have views which were not definite enough to put in an official report, but which might be useful to me?'

'A good idea,' said Weldon, getting up ponderously. 'If I know anything of Dagg, you'll find him very helpful. Give me a hand with this coat, will you, Dagg. I can scarcely get into it without help, and when I'm in it I can hardly move. Well, good morning, chief inspector, and the best of good luck.'

'A good man to work under,' said French when he had gone.

'The best,' Dagg answered without noticeable enthusiasm. 'Never lets you down and if you do make a mistake, doesn't rub it in.'

French chatted for a few moments and then came to business. 'One point arises out of your report, inspector, and that is the deceased's reason for going out into the garden at that hour of the evening. Did you get any light on that?'

Dagg shook his head. 'None, sir. I asked the question as a matter of routine, but nobody could—or would—tell me.'

'I suppose you hadn't time to look through his papers?'

'Only to glance at those on his desk. But I locked his desk and sealed the room. That reminds me, sir; here are his keys.'

'Good. Now another point. Your reports are very clear about what all these people said, but naturally they don't contain your personal opinion of them as witnesses. Did you feel at all suspicious that you weren't getting the truth?'

Dagg moved as if interested. 'Now it's strange that you should ask me that, sir,' almost your first question. As a matter of fact I've been a bit worried about it. I did get that impression, but I didn't learn any fact to justify it.'

'Never mind: an impression may be a useful lead. Who did you think was doubtful?'

'But that's just what worried me. It wasn't one person; it was most of them.'

French glanced at him. 'Most of them? Do you mean that you doubted the truth of most of the statements?'

'Not exactly, sir. I had the feeling—and of course it may have been wrong—that nearly every one of the witnesses knew more than they were telling.'

French laughed. 'Well, that's interesting and no mistake. Who were the exceptions? Or, steady: let's take them one by one.' He picked up the file which had already become the dossier of the case. 'Here's your first: this scientific chap, Harte. Was he one of them?'

'Yes, he was. He was the man who found the body, he and the chauffeur. He was perfectly all right about finding the body: I didn't doubt a word of that. But it was when I began to ask about conditions in the household that he grew sort of cautious.'

'I follow. Did you think he was lying or simply keeping back the truth?'

'I couldn't be sure. He seemed scared, as if there was something he didn't want to come out. And they were nearly all the same. They were perfectly clear about what happened last night: I didn't think there was any question about that. But about conditions in the household nearly every one of them was shy.'

'Suggestive, that. Well, next?' He turned over a page. 'Harold Hawthorne, chauffeur?'

'He was an exception. He just confirmed Harte's statement about finding the body. He knew nothing about household conditions.'

'Then this Jeffrey Elton, the deceased's nephew and junior partner?'

'One of the worst of the lot, sir. Very uneasy.'

'Quite a pretty problem.'

'The same applied to the widow, Mrs Julia Elton, and to her daughter, Miss Mollie Langley. The butler, Croome, was really scared, or I thought so. The cook and the housemaid were exceptions. They seemed straightforward enough. But then they knew nothing about the affair.'

'That finishes with those who lived in the house. What about the guests?'

'Two of them I was a bit doubtful about: Mr Cox, who lives here in Dorkford, and Mr Pegram, who lives in Sutton. All the other guests seemed perfectly normal.'

French sat digesting this for some moments.

'That's extremely interesting, Dagg,' he said presently. 'All the members of the family, including the scientist and the butler, apparently know something which they are keeping dark. The others living in the house, the two maids and the chauffeur, don't know it. That—'

'Excuse me, sir, the chauffeur doesn't live in the house, but in a cottage some quarter of a mile away.'

'That makes it more striking still. All in the house but these maids know it. None of the visitors know it except Mr Cox and Mr Pegram, but about these you were doubtful. I imagine we may rule out Cox and Pegram and confine it to the household.'

'Very likely, sir.' Dagg seemed a little uneasy. 'I'd rather you didn't build too much on it, you know. It was only my impression and it may have been wrong.'

'I recognize that, but it seems too circumstantial to be just imagination. Now what about the deceased? What sort of man was he?'

'A good lawyer. Very good reputation. Upright and so on and a good man for his clients. Drives a hard bargain.'

'His family life?'

'I know nothing of that, sir.'

'And Mrs Elton?'

'I don't know much about her except that she's a lady of position in the place.'

'You don't happen to know who was the deceased's heir?'

Dagg shook his head. 'There wasn't time to get that, sir.'

French saw the man was getting annoyed. 'Naturally,' he said easily, 'I only asked on spec. I think you've done extraordinarily well in the time. Did you happen to find out what that scientist was doing there? He wasn't one of the family?'

'No, sir. He said that the deceased made a hobby of chemistry and he was helping him with some experiments.'

'Paid?'

'I believe so.'

'That's all admirable: the greatest use to me. Now, Dagg, just one other question. Have you any theories or suspicions as to what might have taken place? If so, don't hesitate to mention them, even if they have no backing in fact.'

But Dagg was not going to commit himself further. French, thanking him again for his help, stood up.

'Can you spare the time to come out and introduce me to these people?' he asked. Dagg was evidently gratified and five minutes later they were on the way.

French had a regular routine for investigations in cases in which, like the present, he had a draft of the preliminary evidence. It was: become familiar with the place and house; look for physical traces; take again the evidence of those concerned to check the previous statements and form estimates of character; obtain information and evidence from a distance; and finally, settle down to worry out a theory. Usually he was unable to keep these inquiries in separate watertight compartments and there was overlapping, but these were his aims. As a result, when Dagg introduced him to Jeff and had returned to Dorkford, he began by having a walk with Rollo through the grounds.

As has been said, Chalfont was a little estate of about four acres, situated on the lower slopes of the hills on the north-western side of Dorkford. The road ran above the house and the drive, winding in an easy S-curve, fell continuously to the hall door. About half-way between the gate and the house a branch led to the garage, which was hidden from both house and drive by trees. At the back of the garage was the laboratory.

The house was situated on a shelf on the hillside. The ground still fell, though less steeply, and the lower floor, level with the surface at the north side of the house, was some five or six feet above it on the south. In the centre of this south side was a loggia from which a flight of stone steps descended to the terrace. Below the terrace came a tennis court and then the boundary fence, from which the ground again fell sharply into the valley.

To the left of the terrace was a rock garden, and though French's knowledge of rock gardens was slight, he was able to appreciate that this one was exceptionally well laid out and stocked. The only thing he did not admire was a number of small stone animals placed as if moving among the rocks, and he wondered whose taste they represented.

In the two lower corners of the estate were two charming areas. That to the right contained the flower garden and greenhouses. This was Julia's special interest and she had made the place a picture. French was struck by its beauty, and with the amateur's interest in other people's efforts, decided that before leaving he must ascertain how the effect had been achieved. For the moment he was more interested in the left-hand corner: that in which the murder had taken place.

This was a sort of inner grass lawn and shrubbery, separated from the terrace and tennis court by a yew hedge. There anyone who wished for quiet could find it, even when a game was in progress. At the top, with its back to the cross hedge, stood the summer-house, an open shelter facing south-west, with a delightful view along the valley. Flowering shrubs made a protection from the winds and broke the hard outline of the hedge.

Rollo produced the flashlight photographs of the body, and from these and from Dagg's pegs they saw that Richard had fallen on his face at the farther end of the summer-house. The feet were practically at its corner and the remains lay stretched out at right angles to its front.

'Now, young man, can we get anything from that?' French asked, eyeing the place speculatively. 'Looks to me as if he had been standing just outside the summer-house, facing forwards, and someone coming round from the back had hit him over the head and knocked him out. Can we find any prints along that side?'

Rollo shook his head. 'I'm afraid the ground's too hard, sir. Besides, the dew has fallen since they were here.'

French had seen this for himself, but his nursery-maid's job could not be entirely neglected.

'Let's try if my theory works out,' he went on. 'You stand here, just screened from an occupant of the building by the side, and I'll smash your skull from behind and you go limp and fall forward.'

Grinning appreciatively, Rollo took up his position. French gave him a calculated push and he fell—almost exactly in the position Richard had occupied.

'That seems right enough,' said French. 'Now can we get any more? Why would he stand in such a place? Eh, Rollo?'

'To overhear someone inside?'

'You've said it, I think. And if someone was speaking, it wouldn't be to himself. Two people postulated.'

'Then do you think, sir, that they got wise to what was happening, and while one talked on, the other slipped round the back and did the needful?'

'My dear Holmes!'

French was impressed: it was just the idea which had occurred to himself. 'Just keep it up and perhaps we'll get somewhere?' he went on. 'Next point: if the deceased played Peeping Tom under such conditions, it shows he was pretty keen to learn what was said.'

Rollo this time contented himself with an expectant nod.

119

'Now: what might a secret meeting be about, probably between two people, at a place like this, and in which Richard Elton was desperately interested, for I don't think that's putting it too high?'

'Some business trick? A burglary? Blackmail? It's hard to say, sir.'

French paused. Yes, it might be any of these things. What had been in his own mind had been unfaithfulness on the part of the man's wife. But now he saw that was unlikely for two reasons. First, in these days of easy divorce a lover does not need to murder an unwanted husband in order to marry his wife and second, at the time of the crime the lady in question was dressing for a dance. At such a moment he imagined she would have neither time nor thought for anything else. All the same it was a theory to be kept in mind.

'Well,' he said, 'that's one of our principal lines. If we can find out what the meeting was about, we're half-way to our solution. Now, Rollo, a step further. According to those photographs, the murderer didn't hit Elton with his fist. What did he use?'

'Dagg said nothing about that.'

'Which means he didn't know. Put it this way. You're out here in the dark with a—er—blunt implement, a bloody blunt implement, in your hand. What would you do with it?'

'Throw it into the bushes if it couldn't be traced to me. If it could, take it away and perhaps bury it.'

'In the dark you couldn't see the bushes.'

'Then I suppose I'd stick it in the ground somewhere.'

'There being no convenient pond? Probably you're right but I think we'll have a look in the bushes all the same. And if it's there, Rollo, what will it teach us?'

Rollo thought this over, then shook his head.

'Why, that the murderer knew the place intimately. Knew in the dark which direction to throw.'

'He must have known that to come here at all.'

French laughed. 'It's not impossible. Now before we leave the blunt implement, anything else that we should do?'

This time Rollo was equal to the situation. 'Look if any handy tool is missing.'

'That's it. And of course we must search in the summer-house and all round it for clues. I think we'd better do that now. We can get Dagg to do the shrubbery later.'

A minute inspection having obtained only a negative result, French moved to the opening in the hedge and stood looking round him.

'From the house you could get here by three converging routes,' he remarked; 'round either side of it or from that loggia place in the middle. Let's stroll over them. We might get a footprint.'

Here again they found nothing and then French made a scintillating remark. 'Those folk in the house will be at lunch now, so we can't get their stories till later. We had an early breakfast. What about it?'

In profound agreement they returned to the car and drove into Dorkford.

9

The Initial Inquiry

During lunch French changed his mind as to their next step.

'I think after all we'll postpone the interviews,' he told Rollo. 'The folks would only repeat what they told Dagg. We'd put their backs up and learn nothing fresh. Better to wait till we have theories to be tested.'

'I wondered about that, sir.'

'I'd like to know what brought Elton out to the garden. When we've seen the house we'll have a search through his papers.'

'You think he had a letter?'

'Well now, what do you think yourself? Let's hear your views as to what could have taken him out.'

'I should think he had some sort of message, either a letter or telegram or phone call.'

'Sent by whom?'

'Sent by the murderer.'

'Right; we'll call that Number One Possibility. What else?'

'Well,' Rollo did not seem so confident, 'the murderer might have been meeting someone there and Elton might have got to know of it—overheard them arranging it or intercepted a message or something—and gone out to listen to their talk.'

'Less likely, but still possible. We'll call it Number Two. Next one?'

Rollo shook his head. 'I don't think I—'

'Oh, come now; there are at least two others, and probably a lot more.'

'I suppose he wouldn't have invited them to meet him?'

'Why not? It's as likely as the last. We'll call that Number Three. Now another.'

But these three proved to be Rollo's limit and French went on. 'What about a third party discovering that two others were going to meet and advising Elton, hoping that he'd want to overhear what they said?'

'I thought of that, sir, but it didn't seem to be likely.'

'You surprise me. Take the obvious case. Suppose Mrs Elton had a lover and was meeting him in the summer-house? Suppose someone discovered it and wanted to put Elton on his guard, perhaps to make trouble in the household, or to blackmail somebody? Wouldn't that meet the facts?'

'My word, sir, that's good! It would account for where he was standing too—outside the summer-house.'

'No doubt. But there's still another possibility, quite as likely as any of them. Can't you think of it?'

''Fraid not, sir,' Rollo admitted after a short silence.

'Then that's something you've got to work up. I don't want to preach, but if you're going to make good on this job you'll have to be quick at seeing possibilities. I think this is where the reference to Napoleon comes in.'

'Napoleon, sir?'

'Napoleon, Rollo. According to tradition Napoleon thought out all the possibilities of his military situations and what should be done in each. Then no matter what happened, he was prepared for instant action. Same with us. If we think out all the possibilities, we'll see the significance of clues we might otherwise have missed. Got the point?'

'Yes, sir, and thank you.'

'That's all right. Now the other obvious possibility is that the murderer might have invented a tale to bring Elton out: perhaps that Mrs Elton was meeting another man. The tale would be false and there would be no one in the garden but the deceased and the murderer.'

Rollo was impressed and continued discussing the suggestion as they drove back to Chalfont.

The house was long and narrow, plain and dignified, built of old grey stone with heavy overhanging eaves. At the corners returns projected in front, but save for the one-storey porch, the façade was otherwise unbroken. On the south side it was entirely unbroken except for the loggia in front of the lounge. The two men got Croome to show them over the interior, as if the murder were to prove an inside job, the lie of the rooms might be important.

On both ground and first floors a wide corridor ran down the centre from end to end of the building. Downstairs it ended in porches with doors to the garden, upstairs in windows. Both corridors were divided by doors separating off the service part of the house, which was at the west end. The west return consisted of four servants' bedrooms upstairs, with cellars below, caused by the projection into rising ground. The east return, reached for the same reason by a short flight of steps, contained the billiard room.

The library was in the south-east corner of the house, and dismissing Croome, French broke the seal and entered. As might be expected, it was large and well furnished, though as a sitting-room rather than a library, for books were not much in evidence. Most of those in the few shelves were technical, referring either to chemistry or law. There were the usual easy chairs, tables with magazines and a tantalus, and in one window a big flat-topped desk and a steel filing cabinet. In the east wall was a door leading to a small room containing stocks of paper and such like. It was all very tidy, and after a general glance round, French was sure that papers would be found only in the desk and file.

'There aren't a lot of those books,' he told Rollo. 'While I'm doing the desk, I wish you'd look through them for loose papers or something hidden behind them.'

The top of the desk was clear and there was not much stuff in the drawers. Obviously valuable papers had been immediately filed, the remainder being destroyed. French found nothing in the slightest degree helpful. The letters were all on normal subjects, there were no suspicious entries in the bank book, and none of the filed papers suggested intrigues, blackmail or other promising activities. Nor did Rollo make any discoveries.

One thing that French had noticed was that Richard had taken his chemical hobby seriously. Stacks of sheets were devoted to it, some written in Richard's hand—that of the cheque counterfoils—the rest typed, but with occasional manuscript notes, presumably Harte's. The typescript seemed to be a record of a systematic series of experiments, but they were of an advanced type, far beyond French's comprehension. He was not interested in the sense that he expected the work had any connection with Richard's death, but as a matter of routine he decided to ask Harte what it was all about.

'Now, Rollo,' he said when they had been over everything, 'seeing we've failed to find a letter, what's our next step?'

'It doesn't follow, sir, that he didn't get a letter. He might have destroyed it. I should ask the butler.'

'Right. Then call him in.'

Croome had lost a great deal of his superciliousness. Standing before French, he looked anything but self-satisfied. He did not cringe, but his attitude suggested cringing. French glanced at him sharply and at once he felt that same doubt which Dagg had expressed. For one thing, the man was frightened. French decided to handle him gently, in the hope that he might give away the points he considered dangerous by showing relief when they were passed.

'Now, Croome,' he said pleasantly, 'sit down on that chair and answer a few routine questions. I have your previous statement,' he indicated the file, 'about when you came here and so on, and I don't want to go over the ground again. That is, unless you wish to modify anything you told Inspector Dagg.'

'No, sir, it was all quite correct.'

'I'm sure it was. Now let's see. What was the last time you saw the deceased alive?'

'The inspector did ask me that, sir. It must have been between five and ten minutes past seven last night.'

'Where?'

'In the hall, sir. He came out of this room and saw me. "Croome," he said and he handed me a letter, "I want this letter to go tonight. You might take it down to the letterbox. If you hurry, it'll be in time for the last collection." I set off at once.'

'Where did he go?'

'Upstairs to his room, sir.'

'I don't quite follow that. Do you mean that as you went out you saw him going upstairs?'

'Precisely, sir.'

'Then how can you be sure he went to his room? You didn't see him, did you?'

For a moment Croome seemed disconcerted, but he quickly replied: 'Because of his coat, sir. He was wearing a dress overcoat when found. It was kept in his room and I happened to notice earlier in the day that it was there.'

'I understand no hat was found near the body. Was there a hat in his room?'

'No, sir.'

French nodded. 'Now this letter that he gave you. Where is the letter-box?'

'About a hundred yards from the gate in the direction of Dorkford.'

'And when did you get back into the house?'

'In five or six minutes or less.'

'What did you do then?'

'I was occupied in the service rooms preparing for dinner.'

'Did you see the party coming down before dinner?'

'I happened to see some of them, but I wasn't looking out for them.'

'Quite. Now I'd like to know just what happened from then on. You could perhaps tell me in greater detail than Inspector Dagg required.'

'Well, I was preparing for dinner; you don't want to hear about that. I opened the door first for Miss Crawford and then for Mr Cox: they came separately. Dinner was ready on the stroke of eight, for Mr Elton always liked punctuality. I went to announce it when Mr Cox arrived and then I saw that he wasn't in the lounge. I hesitated whether to make the announcement, then I thought I should wait till he came down. I went up to his room to remind him of the time. He wasn't there, so looked in here and then all over the house. Then I went back to the lounge and asked Mrs Elton if she would proceed with dinner. She said yes and I announced it.'

'That's very clear. What happened then?'

'I was a bit relieved at first, for I had been worrying whether he hadn't been in the lounge all the time and I had overlooked him. But when he didn't turn up I began to think something must be wrong. Then I was sure of it, for when I went back into the dining-room after carrying out some of the dishes, Mr Harte had gone too. Then later I heard Mr Harte phoning for the doctor and I knew it was something pretty bad. Mr Harte then told me they'd found Mr Elton dead outside.'

'It must have been a shock to you.'

'It was, sir, and no mistake.'

French's manner was matter-of-fact as well as pleasant, and he was interested to notice that Croome's uneasiness was not lessened by his mildness. Evidently the delicate subject had not yet been reached.

'Now tell me about Mr Elton. Had you noticed anything abnormal about him lately?'

'Nothing, sir.'

'No irritation or abstraction or signs of worry?'

Croome hesitated. 'Now that you mention it, I did think he was a bit preoccupied. But I scarcely like to say so, for I wasn't sure. If there was anything, it was slight.'

'Had he gone out into the garden in the evening on previous occasions?'

'He sometimes went out, sir, but I always supposed it was to the laboratory. Of course I can't say he didn't go to the garden.'

'Very well. Now I want a note of all the messages he received during the last three or four days. Take letters first. When did they come?'

'The morning delivery's about half-past eight, the evening about six-fifteen.'

'Do you see the letters on arrival?'

'Yes, sir; I take them out of the box and in the morning leave them on the hall table, where the family get them as they come down for breakfast. In the evening I take them round and deliver them.'

'Did you notice any unusual looking letters for Mr Elton?'

'No, sir.'

'None for instance with an address in what might be a disguised hand or written in block letters?'

'No, sir, they were mostly typed and all perfectly ordinary looking.'

'None without a stamp: delivered by hand?'

'None, sir.'

Had the man's uneasiness increased? French obtained that impression, though he was by no means certain.

'What about telephone messages or telegrams?'

'There were no telegrams and no phone calls within the last three days. But Mr Elton made some calls. He did most evenings.'

'Any callers?'

'To see him, sir? None.'

This was not very encouraging. So far French had learnt from Croome absolutely nothing. With more hope he turned to the subject which Dagg had thought embarrassed the witnesses. He decided that a little preparation was desirable.

'Now, Croome, I'm going to ask you some rather awkward questions.' He paused, unobtrusively eyeing the man. There was now no doubt of his increased anxiety. 'I want to know about household and family dislikes and disagreements. We'll take everyone in turn. Whom had Mr Elton reason to dislike or distrust?'

Croome, French thought, looked slightly relieved. 'No one that I know of, sir,' he answered with more confidence. 'And there were no disagreements to my knowledge.'

'Then take yourself. Whom in the household did you dislike?'

Croome, almost with a show of indignation, denied that he had such feelings about anyone. Though French persevered, he saw he was going to make nothing of it.

'Now this last question is purely routine: everyone will be asked it. I want a detailed note of who saw you between 7.10 and 8.30 last night. Obviously I must know who could or could not have slipped out for five minutes to the summer-house.'

Croome was now much more master of himself. 'Are you suggesting I murdered Mr Elton?' he asked.

'Don't be a fool, Croome. Everyone in the house is a suspect. What I'm asking may take you off the list.'

Croome made no further difficulties. With a little prompting he was able to give French a timetable of his movements. It sounded as if it were true, though it did not prove an alibi for the entire period. One of the items was fifteen minutes selecting and bringing wine from the cellar, during which Croome said he had been alone. There was no reason, so far as French could see, why this work could not have been done beforehand, leaving Croome ample time to go out, commit the murder and return. At the same time there was no indication that Croome had done so.

'There it's beginning,' French grumbled to Rollo when the butler had gone. 'In this sort of inquiry you don't often get certainty. Usually all you can prove is that a thing might have happened.'

'I suppose Croome remains theoretically a suspect, but I don't think he did it all the same.'

'You don't? Now just why?'

'His manner, sir. He was nervous when you began and when you were asking him about letters and all that; things he had actually to do with. But about being guilty of the murder he seemed quite sure of himself.'

French was impressed. For a beginner this was not so bad. His own feeling had been precisely similar. However, he took occasion to point out that feelings were not evidence and that till they knew more, Croome must be retained on their list of suspects.

'Not very hopeful about the deceased having had a letter,' went on Rollo.

'He might have without Croome knowing: might have been sent to the office, for instance. Besides, Croome may have been lying. Now, Rollo, suppose you were here on your own. What would you do next?'

'If Elton went to his room, that housemaid, Ada Perkins, might have seen him later than Croome. I suggest have her in.'

French nodded. 'Right. We want to know something else from her too.'

Ada was a rather pretty girl, not in the least obsequious, but with a quiet, respectful manner.

'Sit down, Miss Perkins,' French greeted her, repeating with an even pleasanter manner his saga about routine questions.

'Now further to what Inspector Dagg asked you, I'd like you to tell me what you did yesterday evening between seven and eight-thirty. Please don't be in a hurry and put in plenty of detail.'

'I was on duty upstairs all that time,' she answered.

'Yes, I know; but just what were you doing?'

'The dressing-bell rang at seven, and before that I had seen that the bedroom fires were all burning brightly and curtains drawn and all that, ready for the party. They began to come up a few minutes past seven and while they were dressing it was my duty to remain in the service pantry in case I was wanted. When they went down I tidied up the rooms and prepared them for the night.'

'I understand. Were you upstairs all the time?'

'Yes, sir.'

'In your pantry?'

'Most of the time. Miss Mollie rang for me twice, but I was only a couple of minutes with her each time.'

'What did she want?'

'It was the same each time. She had torn her dress and wanted me to help her on with it.'

'Did you close the door when you went into her room?'

'Yes, sir, for the minute or so.'

French nodded and passed to another point. 'Did you see everyone coming upstairs?'

'Yes, everyone. I wanted them to see that I was there.'

'And going down?'

She hesitated. 'No, sir. But I heard them passing the pantry.'

'All of them?'

'I can't say that. I wasn't watching them going down. There was no reason why I should.'

'Then any of them could have slipped down at any time, if only they had done it quietly?'

'No, sir, that's not quite correct. Someone from the right

132

wing might have, but no one from the left, for they would all have had to pass the pantry and the door was open.'

'Except while you were in Miss Langley's room?'

She thought this over. 'I suppose that's possible.'

'Very well. Who were in the left wing?'

'Mr Jeff, Mr Harte, Mr and Miss Pegram, Sir John and Lady Alingham and Miss Alingham.'

'Then only the members of the family were in the right wing, Mr and Mrs Elton and Miss Langley?'

'That's correct.'

'Of those three, how many did you see going down?'

'Only Mrs Elton.'

'What time was that?'

'About five minutes to eight.'

'And Mr Elton and Miss Langley slipped down unheard: I follow. Now, Miss Perkins, I've been upstairs, but I'd like to have another look at your pantry and the various rooms.'

On French's instructions Rollo made a sketch of the layout. He did such work well, better indeed than French himself. The pantry was to the left at the head of the stairs and the corridor past it led on to a window giving on the flat-roofed porch below. At the extreme end were the rooms of Jeffrey Elton and Philip Harte, Elton's looking out over the valley and Harte's towards the drive. Then came the Alinghams' and Pegrams' rooms. French put Ada in the pantry while he and Rollo crept downstairs from these rooms, and on each occasion she heard them. But in Mollie's room with the door shut she did not hear them.

The two remaining bedrooms, occupied by Richard and Julia respectively, were a different proposition. They were at the end of the right wing, Julia's in the corner of the house with a charming view along the valley to the west, Richard's abutting on the return and overlooking the drive. Either of the Eltons could have reached the stairs without passing the pantry, and as tests showed, without being heard by Ada. But for them there was a second and more secret exit. A door across the corridor just outside their rooms led into the servants' quarters in the return. A service staircase connected these with the passage leading to the cellar, from which there was a side door into the grounds. French tested these doors and found they all opened silently.

It was true that anyone using this side door ran the risk of being seen by the servants below. But when French called Croome and went into this question, he found that the chance of discovery was remote. Moreover the passage was tiled and the sound of approaching footsteps would give ample warning to anyone doing so.

'I take it you're satisfied that's the way Elton went out?' Rollo asked when he and French were back in the library.

'Now, Mr Inspector Rollo, just answer your own question. Why should I think so?'

Rollo stared, then made a gesture of comprehension. 'His coat. I didn't think of it till now.'

'His coat of course and the absence of a hat. If he had gone down through the hall he could have got both. He avoided the hall. And we learn something else from that?'

'That he wanted to keep his movements secret?'

'That's it. But there's another reason why it's interesting to know that he used the back stairs.'

Rollo gave his impersonation of a man thinking. This time it produced no results.

'Well, don't you see?' French went on, 'if he could do it, Mrs Elton could also.'

'That's good, sir. I didn't twig what you were after.'

'There's another point. That girl Perkins was in Miss Langley's room twice. Anyone could have gone out during the first visit and returned during the second.'

'If they had known the girl was going there and would be there long enough.'

'I know that's a snag. All the same we note the point.'

French glanced at the clock on the chimney-piece. 'I think that'll do here for today. I want to see the body and the doctor and there'll just be time before dinner. Then we'll go over what we've learnt and fix up a programme for tomorrow.'

Dr Winn saw them in his consulting room. He was rather official and distant at first, but under the influence of French's quiet, unassuming manner he thawed.

'Death was caused by the blow,' he declared. 'As you know, in these cases one can't be absolutely certain without an autopsy, but Dr Grahame and I were both satisfied that otherwise he was in very good health.'

'The injury was at the back of the head, sir?'

'At the back and rather to the right. There was a compound fracture of the right parietal, caused by a heavy blow with—I don't like to say it, but it really was—a blunt instrument.'

French smiled. 'Does that mean that the blow was struck by someone standing behind him?'

'I think so, if he were right handed.'

'Of course, sir. Would the blow tend to throw the deceased forward on his face?'

'As he was found? Yes, I'm sure it would.'

They learnt little from an inspection of the body, but took prints from the fingers and rubbings from the shoes. Then they examined the contents of the pockets, though as Dagg had reported, these were just the articles which a man like Elton would normally carry. There was an engagement book with a page for each day, very fully entered up, but the only entry for Friday evening was the one word 'Dance'.

'Nothing there,' said French as they walked to their hotel. 'I shan't be sorry to see dinner. After it we'll have our conference, and if you don't put up some good points, you may go home and send Carter back in your place.'

Rollo, by this time knowing his temporary chief, grinned happily.

10

The Emerging Alibi

The conference proved sadly unproductive. No brilliant flashes of insight occurred to either man, and French at last regretfully decided that the case was one for ordinary humdrum and uninspired methods. Of these the first was obviously to interview the members of the household, and early next morning he and Rollo returned to Chalfont for that purpose. On the way they called at the police station to ask Dagg to have a search made near the summer-house for the weapon.

They were too late to see Jeff, who, though it was Sunday, had gone down to the office, ostensibly to see yesterday's letters, but really, French imagined, to consider his future actions as head of the firm. Not wishing to worry the women-folk so early, French asked for Philip Harte.

'I'm sorry, Mr Harte, to trouble you so soon after Inspector Dagg, but we now require a little more detailed information than was necessary at first.'

Harte was polite though not cordial. 'It's all right, chief inspector,' he said. 'I realize you have to do your job and I'm out to help as far as I can.'

'Thank you. Now first let me read over Inspector Dagg's notes, in case any error may have crept in that you would like to correct. You said: "My name is Philip Lionel Harte and I am aged twenty-eight. My parents are dead and I have no near relations. I was educated in the Midlands and took my degree at Leeds, specializing in chemistry. I had one or two small jobs, then got a start with Chemical Agencies Ltd of Sutton. Mr Pegram, who was here on Friday, is the managing director. Recently, owing to a reduction of staff, I was told to look out for another job, but before I heard of one Mr Pegram called me into his office and said he had had an inquiry from Mr Elton for a chemist to assist with some experiments and would I like the job? I said yes and he arranged it for me. The work was to experiment on a half-developed water softening idea he had obtained as a legacy from some friend he had helped earlier." Is that correct, Mr Harte?'

'Quite.'

'Can you tell me a little more about the deceased's idea? What put him on to chemistry in the first place?'

'He explained that. He said he had always been fond of it, and had wanted to be a chemical engineer, but his father, who was then head of the business, thought he'd do better in the law. Then a few years ago his firm acted for Chemical Agencies Ltd in a dispute about the ownership of a chemical process. For this he had to take up the subject again. This revived his interest and he began some experimental research. During the work he received his legacy of the water softening idea. He hadn't time to develop it himself, so he decided to do it by proxy. He approached Mr Pegram and I arrived.'

'Is it possible to explain what the idea was? I'm afraid I'm not a chemist, but perhaps you could put it in popular language.'

Harte smiled sardonically. 'Well, I think you've got me

there,' he answered. 'Do you know what positive and negative ions are?'

French shook his head, then glanced questioningly at Rollo, as one with a more modern education.

'I think ions are the parts of atoms which go to the electric poles in electrolysis,' Rollo answered doubtfully, 'but I'm afraid I don't know much about it.'

'That's right up to a point,' Harte returned. 'The present theory is that when a salt dissolves in water it separates into two ions; that's founded on recent discoveries. By the use of certain resins you can extract one or other or both of these ions. If you extract them both you soften the water. The testator's idea was that this could be done more easily and cheaply by the use of a catalytic agent, and he thought some natural deposits like hornblende would do the trick.'

'Now, Rollo, define a catalytic agent.'

'A substance whose presence helps chemical action between other substances, without itself undergoing chemical change.'

'That right, Mr Harte?'

'Yes, that's all right.'

'Then the testator's process wasn't complete?'

'That puts it very well. And that's what I was for: to complete it.'

'But you didn't succeed?'

'I certainly did not.' Harte's voice was contemptuous.

'You seem surprised at my asking. Did you not expect to?'

'If you want to know, I thought the thing was either a leg pull or completely potty. But why should I say so to Mr Elton? I was getting a good salary and living in a comfortable house. Besides I was giving him value for his money. I really worked and carried out the experiments he suggested. It was an amusement for him and he seemed quite satisfied.'

'I'm not questioning your conduct, Mr Harte: only trying to understand the position.'

'I realize that, though I confess I don't see what it all has to do with the murder. But of course,' he added as an after-thought, 'that's not my business.'

'Very well, let us turn to what has to do with the murder. Will you tell me about finding the body and so on. Perhaps you'd better do as everyone else is doing and tell me all you did from seven o'clock on?'

'In other words, have I an alibi?'

'If you like to put it so.'

'Well, I haven't really, or not a very good one. But I didn't kill Mr Elton, if that's what's in your mind.'

'I made no such suggestion. Now please answer my question.'

'Right. From seven.' He paused for a moment. 'At seven I was with Mr Elton, Sir John Alingham and Mr Pegram in the billiard room: the gong went when we were there. We went upstairs a few minutes later, Sir John first and Mr Pegram and I together. I don't know what Mr Elton did. I had a bath and dressed and came down about ten minutes to eight. I was first into the lounge, but Mrs Elton came in almost at once and then the others followed, all but Mr Elton.'

Harte then described the delay over dinner and his being asked by Julia to look for Richard in the laboratory. 'I didn't find him of course,' he went on, 'so I rang up Hawthorne, the chauffeur, to tell him to search the grounds, as Mrs Elton had suggested. I joined him when he came and we walked round with our torches till we found Mr Elton.'

'And what then?'

'I saw instantly that he was dead. I left Hawthorne to watch and hurried in and rang up Dr Winn. Then I told Croome to bring Mrs Elton and Jeffrey here. Mrs Elton came first and Jeffrey followed. I told them and Jeffrey took charge.'

'Thank you, that's very clear. Now, Mr Harte, here's a more difficult question. You were a stranger in the house, and a stranger often notices things that the members of the family miss. I want you confidentially to give me your impressions of the household.'

For the first time Harte hesitated. 'That's rather a tall order, isn't it? I found it very pleasant. Everyone was very decent to me and I've enjoyed being here. But I don't suppose that's what you want. Perhaps it would be better if you'd ask definite questions.'

'I'll do so,' and French began with Elton's recent frame of mind.

Like Croome, Harte had noticed some abstraction and irritation within a short time of the man's death. He also had thought he had something on his mind. 'It was not very noticeable,' Harte went on, 'for Mr Elton was always reserved and dry in manner. In fact I may have been mistaken.'

'Do you think Mr Elton was happy?'

'He had every reason to be and he seemed all right, but of course I couldn't possibly tell.'

'Did you think he was in complete harmony with his wife?'

'Oh come now, chief inspector,' Harte protested, 'I can't answer questions like that. How should I know?'

'I'm going to ask you also whether in your opinion Mrs Elton was happy and in harmony with her husband?'

Harte shook his head. 'I don't think they're fair questions,' he was beginning, when French cut him short.

'Mr Harte, this is a murder case. I must ask, and you must answer, everything that may help to clear it up.'

Harte looked troubled. 'Mrs Elton was always exceedingly

nice to me,' he said after thought, 'but of course I was an outsider and she didn't take me into her confidence. I don't know what her feelings were towards her husband.'

French thought his question had been answered. Harte would surely have said that Julia seemed fond of the deceased unless he had known that the contrary was the case.

'How long are you remaining here?' was French's last question.

'A few days longer. Mrs Elton is paying me for this month and I'm dismantling the laboratory so that the apparatus can be sold. When that's done I'll go.'

'Are you going far? I'd like to keep in touch with you till this matter is settled.'

'Only to Town. I'll be staying with Mrs Harper, 170 Beechwood Crescent, Camden Town.'

The interview had been anything but illuminating, and yet French thought they had got as much as they could have hoped.

'Well, young Rollo, what did you think of him?' he asked when the chemist had disappeared.

'Dagg was right, sir. He's on edge about something. He carried it off well, but he knew something.'

'Exactly my impression. Didn't want to give the woman away, I thought.'

'So did I, but can you blame him?'

'I can, though that won't help matters. Whom shall we have now?'

'Mrs Elton, I should say.'

'I think not. I think we'd better keep her to the last in case we get a lead from someone else.'

'Right, sir. Then what about Miss Elton; I mean, Miss Langley?'

French agreeing, Mollie was sent for. French handled her

very gently, but he learnt even less than from Harte. She scouted the idea that her mother was unhappy in her married life and seemed surprised that French should ask such a question. She admitted that she had not greatly cared for Richard, though asserting that he had been kind to her and that they had been good friends. She had been distressed and amazed at the murder and could not imagine why anyone had done such a thing. Her mother had been terribly upset, but was bearing up wonderfully.

French felt slightly sceptical about her evidence, though he concealed his doubts and dismissed her with a word of thanks.

'Jeffrey Elton next, I think,' he went on to Rollo. 'We'll see him at the office and have a look at the deceased's papers at the same time.'

Jeff was alone in the old Georgian house in which the firm carried on its business. After a delay he opened to their repeated knocks.

'Oh,' he said, 'it's you, is it? I wasn't expecting callers on a Sunday.'

'We also regret working on a Sunday,' French said dryly, 'but I'm not able to shut down on the inquiry. I want to ask you some questions and also to run over the late Mr Elton's papers.'

'Come up to his room. Unfortunately there's no fire.'

'I don't mind that.'

'With regard to his personal papers,' Jeff went on, 'you are entitled to see anything that you want. But professional papers were not his secret and are not mine; they're our clients', and if you want to examine them I'm afraid you must get a search warrant.'

'That's all right, sir. I only want the personal stuff. But first I'd like to ask you one or two questions.'

'Right,' said Jeff. 'Go ahead.'

French picked up his file. 'Then just to check Inspector Dagg's notes, so as to avoid going over them in detail. Is this correct, please? "My name is Jeffrey Claud Elton. I am aged twenty-eight and am the son of the deceased's elder brother and therefore nephew to the deceased. Shortly after I joined the firm my father died and I then came to live at Chalfont, where I have since remained. Six years ago I was made junior partner. I have always got on well with my late uncle, who though a strict disciplinarian, was invariably kind to me."'

French looked up and Jeff nodded. 'If you look, you'll see that I signed the statement,' he said. 'All that I said was correct.'

'Then let's leave the statement and I'll ask my questions. You got on well with the deceased, but what about other members of the household: Mrs Elton, for example?'

Jeff seemed surprised at the question. 'I don't know what that has to do with the murder,' he said, 'but of course I'll answer it. I liked Mrs Elton greatly, and though we were never very intimate, we were excellent friends. She was always pleasant and kind.'

Jeff, it appeared, got on well with everyone. He admitted that be didn't care much for Croome or Harte, but said this was mere personal preference and he had nothing against either. French then turned to relations generally between members of the household. But here again he learnt nothing. According to Jeff, every member was a model of amiability.

'Now another point,' French went on. 'Can you tell me the provisions of the deceased's will?'

Jeff frowned. 'That's a question as a solicitor I couldn't normally answer, but seeing that I'm the chief beneficiary, I'll do so. I looked up the will just now. My uncle left me the bulk of his money, subject to a life payment to Mrs Elton of a thousand a year. I know he would have left her more only that he wanted his money to be at the disposal of the firm.'

'Very roughly, what did he die worth?'

'Quite a lot in a small way: I don't know, but I should think at least fifty thousand.'

'Mrs Elton's legacy wouldn't enable her to carry on Chalfont?'

'No: besides, the house was left to me. Of course I might keep it on and she might be willing to stay. But I shouldn't talk like this: I don't really know what may be settled.'

'I appreciate that. Did anyone else in the household benefit?'

'To a small extent. Miss Langley was left a thousand and Croome two-fifty. Hawthorne gets a hundred. I think from memory that's all.'

'Did you know before this morning of your own position?'

'Approximately. My uncle has spoken of it on various occasions.'

'Did the others know?'

'I really couldn't say.'

'Thank you. Now just one other question, the routine one which as a solicitor you'll know is asked in all these cases. Will you please give me an account of your movements between seven and eight-thirty on Friday evening?'

'It's not a pleasant question, even though I know it's asked,' Jeff said rather grudgingly. 'However, I suppose I'll have to answer. I was delayed at the office till after half-past seven. I had my car and drove home and got there about twenty to eight. It took me all my time to have a bath and dress and be down by eight, but I just managed it. For the rest of the time I was in the lounge and at dinner.'

'I'm afraid I shall want details about your being kept at the office. Were you alone?'

'Yes, and I can't prove I was there. I've no alibi. I suppose that's what you're after?'

'Of course, sir, as a necessary bit of routine. Perhaps you'd let me have the details?'

'They're simple enough. We're acting in a case of a disputed will, which is shortly coming before the courts. It's Sandford versus Emery, if you must know, and Mr Julian Greer is counsel on our behalf. He had raised some points and certain revised figures were necessary. These I discussed with my uncle after lunch and he gave certain rulings. I spent same time putting the results in order and then gave them in the form of a letter to Miss Ridley, our stenographer. She had to stay late to type it and I had to stay to sign it. She finished just before seven and I signed and started for home. But I had only got as far as the car when I realized that I had made a mistake in one figure. I raced back, but Miss Ridley had left and I knew that she would have posted the letter. I was very much tempted to let it slide until the morning, then I thought that Greer would want to go over the stuff during the weekend and a letter written on Saturday morning might not reach him till Monday. A telephone call would not be satisfactory, even if I was able to get on to him, so there was nothing for it but to write a second letter. I did this, typing it so as to get carbons for the files. I didn't get it finished and posted till just after half-past seven. That all you want?'

'As I'm sure you know, I'll have to go into that. Did anyone see you going back to the office?'

'Not that I knew of.'

'And no one was there? A charwoman, for instance?'

'No one.'

'Where did you park your car?'

'In the municipal park across the street.'

'Did anyone see you taking the car out?'

Jeff hesitated. 'I don't think so. Someone may have heard me, but I didn't see anyone.'

'And where did you post your second letter?'

'At the pillar-box in Cross Street.'

French closed his notebook. 'Thank you very much, sir. If you'll just let me see the carbons of those letters, that'll be all.'

'My word, chief inspector, you're not leaving much to chance. All right, I'll get them for you.' In a few moments he was back. 'Is that everything?' he asked as he passed over the carbons.

'Everything except Mr Elton's papers. I suppose this is his desk?'

Jeff nodded and again left the room, this time unwillingly, as it seemed to French. French glanced at Rollo and put his finger on his lips. 'Go through those books on the table,' he said, 'while I do these drawers.'

Quite a long time passed before French looked up.

'Any luck?' he asked, and when Rollo had shaken his head he added, 'Nearly one! The time does slip by. I dare say you're ready for lunch?'

When they reached the street Rollo discovered that this remark was intended for Jeffrey, working in the next room, for French continued: 'No lunch for you yet, young Rollo. A call first. Two calls indeed. Back to Chalfont.'

'What's the point, sir?' Rollo asked as he started up the car.

'You should know,' returned French. 'Don't tell me you've noticed nothing that wants looking into?'

'About Jeffrey's return on Friday evening?'

'Yes; don't you see? The maid said she saw everyone coming

147

upstairs, but she gave me the impression it was just after seven. If so, what about Jeffrey?'

'I don't think she said it was just after seven.'

'No, she didn't. All the same if Jeffrey wasn't with the others, she should have mentioned it.'

This evidently was not Ada's view, for when they asked her she said immediately that Jeff had been very late. She had noted the hour he arrived because she thought he had not left himself much time to dress. It was just twenty minutes to eight.'

'Did he speak to you?'

'Yes, sir, he said, "Bit late, but I think I'll make it".'

'Now when I asked you for particulars of what happened that evening, why didn't you mention this?'

'You asked me if I had seen everyone coming up and I said I had. You didn't ask me when they came.'

This was so unanswerable that French did not attempt a reply. He merely smiled at her and said he must try to do better next time, a remark which to Rollo's joy she took seriously and answered politely, 'Yes, sir.' They returned to Dorkford without comment.

'Well,' French went on presently, 'we've learnt that Jeffrey was absent from the house at the critical time, but whether he was typing business letters or murdering his uncle we don't yet know. Let's pay our second call. 16 Heather Lane. It's up here.'

'What are you on to now, sir?'

'That typist. Found her address in Elton's staff book. Found Heather Lane on a directory map of Dorkford.'

Dora Ridley proved to be a young woman with the sharpened type of face which suggests a fox. She was more elaborate as to dress and make up than French would have associated with Richard's office.

'We've just come from Mr Jeffrey Elton,' French told her,

after showing her his card. 'We're interested in the two letters he wrote to Mr Greer on Friday afternoon. He could not remember the times they were done, but he mentioned your name and I thought you might be able to tell me.'

'He knows very well I'd remember the time,' she answered pertly. 'I was kept an hour late over it and I had a date to go to the pictures.'

'Hard lines,' said French sympathetically. 'What time do you usually stop?'

'Six, and that's too late. It's not fair. Other offices close at five-thirty and I don't see why ours shouldn't.'

'It certainly doesn't sound right. Then on Friday it was nearly seven, was it?'

'*Nearly* seven! It was two minutes past seven when I pulled the door after me. I know, for you can see the town hall clock from the door. And then I had to go to the post office to post the letters: another three minutes.'

'You were the last out of the office?'

'Yes.'

'When did Mr Jeffrey Elton leave?'

'Just before me; not three minutes.'

'He tells me he went back and typed another letter on your machine?'

'That's right. At least the carbons were there in the morning and someone had been at the machine. The carriage wasn't centred and the lid was jammed on. If I had done that there'd have been no end of a fuss, but it was all right because Mr Jeff did it.'

'Ah, but then he hasn't your skill,' French pointed out smoothly. 'Thank you, Miss Ridley, for your help.'

Doubtfully, as if not sure whether her leg was being pulled, the girl said that that was all right.

'Sharp enough to cut herself, that one,' French remarked as they left the house. 'A spiteful eat, but a good witness, I think.'

'If the alibi's correct, she won't be wanted.'

'That's the way with good witnesses. Haven't you noticed that? Now, Rollo, what were your impressions of the morning? Let's hear what you've learnt and what you'd do next?'

'Sounds a bit formidable, put that way,' Rollo returned. 'I was impressed with Jeffrey Elton's statement. I thought it sounded true, and if so, it lets him out. I would suggest trying to check it further.'

'How?'

'I'd examine that second letter and estimate how long it took him to do it. Then I'd try and find if anyone saw him posting it or going home in the car. Perhaps it would be wise to find out from Greer if the whole thing was genuine.'

'I agree. What else?'

Rollo shook his head.

'Then I'll put up a different approach,' French continued. 'The first thing that emerged this morning was that Jeffrey had a motive for the crime. Richard's death. makes him master of Chalfont and gives him some fifty thousand, less death duties and the payment to Mrs Elton. But it does more. So far as we know, it makes him head of the firm, for the other partner has been dead for many years. All the same I don't think this motive would alone be strong enough for murder.'

'I shouldn't either.'

'But there may have been another factor. If Jeffrey was hard up or in some kind of trouble and wanted Richard out of the way, it might make the motive overwhelming. So we've got to investigate Jeffrey's life.'

'You think testing the alibi wouldn't be enough?'

'Well, you know,' French smiled, 'the emergence of the alibi makes me doubtful. Nothing is easier to fake than an alibi. I've found several that looked absolutely watertight, and they weren't.'

'A bit of work in that, sir.'

'What do you think you're here for?'

Rollo grinned. 'I'm on all right.'

'Oh, you are, are you? Well, that's not the only line we've got to work. I made another discovery in that office. The deceased's staff book showed that there was a clerk named Underwood who had just been dismissed for theft. And what's more, he'd been given till tomorrow to pay up: otherwise prosecution. What about that for a motive?'

'That looks more hopeful.'

'More work for Mr Inspector Rollo.'

'Only too glad, sir.'

'Don't worry: you'll get your wish.'

11

The Catalytic Agent

After lunch the two men drove to police headquarters and had a chat over the case with Dagg. They had not seen him since the inquest, about which French's scorn was unmeasured. As he pointed out disgustedly, not one point of the slightest novelty or interest had been brought out. What he did not add was that this was none the worse for the inquiry, avoiding, as it did, any indication as to the direction which their investigations might subsequently take.

'I've got a bit of information for you,' said Dagg when the subject was exhausted. 'We've found the weapon. Constable Vickers went up to the house to tell you, but you weren't there, so he brought it to the station.'

'Oh,' French returned. 'I'm glad to hear that. What was it?'

'A small stone owl standing on a base. Ornamental, I suppose, though I can't say I admire it myself. Vickers thought the murderer had picked it up on his way to the summer-house, for there are several of the same kind, a squirrel and a rabbit and a toad and so on, in that patch of rockery at the end of the terrace.'

'Likely enough. Where did he find it?'

'In the thick grass outside the Chalfont grounds. It had evidently been thrown away after the crime.'

French stared. 'Now why did the murderer do that? Wouldn't it have been safer to put it back where he found it?'

'It might and it might not. There was a reason against it anyhow. It was badly stained with blood.'

'H'm; perhaps you're right. He probably thought it wouldn't be missed. Any prints?'

'None; the stone's too rough.'

'Then I don't know that it's going to help so much after all. It shows that the murderer knew the grounds intimately, but we'd already come to that conclusion. Was it identified as belonging to the rock gardens?'

'No, sir; the constable didn't mention that he'd found it.'

'Quite right, of course. Take a note to see into that, Rollo. Tell me, Dagg, do you know a man called Underwood, who used to be in the Elton office?'

'Used to be?'

'Yes, he was sacked a little time ago.'

'I know the man slightly, but I didn't know he'd been sacked.'

'What sort is he?'

'Quite all right, I think.'

'I see the head clerk's a man named Moffat. Do you know anything of him?'

'Mr Moffatt? Oh yes, he's a sound man; well respected and popular in the town.'

'I thought I'd go round and get the dope about Underwood from him.'

Dagg looked startled. 'You don't mean—?'

'No,' said French, 'but we ought to be sure.'

'Underwood's not likely to have known about the stone owl,' Dagg remarked thoughtfully.

'That's certainly a point. I'll bear it in mind.'

An inspection of the 'ornament' yielded nothing of interest. The owl was in a perching position with its wings closed. About fifteen inches high, it stood on a heavy base about eight inches square. It formed a mallet with the bird for the handle and the base for the head. It made a formidable weapon, and the blood on the base showed how it had been used.

'By the way,' said French, 'there's another job I wish your men would do. Jeffrey Elton has put up an alibi,' and he gave the details. 'Could you find out if he was seen on the way home? If so, I think it would let him out.'

Dagg promised to make inquiries and French and Rollo went out to a house in a suburban terrace and asked for the owner. Moffatt proved to be an elderly man with a pleasant Scots burr in his voice. French recognized him as having been one of the most interested auditors at the inquest.

'This must have been a shock to you, Mr Moffatt,' French began. 'I expect you'd be glad to hear of our getting the guilty man.'

'I would, Mr French; I certainly would. Mr Elton had his little peculiarities like everyone else, but he was a good friend to me. The office won't be the same without him.'

'I'm sure of that. He was popular among the staff?'

'Well,' Moffatt was evidently thinking how to frame his reply, 'popular perhaps mightn't be just the word. He was well respected and all that, but he was too reserved to be exactly what you'd call popular.'

'But no actual enemies among the staff, I suppose?'

Moffatt shook his head. 'Enemies? Oh no, no enemies. Nothing of that sort.' But his voice seemed to lack conviction.

'Let's see,' said French, opening his notebook, 'just whom did your staff consist of?'

Moffatt mentioned a number of names, which French wrote down, and each was duly discussed.

'That all?' said French at last, continuing when the other agreed, 'I thought you had a clerk named Underwood?'

'We had, but he's left.'

'That long ago?'

'About a month.'

'Why did he leave?' French's voice was casual.

Moffatt hesitated. 'He and Mr Elton didn't exactly hit it off.'

'I follow. How long had he been with the firm?'

'A good long time,' Moffatt answered with obvious unwillingness; 'getting on, I suppose, for twenty years.'

French looked at him in apparent surprise. 'It must have taken something serious to make him leave after all that time. I wish you'd tell me the details.'

Presently it all came out, just as Carrie Underwood had told it to Julia. And Moffatt minimized it to just the same extent. Clearly his sympathies were with the clerk.

'What will happen now?' went on French. 'Will Mr Jeffrey prosecute?'

'I couldn't say, but I think it unlikely. Mr Jeffrey was very good to Underwood: used often to give him a lift home in the evenings. They lived in the same direction.'

'Underwood was a little excitable, I understand? Is that so?'

'He was shell-shocked in the last war. But he was much better. Normal, or practically normal, I'd say.'

French assumed a disinterest in the matter which he did not feel. He continued questioning Moffat about possible disgruntled clients, of whom there appeared to be none. Then when the Underwood episode had suitably retreated into the background, he took his leave.

'Better go and see that gardener at Chalfont when we have the chance,' said French as he started up the car. 'What's his name, I forget?'

'Moggridge.'

They found the man working among the flowers surrounding his house. French introduced himself, and having admired the garden, chatted about some of his own gardening feats.

Moggridge, who was at first strongly on the defensive, gradually thawed.

'Now,' said French, presently working round to business, 'I have to get a report from everyone about this unhappy affair. I understand from Inspector Dagg that you left work about five-thirty on last Friday evening, came home, and were in your house all the rest of the evening. That correct?'

'Correct, sir.'

'Did you see anything unusual about the place or garden recently? I mean, within the last week or two?'

'No, sir, I noticed nothing.'

'Or since the tragedy? No footprints? You picked nothing up?'

'Nothing, sir.'

'Nothing out of its place or disappeared?'

'Nothing, sir.'

French insisted on his accompanying them to the Chalfont rock garden, where he told him to have a good look round.

The man, obviously honest and obviously completely puzzled, stood running his eyes slowly over the area. He shook his head, then his eyes stopped and goggled.

'That there little stone bird's gone, sir,' he exclaimed. 'An owl, it was, about the size of that squirrel. It stood beside that stone.'

Here at last was proof of at least one item in this so far nebulous case.

A little later as he and Rollo sat over dinner, French remarked: 'I had rather wanted to go over the deceased's chemical stuff tonight, but I suppose with such a hot iron we must do some striking.'

'A call on Underwood being indicated?'

'True, Sherlock. Let's go to it.'

Half an hour later they knocked at the door of a small terrace house in the suburbs. Carrie Underwood, opening it, explained that her husband was out, she did not know where. He might not be back for some time. Would French come in and wait or return later?

French, smiling, said it wasn't so urgent as all that and that he would call again next morning.

'I'll see that he's here.'

'Thank you, madam. Good night.'

A hundred yards from the house French stopped. 'Now, young Sergeant Rollo, you may do a spot of work for a change. Keep an eye on the house. Let Underwood enter, and if he comes out again, shadow him. Got the idea?'

'Okay, sir. As a matter of fact it explains what was puzzling me: why you were giving him such a chance.'

'More likely to get something if he's off his guard. I'll send a man to relieve you. Then come round to the hotel. We'll be able to look over those chemical notes after all.'

Half an hour later Rollo turned up.

'Here's a chance for you to display your chemical knowledge,' French greeted him. 'All this stuff,' he waved vaguely at the papers which surrounded him, 'is about things which were discovered since I was at school, but you've no such excuse.'

'What is it, sir?'

'Ions. Ions and anions and cations and synthetic resins and whatnot of that kind. Worse than Greek to me.'

'I'm afraid it's not much better than Greek to me. May I see?' He picked up one of the papers.

'Steady a moment,' said French, 'don't mix 'em. I've been marking them to keep them separate. You see, I found two lots. The greater number were in folders in that vertical file, which was unlocked. But there were others in the safe: locked up. What does that suggest to you?'

Rollo stared at him. 'That the deceased had a real secret?'

'I don't know what an unreal one's like, but yes, so far. What else?'

'I mean that it was valuable.'

'I realize that. But you haven't got my idea. What about his keeping it from Harte?'

Rollo thought this over. 'It might be that of course. But might it not just be a precaution against outsiders?'

'From the letters I don't think so, but there I'm handicapped by not knowing what these darned things are. Cations, for instance. What under heaven is a cation?'

'I'm afraid you've rather got me there. Anions and cations.' He paused in thought. 'I *think*, but I'm not sure, it's connected with the electrolysis of a liquid and the parts of the atoms that go to the different electric poles. It's something of that kind, but I don't think that's exactly right.'

'I'm appalled at your ignorance. Very well, let's take these papers and see what we can make of them. First those in the file, which Harte had access to. Here's a letter setting out Elton's agreement with Harte. Just read it aloud.'

'"Chalfont, Dorkford, Surrey, 5th October, 1939,"' read Rollo. '"Philip Harte, Esq.; Dear Mr Harte, This letter is to place on record the agreement at which we have arrived. In consideration of the sum of £6 (six pounds sterling) per week together with full board and lodging at my house, Chalfont, i.e. living here as a member of my family, you will carry out chemical experiments under my general direction and in my laboratory with a view to discovering a catalytic agent which will act as that described in the attached copy of letter from my friend Andrew Mackintosh. The results of your work to be my absolute property, though this does not preclude my offering you a bonus, should these prove profitable. One week's notice on either side to end this agreement, no reason being necessary. If you find these terms satisfactory, please sign and return the copy enclosed herewith. Yours faithfully, Richard Elton." Harte hasn't signed this carbon, so there must be another copy elsewhere.'

'That's all right. It was in the safe, stamped as well as signed.'

'A copy of the letter from Andrew Mackintosh referred to is attached. It reads: "Cairo, 29th July, 1939. Dear Richard, I have met with an accident and the doctors tell me it is all up with me. Well, I have had a good innings and I'm not complaining. Thank God I've been given time to make my will, which I had neglected. This letter is a part of it. I am leaving you the most valuable thing I have, partly because I know no one but you who could use it, and partly in remembrance of your help to me when I was down. Only for that I should have gone under. The legacy is a partially worked out chemical discovery: a new way of softening water which, if you can complete it, will supersede all the present methods. I discovered it by accident, but there's no time to tell you about that. Here's the method, and I wish you the best of luck with it. You probably know that it has recently been discovered that the anions and cations of a limited quantity of hard water salts dissolved in water can be removed by passing the water through beds of different synthetic resins. This exhausts the resins, though they can easily be regenerated. My discovery is that this result can be obtained without exhausting the resins. By my process these will act continuously, thus removing, not a limited amount of the salts, but the whole of whatever quantity is present, and once the plant is set up, at practically no cost. It is brought about by the use of a catalytic agent, which is crushed and mixed with the crushed resins. The process obviously depends on the catalytic agent and that is the snag. It is a crystalline stone I picked up out of a bed of hornblende slate when excavating in Upper Egypt. I have since been trying to find more, but without success. If you can succeed, you will have a process worth a fortune. Goodbye, my dear Richard, and best wishes for your success. Andy Mackintosh."'

There was silence for a few seconds and then French asked Rollo what he thought of it.

'Well,' Rollo hesitated, 'I'm not sure that I don't agree with Harte. It doesn't seem to me to make sense. More like a leg pull or completely potty, as he said.'

'Can you say just why you think so?'

'I don't know that I can, sir. It just doesn't seem to ring true. Why would Mackintosh have picked up that particular stone which afterwards turned out so wonderfully? And if it was so extraordinarily valuable, why didn't he get it analysed?'

'I suppose he'd used it in his experiments.'

'Then couldn't he have gone back to the quarry or wherever it was and got another?'

'Perhaps he was going to when he met with his accident.'

'If a chap was dying, would he be able to concentrate on all technical stuff?'

French laughed. 'I see you won't have it at any price. Very well, I'll tell you now that you're quite right.'

Rollo stared.

'No one found a stone in Upper Egypt,' went on French. 'Andrew Mackintosh never went there; in fact, I doubt if any such person ever existed.'

'Then what's it all about?'

'A trick of Elton's. There were some notes about it in his safe. Perhaps I'd better give you an idea of it and then you can read the stuff at your leisure. It appears that four years ago there was that case of Sandford versus Chemical Agencies Limited, in which the firm acted for the defendants. It was about this business of softening water by resins and Elton had to make it all up. That started him on to chemical work, which he had always liked. He fitted up his lab and began working on this same problem.

'Well, that was the position when a very strange thing happened: an accident which gave him a clue. They had some friends staying in the house, and one night after dinner Elton took them to see his lab. At bedtime there was a terrific shemozzle in the house of Elton, for the lady found she had lost a large emerald. It was in a brooch or clasp she was wearing about her neck and it had dropped out of the setting. They roused the servants and searched everywhere, but not a trace of it could they find.

'Later Elton discovered that the very hard water in one of his experimental dishes had become soft. It was one in which he had put both kinds of resin, that which removed the positive and the negative ions respectively. He had been trying to get rid of both at the same time. Then he found the emerald lodged under a fragment of crushed resin, touching both kinds. It was undamaged and Elton with joy returned it to its owner.

'He couldn't understand what had happened, but he felt it must somehow be connected with the emerald. So he bought a small stone and began experimenting. There are details of the experiments which you can read if you think them entertaining, but to make a long story short he found that the emerald acted on the resins as a catalytic agent and that precipitation continued while they were in contact.'

'I say, sir, but that's a marvellous tale.'

French glanced at the young man suspiciously, but his enthusiasm seemed genuine.

'All that is given in elaborate notes, though there the record stops. But I think we can reconstruct what follows. Let's hear you now, Rollo, making a shot at it.'

'Well,' the young fellow spoke up eagerly, 'Elton saw he was on to something big and he wanted to follow it up: that seems pretty clear. Also that because of his business he wouldn't have time to do it himself. So there follows the inquiry to his chemist friend Pegram, which produced Harte.'

'Right. Go on.'

'Elton had discovered that he could do the trick with emeralds. But no process run on emeralds could be more than a laboratory experiment. He must find something cheaper. I take it that was Harte's job.'

'That's my reading of it,' French approved, 'and I think it's borne out by the evidence. Now, Mr Just-from-school, where are emeralds found?'

'I don't know, sir, except that it's in rocks.'

'Well, I, not having been to school for many years, didn't know either. But by a stroke of luck the hotel proprietor had an old encyclopaedia in his office. I borrowed it and read, marked, learned and inwardly digested its contents. Emeralds are found in clay slates, hornblende slates and granites, and one of their special birthplaces are the hornblendes of Upper Egypt.'

Rollo looked puzzled. 'You mean that was what suggested the faked letter story to Elton?'

'Yes, but I fancy there's more in it than that. I imagine he reasoned this way. Emeralds are composed of certain chemicals. Those chemicals must be found in hornblendes, or else the emeralds wouldn't be there. Perhaps some ordinary bits of hornblende, obtainable at small cost in countless areas all over the world, would do the trick?'

'Ah yes, I've got you now. We could check it up by finding out if Harte was using hornblendes.'

'He was. That's the evidence I was referring to. I came across letters about it and bills for it in Elton's desk. Samples had been sent from the Grampians and North Wales and other places.'

'I wonder if he had made any progress?'

'I don't think so. But there's a detailed record of his experiments. We can find out just what he had done.'

'That's true.' Rollo smiled. 'I have a friend, a chemist. I'd like to put him on to it. What about it, sir? A third each of the millions he makes?'

'Then we'd have to run ourselves in for theft, which would be bad for our respective careers. Pity your friend's not our authorized expert. We'll send all these papers up to the Yard and get a report from Professor Kennedy.'

'I'm afraid, sir, I don't understand the thing yet. What was the point of the fake letter? I mean, why shouldn't Elton have told Harte the facts? Harte would have been able to help to much better advantage if he knew.'

'Well,' French returned, somewhat doubtfully, 'it's not hard to make a guess at that. It's obvious that Elton wanted to keep the matter of the emerald from Harte. Now why should he?'

Rollo thought, then shook his head.

'Because, don't you see, it was a considerable discovery: something new which would be bound to create a stir in the scientific world. Now suppose Harte succeeds in his job: well, Elton is all right. Harte daren't go back on him or Elton will prosecute at once. But suppose Harte fails. If Elton has kept the emerald process secret still he can read a paper about it and get fame and kudos. But if Harte knows of it, he may sell the information. In other words, Elton holds on to his secret as a next best thing, because he does not trust Harte. And quite reasonably: he knows nothing about Harte.'

Admiration shone in Rollo's eyes. 'My word, sir, that's very neat. I'm sure you're right.'

'Well, make up these papers for Professor Kennedy and post them tonight. Then I don't know what you're going to do, but I'm for the hay.'

12

The New Lead

Shortly after nine o'clock next morning French and Rollo were once again at the Underwoods' door. Underwood opened it himself. He was a tall, big-boned man of between forty and fifty, but his flesh had fallen away so that he was by no means the fine figure which such a frame should present. He looked pale and anxious and his fingers twitched nervously as he talked.

'Come in,' he said jerkily. 'My wife said you wanted to see me.' He led the way to a small sitting-room and indicated chairs.

French's manner was smoothly courteous. 'We're looking up everyone who knew the late Mr Elton,' he explained, 'in the hope that somebody will drop a hint which may help us. Now I understand that you were in his office for many years, so you should know a good deal about him.'

Underwood seemed slightly reassured. He said hesitatingly that he would be glad to answer any questions.

'There are three lines which I usually find helpful in cases like this,' went on French. 'First, anything you may have noticed unusual or suggestive about the deceased; second, your own personal relations with him; and third, any third person or persons who might have had a grievance against him. Now let's begin with the first.'

French made a good deal of this, though he did not expect to get anything from it. But his apparent eagerness about something not connected with Underwood quieted the latter's uneasiness and tended to put him off his guard.

'Very well,' said French at last. 'I'm afraid there's not much there, Now the second item.' He looked up his notebook as if he had forgotten it: 'Yes, your own relations with the deceased. You may, for example, remember some remark he made which would indicate a line of research?'

Underwood shook his head.

'Then I suppose we'd better go over the circumstances of your leaving. I know of course about the money and all that and I'm sorry to refer to what must be painful, but I shall have to have the details in my file. Just tell me about it, will you?'

The man's nervousness grew again more marked as he realized the extent of French's knowledge, though he presently gave what seemed a very fair account of the entire episode.

'Quite,' French returned in matter-of-fact tones. 'That confirms what I had heard. Now my Number Three point. Can you think of anyone who had a grievance against the deceased?'

Here again French expected nothing, pressing his questions merely to discover the clerk's reaction. A great relief showed in the man's manner. Obviously he had realized his equivocal position.

'Thank you,' French said in due course. 'I don't think I'm going to get much after all. Now my last question, the one I have to ask everyone connected in anyway with the deceased: please say where you were from seven to eight-thirty on last Friday evening.'

This touched a chord. Underwood grew more distressed.

'I expected you'd ask that,' he said, 'and I've been thinking. I can't give you an alibi, if that's what you want.'

'Never mind: answer the question.'

'I—I—' he twitched about, 'was worried that evening about having to pay the money on Monday and I—thought I'd have another word with Mr Elton about it; perhaps he'd agree to give me a little more time. I thought I'd call at the office on Saturday, then I felt I couldn't stand that, with the typists and everyone knowing what I'd come about. Then it occurred to me that perhaps he'd be easier to approach at home and I suddenly decided to go and see him then and there. That was just about seven, for I looked at the clock and thought I'd have time to see him before his dinner, which I had heard was at eight.'

His nervousness was again subsiding. A brief pause and he continued: 'It's about ten minutes' walk to Chalfont, so I suppose I got to the gates about ten past seven. But I didn't get as far as the house. I met Mr Croome on the drive. I asked him could I see Mr Elton, but he said no, that there was a dance on and that he had just gone up to dress. Then when I was turning away he said he was taking a letter to the pillar-box and if I was passing that way he'd be grateful if I'd slip it in. I did so of course and he went back towards the house.

'I was a bit upset about not seeing Mr Elton, for it meant still bearing the uncertainty. I felt restless and I thought a good walk might quiet me down. So I took a round of six or seven miles. This made me thirsty and I went into the Green

Pig for a drink. It was pleasant there and the talk took my mind away from myself. I stayed till closing time and perhaps— took a drop too much.'

'Thank you,' said French, 'I think that's all I want. Did anyone see you between the time you parted from Croome and your reaching the Green Pig?'

Underwood shook his head.

'Whom did you talk to in the Green Pig?'

'Well, I knew a number who were there. I was sitting beside a man named George Jenkins. He's servant to a Mr Cox who lives not far away.'

'I've heard Mr Cox's name. Got all that down, Rollo? Then read it over to Mr Underwood. Just listen if it's correct, Mr Underwood, as I shall want you to sign it. By the way,' he suddenly fixed Underwood with an intense gaze, 'the really important thing in this case is the stone owl. Can you tell me anything about that?'

But the little trap failed in its purpose. Underwood stared back with an expression of such complete mystification that French felt it must be genuine.

'All right,' he said. 'Get on with the reading.'

'A couple of interesting points about that story,' French went on when they had left the house. 'How does it strike you?'

'Underwood admitted he was at Chalfont about the time of the murder,' Rollo answered. 'I was a bit surprised to hear that. He might have gone to the summer-house as soon as Croome had left him.'

'On the other hand, is that admission evidence of innocence?'

Rollo hesitated. 'I don't think so. If the story's true, and I suppose that part must be, Croome met him on the drive. He therefore couldn't deny he was there and to volunteer it might have seemed his best policy.'

'That raises the most interesting point in the whole statement.'

'That Croome saw him?'

'No: that Croome didn't mention it.'

Rollo nodded. 'Looks as if Croome suspected him and didn't want to give him away?'

'That occurred to me. We'd better go and put it to Croome. What's your next most interesting point?'

'That he took too much drink. That might have been to account for his excited manner after the murder.'

'Equally easy to argue that if he was guilty he would have avoided drink to avoid giving himself away.'

'It certainly cuts both ways.'

'There are a lot more problems,' went on French. 'Whether Underwood could have known that Elton was in the garden, and if so, how? Was there a leakage of information from the house? If so, who in the house had that information? If not, had Underwood already made an appointment with him and was he coming to keep it? If so, what business could have induced Elton to do such a thing? If so again, was Underwood's story to Croome an invention made on the spur of the moment to account for his presence?'

'Perhaps Underwood really didn't know where Elton was?'

'If Underwood didn't know, his story's obviously true, and he's innocent. So that's something to find out: could Underwood have known Elton was in the garden? Note that, Rollo.'

Croome seemed anything but pleased when French intimated that he wished to ask him some further questions. With a bad grace he led the way to the library.

'You told us,' French began, speaking much more sharply than on the first occasion, 'that at a few minutes past seven on last Friday night Mr Elton asked you to post a letter, which you did. Did you post that letter?'

The butler was evidently taken aback. 'Well,' he stammered, 'yes and no. I got it posted all right, but I didn't actually put it into the box with my own hands.'

'We have your signed statement, in which you clearly conveyed that you did it yourself.'

'I don't think I said so, sir.'

'You certainly conveyed it. However, I'll give you the benefit of the doubt and assume you did not intend to mislead. Remember, Croome, that any hedging in a murder case is a very serious matter and make quite sure you say what you really mean. Now tell me what actually occurred.'

Croome was obviously terrified. French did not believe this could be due to his inaccurate statement, and if not, it pointed to something more serious. Did the man fear he would be suspected of the murder, or was he in point of fact guilty? Or was it that he knew the identity of the criminal and feared his discovery?

'I'm sorry, sir,' he said, and there was something of cringing in his new found respect. 'I assure you I wasn't trying to hide anything. On my way to the post I met Mr Underwood. He was passing the box and I gave him the letter. That's the whole truth.'

'Why did you not mention this when I first asked you?'

'It never occurred to me that it could matter. I mean, I didn't think the posting of the letter had anything to do with—with Mr Elton's death.'

'I don't say it had. The point is that when you were asked to describe in detail what took place, you should have done so.'

Without hoping for much result, they next interrogated Hawthorne, the chauffeur. Beyond corroborating Harte's account of the finding of the body, he had nothing of interest to tell. Neither had the cook nor the kitchen maid. Then to complete the interviews with members of the household, they asked to see Julia.

French had few questions to ask her which she had not already answered to Dagg, though he did touch on her relations with her late husband. It was really to study her personality that he wanted. He was favourably impressed by what he saw of her, though her manner puzzled him. Like Dagg, he formed the opinion that she knew something which she was keeping back, and as a result was acutely anxious. Again the possibility of an intrigue occurred to him, though he felt that this was not the occasion for developing the idea.

'This case is running true to type,' he grumbled as he left the house with Rollo. 'One possibility opening up after another and no certainty anywhere. Mrs Elton appears to be hiding something, and at the time of the murder both Croome and Underwood were close to the summer-house and neither has an alibi.'

'For the matter of that,' Rollo answered, 'no one that we've yet considered has an alibi, except perhaps Jeffrey Elton. That letter business does seem O.K. But Mrs Elton might be guilty and so might that head clerk and the chauffeur.'

'What about the maids' evidence about Harte, the three Alinghams and the two Pegrams? Does that clear them?'

'Yes, I suppose that does. But I've been thinking, sir. Croome may be innocent after all. That letter business is likely enough. Elton may have wanted to get him out of the way while he was slipping out to the garden.'

'Then what about Croome's uneasiness?'

'Afraid of being suspected.'

'You may be right. Certainly what we know of motives backs up your view. Jeffrey Elton and Underwood had motives for the crime. Croome probably wished to keep the deceased alive lest his job should end at his death. Same doubtless with Harte. If you were in charge, what would you do next?'

'I think I should ask the Yard to check up with Julian Greer whether all that stuff about Jeffrey's letter was okay. If it is, I think he might be eliminated, which would be one thing to the good. Then I'd suggest calling on the landlord of the Green Pig to find out about Underwood's condition on Friday night. If he'd just committed a murder he could scarcely have been quite normal. I think also it's important to learn what took the deceased to the garden, but I don't for the life of me see how we're going to do it.'

'Not too bad. I agree. There's a call box on the way to the Green Pig and we'll ring up about the letter as we pass. Would you like to try your hand with the landlord?'

'Yes, I should, sir.'

'Then go ahead. If he seems a reasonable sort of man treat him as a friend, anxious to help. You get far more out of people in that way. Throwing your weight about only puts their backs up.'

Joseph Giles, landlord of the Green Pig, seemed not only 'reasonable', but a very superior type of man. Rollo courteously introduced French, and after they had lunched off bread and cheese and beer, he explained their business and asked for help. 'We're checking up on everyone connected with the deceased, as you'll understand is our duty,' he went on, 'and one of these is William Underwood, a former clerk in the firm. Our information is that he was in here on Friday night and we wondered if you could confirm that?'

'The night of the murder,' said Giles. 'That's correct. He was here.'

'Lucky for us that you've a good memory, Mr Giles. Can you give an idea of when he came in and when he left?'

'He left at closing time: I remember that clearly. He came seldom and drank little, but on that night he took more than usual. In fact, at closing time it was just beginning to show on him. Not drunk, of course; just a little light-hearted, as you might say. I'm not so sure when he came in. Let's see, I'll have a word with Miss Wilks.' He vanished for a moment. 'She says about half-past eight, and that's my own recollection.'

'Did he drink alone or with others?'

'Ah, that's not so easy. I saw him sitting with a man named Jenkins, he's manservant to a Mr Cox that lives not far away and—No, I'm wrong there. It was on his previous visit that he sat with Jenkins; on the Saturday before. They had their heads together the whole evening. On last Friday he was just with the crowd.'

'Was he excited at all?'

'Not more than usual. He was always a bit excitable. Shell-shock, they tell me.'

'Thank you, Mr Giles, that's all been helpful. Just one more question. Could you give me the names of one or two of the crowd he was with?'

Giles considered. 'John Wilton and Peter Holmes. They both work at the Claremont Flour Mill.'

Rollo got up to go but Giles stopped him. 'I'm not so dense as not to see where your questions are tending,' he said with some hesitation. 'It's not my business, of course, but I hope you've nothing serious against Underwood. Though he doesn't add much to my revenue, he's a good fellow and his wife's one of the best. I can't see him committing a murder and I'd be sorry to know he was suspected.'

'That in itself is valuable information, Mr Giles, and I'm grateful for it. In confidence I may tell you that we've nothing against Underwood except that he could have done it. What

I said was true: we're checking up everyone in the same way.'

'Did I butter him up enough, sir?' Rollo grinned when they were once more on the road.

'Don't you jeer at my advice, young man,' French advised. 'Giles is just the type that would react to that sort of treatment. If you had gone in blustering, he'd have shut up like a darn. Now if he thinks of anything, he'll drop you a note.'

Interviews with Wilton and Holmes at the flour mill brought corroboration of Giles' statement. Both men said that Underwood seemed depressed and anxious, though not excited or frightened.

'It's in his favour as far as it goes,' French commented. 'Next step, Inspector Rollo?'

'What about a word with Jenkins? If he and Underwood had their heads together for a whole evening he ought to know what was in Underwood's mind.'

'That's right. We'll do it now.'

Linden Cottage, Frank Cox's luxurious bungalow, was on the south side of the valley, facing Chalfont. Its situation, though charming, was not as good as Chalfont's, as the view looking north was not as good as that in the opposite direction.

Jenkins was a middle-aged man, small, wiry and red-haired. His round eyes gave him a sort of surprised, puckish expression, and French thought he might prove to be what is, for some reason, called a 'character'.

'Mr Cox has gone to Town,' he answered French's inquiry, an accent which immediately recalled the North of Ireland. 'He'll likely not be back till six or seven. Can I take a message?'

'Yes, I expect you could. But now that we're here, I'd like to have a word with yourself first. You're Jenkins, aren't you?'

'I am. Will you come in?'

It was a question rather than an invitation, and when French agreed, the man seemed a little surprised. He took them to what was evidently the lounge, a long, low room with deep saddleback armchairs and windows looking out across the valley. He asked them to sit down and did so himself.

'It has nothing to do with you personally,' went on French. 'We want a bit of information about a visit you paid to the Green Pig on last Saturday week. Do you remember it?'

The man nodded. 'I do surely.'

'Do you happen to remember whom you saw there?'

Jenkins' manner changed subtly. He looked appraisingly at French, then after a slight hesitation replied: 'I do; a man named Willie Underwood. We had a table between us.'

'I'm anxious to know what you talked about. Can you remember?'

The man's hesitation grew into embarrassment. 'I don't know that I could rightly tell you. We spoke of many a thing.'

'Was Mr Elton's name mentioned?'

Jenkins' embarrassment increased. 'I suppose it might have been,' he muttered at last.

'Well, that's the reason,' and French's manner was sharper. 'And if you had thought for two seconds you might have guessed it.'

'Well, so I did, but I wanted to be sure.'

'All right: you're sure now. I want an account of that conversation; what was said on both sides.'

Jenkins made a show of unconcern. ''Deed if I could tell you after all this time. You don't be remembering every word you would let slip in the course of an evening's conversation.'

'As you wish. Then I'll ask you questions. Did Underwood mention his trouble about the money he had taken and about Mr Elton wanting to be repaid before the end of the month?'

Jenkins' round eyes contrived to look both surprised and exceedingly shrewd. 'Since you're asking, he did pass a remark about that.'

'Did he seem much upset?'

'Not more than you or I would'a' been under the same circumstances.

'That would have been a good deal in my case. Did he think Mr Elton had been unduly hard with him?'

'Well, of course he was a hard man. Everyone knows that.'

'Yes, but that doesn't answer my question. What did Underwood think about it?'

'He thought it was hard right enough. He wondered whether if he asked him again, Mr Elton wouldn't maybe extend the time.'

'And what did you say to that?'

'I said, maybe he would.'

French had been growing more and more interested in Jenkins' manner. He was positive that the man knew more than he had admitted. But he did not for the moment see how to force a confidence. Then he decided to bluff. He bent over and spoke more seriously.

'Now look here, Jenkins, this is a murder case. In investigating that murder I'm asking you certain questions. If you try to mislead me it may be very serious for you. This is not a threat, but a warning. Have you ever heard of accessory after the fact?'

Actual fear shone in Jenkins' eyes. 'I don't know what you're getting at,' he mumbled. 'I haven't done anything.'

'I'm not suggesting you have. I'm asking you about your conversation with Underwood. What else did you say to him when he spoke of a further application to Mr Elton?'

'Nothing in particular. Besides, it couldn't matter, for he didn't act on anything I said.'

176

Joyfully French seized on the admission, though his manner remained unaltered. 'How do you know that?' he asked.

'Because I saw him again last Friday night,' Jenkins said with more confidence. 'I didn't want to tell you, for I'm not supposed to leave the house when the master's out. But my wife was here, so I thought it would be no harm to slip down to the Green Pig for a pint.'

'I'm not interested in that. I'm not going to tell Mr Cox, if that's what you're afraid of. Now you state that Underwood didn't act on what you said. That means you said something he could have acted on. What was it?'

Jenkins looked so taken aback that French knew he had at last struck oil. 'Come on, man,' he said impatiently, 'I can't stay here all day. You needn't attempt any denials, for your manner has given you away.'

It was not till French hinted that reticence could only mean guilt of the murder, that very unwillingly Jenkins answered. 'Well, if you must have it, I said that Mr Elton had given a lot of trouble to others, but that if I wasn't mistaken, he'd a big spot of it coming to himself one of these days.'

'Oh, and what did you mean by that?'

Jenkins shrugged as if giving up a further struggle.

'I hope you won't be mentioning it, sir,' he said urgently, 'for if the master got to know it would be the boot for me and no mistake. It was when Willie Underwood was grumbling about Mr Elton making him pay.' He paused, wriggled uneasily in his chair, and looked in every direction but at French. Then finding no escape in these evolutions, the story at last came out.

It appeared that some months earlier Cox had brought some historical prints of the neighbourhood and Mrs Elton came up to see them. There was a large mirror on the lounge wall—Jenkins pointed it out—and when the end. window was open those passing outside could see down the room through this while remaining hidden themselves. The window had happened to be open that day and he had happened to pass. Glancing in, he had seen Mrs Elton in Cox's arms. It was none of his business of course, but from Cox's absences in Town and his manner before and after them, Jenkins felt sure that he was still seeing her. It was this that he had referred to when he had said that Elton had a spot of trouble coming to him.

Though his manner remained unaltered, French felt a thrill at the news. One of his theories had been that Julia Elton had a lover, and now it looked as if this were correct. His interest in Cox increased a hundredfold. But that could wait. He must now get all he could from this Ulsterman. 'Did Underwood ask you to explain your remark?'

'He did.'

'Did you do so?'

'Well, I did. I shouldn't have; I see that now. But I had a drop too much taken and that's a fact.'

'I see,' said French. He leant forward. 'You mentioned your idea to Underwood. Tell me, did you mention it to anyone else?'

Jenkins shook his head indecisively.

'Come now, I see you did,' French said sharply. 'Who was it?'

It was like dragging a bone from a snarling dog, but eventually French got the information. He had told Croome. He now bitterly regretted it. But he swore, and French was inclined to believe him, he had made no further confidences.

'We're getting to it at last,' French went on, 'but you haven't told me everything yet. What was the action you suggested Underwood should take?'

Jenkins had grown ghastly and drops of perspiration were standing on his forehead. 'That was all there was about it,' he insisted, but brokenly.

'Don't lie,' French adjured him harshly. 'Do you want to be arrested as an accessory? Can't you see that you've given yourself away? Come: out with it!'

The atmosphere in the room grew tense as the man remained silent.

'I'm waiting,' French said grimly after an impressive pause, 'but I won't wait much longer.'

Some more delay, some more prevarication followed by a threat of an immediate adjournment to the police station, and Jenkins threw up the sponge.

'I suggested,' he muttered with a venomous glance, 'that Mrs Elton would be glad to pay the debt to have her affair kept quiet.'

'Oh,' said French, 'inciting to blackmail? They give a good long stretch for that. Anything else?'

The change in the man's manner told French that at last he had the truth. 'Be thankful, Jenkins,' he went on, 'we're not interested in that at the moment. But if you give any more trouble we may change our minds.'

'A worthwhile story at last, sir,' Rollo exclaimed on their way back to the police station. 'We're getting somewhere for a change.'

'But where?' French was less enthusiastic. 'It's not so clear to me. Just let's hear you spouting.'

Rob grinned. 'Well, first you were right about Mrs Elton having a lover. Cox becomes a real suspect and there's something tangible against the lady herself.'

'Yes?'

'Then there are surely several possibilities in the blackmail idea. Perhaps Underwood took the advice: either wanting money from Mrs Elton or Cox or threatening Elton he'd blaze the story abroad unless he let him off the debt. Or—what would you say to this, sir?—Perhaps Jenkins was doing it himself? Or even Croome? I don't know: I'm afraid this isn't very sensible. But it's at least correct that we should look into Cox's doings.'

'We'll do it tonight. I'm not very much impressed by your blackmail ideas, though you may be correct. If so, it might explain one puzzling thing: what Elton went to the garden for. On the other hand, why should a seeker for golden eggs murder the goose?'

'That's a point certainty. Unless Elton went for him and it was done in self-defence.'

'The blow was on the back of the head.'

'I'm afraid I've been talking a lot of rot,' Rollo admitted ruefully. 'All I really mean is that we've still got a good many suspects.'

'It's not so bad if you keep an open mind. Always let the facts lead you. A fixed idea is bad at all times, but in this game it's worse than in most. Cheer up, young Rollo. When you see how we get through this case, you'll be less frightened of the next.'

Rollo smiled gratefully. French certainly was the goods.

13

The First Stocktaking

No further information having come in to police headquarters, French and Rollo discussed their next move.

'The first point,' said French, 'is whether we've got the motive. Was it the intrigue? What do you say?'

'I can't see any proof of it, sir, but on the face of it I should say it was likely. I suggest we assume it and see if it gets us anywhere.'

'Good,' French said approvingly, 'I'm pleased with that. It's standard practice when one's in doubt. Select a likely line, act on it, and see what happens. Very well: if we assume the intrigue was the cause of the murder, we may also assume that it was the intrigue which brought Elton to the summerhouse. From that something follows?'

'From the position of the body it looked as if he went there to overhear conversation. That would mean Mrs Elton and Cox.'

French nodded. 'How do we act on that?'

'Put it up to Cox tonight, I suppose?'

'Of course, but I think we can do better. Would we be likely to get more out of a poor weak woman who has just suffered bereavement, or from a strong silent man whose designs seem to be on the point of succeeding? I think the former. Then all being fair in love, war and detection, let's tackle Mrs Elton.'

Julia was in the garden, but came in and received them in the lounge. She was looking old and tired and French instantly regretted what he had to do. His manner when he spoke to her was firm, but it was also kindly.

'I'm sorry madam,' he began, 'to trouble you so soon again and to touch on a subject which may be painful. You will understand that I can't help myself. It's in connection with your friendship with Mr Cox and I want to know when, previous to his arrival for dinner on Friday, you last saw him?'

That the shot had gone home was apparent. Julia's face went dead white and she sat staring at him with an expression of absolute panic. Twice she tried to speak, but no sound left her lips. To French it suggested that Cox was guilty and that she knew it.

'Mr Cox met Mr Elton in the garden on that evening?' he went on, quietly but inexorably.

'Oh no!' she cried, terror in her tones. 'You're wrong! He didn't! He—he—wasn't there.'

As so often before, it flashed through French's mind that the penalty for normal truthfulness was the inability to lie convincingly. That Julia was lying now he had no doubt whatever.

'You were out there with him?' he bluffed again.

Though she feebly shook her head, he saw that he was right. 'I'll forget those last two answers, Mrs Elton,' he said gently. 'I can assure you that your best policy is to tell me the truth. Please understand that I am aware of the relations between you and Mr Cox. All the same I must inform you that when answering, you're entitled, should you wish it, to have your solicitor present.'

'Oh,' she moaned, covering her eyes with her hands, 'I can't help seeing what you think. But I assure you on my honour both Mr Cox and I are innocent of this terrible crime.'

'Madam, I haven't accused either of you. But you must admit that the circumstances look suspicious. I must have those suspicions either confirmed or removed. If you think your statement will remove them, you'll make it; if you don't, we won't. You can wait if you like for your solicitor, but if you wait to discuss it with Mr Cox, that in itself will be my answer.'

A long silence reigned. French waited patiently. Julia was obviously fighting a mental battle. At last something seemed to give way and her resistance broke down.

'I'll tell you,' she said in a low voice. 'You look honest and I think you won't twist what I say. He was there at the summer-house and I met him: Mr Cox, I mean. But my husband—was dead. Mr Cox found him.'

'Then why did he not report it?'

She turned away her head. 'For my sake,' she whispered. 'He didn't want it to be known that we were meeting. Also he was afraid we might be suspected.'

A few more questions and the whole story came out; the conditions of her marriage, her relations with Richard, her falling in love with Frank, their discussion about a divorce, her decision to remain faithful to Richard, her meeting Frank in the garden to tell him her decision, and his strange manner and subsequent explanation. She spoke with frankness and French's instinct was to believe her. His reference to the stone owl produced no incriminating results. Continuing his questions, therefore, he obtained a large number of designedly

irrelevant details. If Cox's statement coincided on these inci-
dental matters, he thought the entire story might be accepted.

'One other question, Mrs Elton, and I have done,' he went
on. 'Do you know a man named Underwood, a former clerk
in your late husband's office?'

'I don't know him personally. I know his wife.'

'Did you know of the circumstances under which he left
his employment?'

'Yes, Mrs Underwood told me.'

'Mr Elton hadn't mentioned it?'

'No, he never troubled me with the details of his business.
But I spoke of it to him.'

'Oh. And what did he say?'

'He explained his point of view. I could not quarrel with
it.'

'Thank, you. That's everything at present. If you have told
me the truth, as I'm sure you have, I hope that you will not
be troubled again.'

This was not mere politeness on French's part. Except on
one point he really did accept her statement. Whether Cox
was guilty of the murder he did not know, but he was satisfied that Julia believed in his innocence. The doubtful point
concerned Underwood. Though her statement was reasonable
enough, it left French dissatisfied. Her manner while making
it had altered, and he doubted that he had heard the whole
truth.

'A nice woman, that,' he remarked as they left the house.
'I fancy she didn't have too good a time with her husband.'

Rollo dutifully agreed, but his attention was not on Julia.
During the interview he had developed a new theory and was
brimming over with it.

'What about Mrs Underwood?' he exclaimed eagerly. 'She

knew all the details about her husband and the money, so she had a pretty strong motive. What's to prevent her from having written Elton an anonymous letter to get him out to the garden? She'd been there and knew the layout and had probably noticed the owl.'

This had already occurred to French, though he had not been greatly impressed by it. He doubted if Mrs Underwood had the resolution for such a crime. However, an interview could do no harm. He decided he would let Rollo make what he could of his idea.

'You may be right,' he said. 'We'll go there now and you can talk to her.'

Though it soon became evident that the lady was innocent of the murder, French was pleased with the way the young man handled the interview. From it two facts of importance emerged.

The first was that Underwood had been in such a frame of mind on that Friday evening that she feared disaster of some kind. This was an obvious deduction from the fact that she had followed him to Chalfont. The second was the presence of Cox. This she had admitted with the greatest unwillingness, and only when she had been no longer able to parry Rollo's skilful questions.

Once only French put in his oar: when he asked her at what hour Cox had passed into the garden. She was able to answer from the hour at which she had arrived home, which she had noted. It was just seven twenty-five.

'I suppose it's Linden Cottage again?' said Rollo, as they turned away.

'Straight,' French answered. 'We must see Cox before he talks to Jenkins.'

They reached the cottage well before the time Cox was

expected home and took up their position behind some shrubs. When he drove up they were waiting for him on the doorstep.

He seemed neither surprised nor perturbed to see them, and though slightly sarcastic about the apparent urgency of their visit, took them into the lounge immediately.

'I want, sir,' said French after the usual explanations, 'a statement from you as to your movements on last Friday evening, but I have to inform you that you are not bound to answer my questions, and also that if you think it desirable, you can have your solicitor present at the interrogation.'

'That sounds ominous, chief inspector,' Cox spoke lightly, though anxiety showed in his eyes. 'But I've nothing to hide and we can therefore go ahead now.'

'As you wish. Then my first question is: At what hour did you meet Mrs Elton near the summer-house in the Chalfont grounds?'

It was a knockout blow. Cox sat motionless, staring as if he couldn't believe his ears, while his face paled.

'Your reaction is an admission that you did meet her at all events,' went on French. 'Well, sir; at what hour was the appointment?'

Though so much taken aback, he soon rallied and attempted a bluffing denial. But French's quiet, 'Then when Mrs Elton says it was seven-thirty, I suppose she's lying?' broke him down, and somewhat disjointedly he repeated the statement he had made to Julia. French waited till he had regained self-control, then continued his questions.

'Can you estimate how long you were at the summer-house before Mrs Elton arrived?'

'Only a minute or two. I had just time to make sure that Mr Elton was dead. Then I hurried to the entrance at the yew hedge, to prevent Mrs Elton from seeing—the body. She came up as I reached it.'

'Did you know the deceased would be at the summer-house?'

'Certainly not. It was a complete and ghastly surprise.'

'Had you mentioned your appointment with Mrs Elton to anyone?'

'Well, what do you think, chief inspector? Of course not. 'Could anyone have got to know about it?'

'I'm certain they could not.'

'Did you see anyone on your way to Chalfont?'

'No one.'

'Did you move the stone owl?'

Once again this question failed of its purpose, and after some further talk, in which the Box Hill meeting was discussed, the detectives took their leave. Jenkins with chastened mien showed them to the door. French paused on the step.

'One other question, Jenkins,' he said. 'Can you remember at what hour Mr Cox left for Chalfont on Friday night?'

It appeared that owing to his anxiety in the matter of the Green Pig, he had noted it: exactly a quarter-past seven.

'That works in,' said French when the door was shut. 'Well, Rollo, what about the yarn? Acceptance or rejection?'

'Acceptance, I think. It was pretty clear he was lying at first, but I imagined afterwards he was speaking the truth. And that stone owl question is a bit of a test.'

'True. Anything else?'

'His details agreed with Mrs Elton's: in small things, I mean, like the closing of that frame. Then the times worked in.'

French nodded. The young man certainly was no fool. French was growing increasingly pleased with him, and believed he would be able to send in a report which would confirm his promotion.

'Just run through them,' he suggested.

'Cox left his house at seven-fifteen and was seen on the drive by Mrs Underwood at seven twenty-five: both these witnesses disinterested and probably reliable. With the parking of his car the trip would probably have taken him ten minutes; the walk to the summer-house via the rock garden would take three or four minutes,' four when one includes searching in the dark for the owl. Say he reached the summer-house about seven twenty-nine.'

'Right.'

'Mrs Elton left her room at seven-thirty and it would take her about two minutes to reach the summer-house. That works in if their story's true. It would only leave Cox three minutes to find where Elton was, to creep up behind, him, commit the murder, see that Elton was dead, throw the owl into the bushes and get back to the hedge to stop Mrs Elton. I don't think he could have done it, sir. Do you?'

French smiled. 'It's not proof. I'm afraid we must still reserve judgment.'

'A bit exasperating: I mean, not to be sure.'

'Ah, Rollo, I see you're beginning to learn your job.'

They returned to the hotel and after dinner French, wishing to please the young fellow, who had worked hard, suggested looking in at the pictures. The proposal was enthusiastically received, but unhappily for Rollo, as they reached the porch they met Dagg.

'Going out, Mr French?' he asked. 'I have a message for you, if you can wait a moment.'

'Only a stroll to pass the time,' French declared. 'Come in and have a drink.'

They made themselves comfortable in a corner of the lounge, and after a few polite exchanges, Dagg explained his business.

'The Yard were on the phone just now, but I couldn't get through to you, so I took the message. It's about some questions you wished asked of Mr Julian Greer, the K.C.'

'Oh yes, Dagg. Go ahead.'

Dagg read from a memorandum. 'I was to inform you that he had received the two letters by the same post, all correct and as you had said; that the mistake in the first one was reasonable and might easily have been made, and that they were both signed for the firm, but in Mr Jeffrey Elton's hand, which he knew well. I presume you understand what it means, sir?'

'Oh yes, it's very clear. It's about that alibi of Jeffrey's I told you of. By the way, have you people got anything about the car?'

'Yes. Mr Jeffrey took it out of the park at seven thirty-two.'

'How did you learn that?'

'An attendant named Arthurs saw him. He was on late duty that night and went for supper from six-thirty to seven-thirty. He was just stepping into his but as Mr Jeffrey hurried in. Mr Jeffrey started up the car and swung out in the devil of a hurry, so Arthurs said.'

'Arthurs looked at his watch?'

'Yes, because if he'd been late he would have heard about it from his relief.'

French looked from one to the other. ''Pon my soul, Rollo, it looks as if a miracle had happened. Is it possible that we've got certainty at last? I was just saying, Dagg, that in our job you get possibility after possibility, but not certainty, and the words are scarcely out of my mouth till they're proved wrong.'

'You think Jeffrey may be eliminated, sir?'

'Well, what do you both think? Between seven and seven-thirty he types his letter. All that's confirmed first by the typist

189

and now by Greer. He comes out about seven-thirty and drives home. He is seen arriving upstairs at seven-forty and you've just proved he left the park at seven thirty-two. I think that's all right.'

'I should think so too,' said Dagg.

'And so should I,' Rollo added.

'What do you think of the case as a whole, Mr French?' Dagg went on. 'Is it likely to be a long job?'

'We're not ready for a conference yet, I'm afraid,' French answered, 'but I'll tell you just where we stand. In fact I was just wanting to check up our results,' he caught Rob's eye and his own twinkled, 'and if you have time to wait, your views might be helpful. I'm afraid Rollo was wanting to go to the pictures, but he'll have to control his yearnings. Moral tonic and all that.'

'No moral tonic to me, sir,' Rollo grinned. 'I'd much rather check up.'

'Then you'll get your incomprehensible desire. What about you, Dagg? Can you wait?'

'I'd like to.'

'Right. Then just pass me my notebook and we'll go into it.'

He turned over the pages, but before he could go further a constable appeared.

'A letter for Mr French, sir,' he said, passing a note across. 'A car from the Yard was passing and left it in.'

The note contained a preliminary report from Professor Kennedy about the chemical experiments. French explained the affair to Dagg and then read its essential paragraphs aloud.

'The deceased's alleged discovery that emerald acts as a catalytic agent in causing certain synthetic resins to act continuously and without exhaustion in removing the positive and negative ions of salts dissolved in water, is completely novel and previously unknown to science. Should this prove possible with a stone of less value, it is obvious that the discovery would become one of considerable importance, and the holder of the patent rights would doubtless find them profitable.

'The deceased's action in the matter was, in my opinion, not only natural and reasonable, but extremely able. To use emeralds in the process was out of the question: therefore could a cheap substitute be found? Where should this be looked for? Naturally in the rocks and clays in which emeralds were found. Such a search must therefore be undertaken.

'But the deceased could not do the work himself. Therefore he must employ an agent. He was naturally unwilling to trust the details of his secret to an unknown man: hence the adoption of the subterfuge of the letter from Cairo.

'The notes of the experiments returned by Harte are admirably complete. They show that the deceased's plans were being systematically carried out. Harte was testing, and in a highly efficient and competent manner, various crystalline deposits found in granites, hornblendes, and clay slates. He had without success worked through about one half of the various samples the deceased's other agents had sent in. To complete these would have meant several months further work.'

'Damn it, that lets Harte out,' French commented. 'If he hadn't found the answer and had several months' work before him, he'd want to hold the job and therefore to keep Elton alive. That's two of them cleared as far as we're concerned. Well, even negative progress is better than none. But we should have eliminated half a dozen of our suspects by this time. We've been too slow.'

Rob protested. 'Of course I know I've had no experience

in murder cases, but I thought we hadn't done so badly in the time: only three days, sir. What do you think, Mr Dagg?'

'Don't ask embarrassing questions,' French retorted. 'It depends on your criterion. If you mean work, yes: we've been quite busy. But if you mean reaching a solution, there's not much to make a song about. Well, let's take stock.' He turned to Dagg. 'Rollo's learning the job, you know, so I let him keep the notes and do the spouting. Go ahead, Rollo. Take Julia Elton first and let us have our conclusions to date.'

Rob grinned at Dagg. 'Embarrassing for me this time, Mr Dagg, but I'll do my best.' He grew serious as he paused to collect his thoughts. Then he recounted what had been discovered to Dagg, continuing, 'Mrs Elton is a possible. She had a strong motive in her love for Cox, coupled with the difficulty about a divorce. She also had opportunity. She went secretly to the scene of the murder, and denied that she had done so. On the other hand she does not seem the kind of woman to commit a murder, though obviously there's not much in that. Further, she probably did not know about the stone owl. If guilty, therefore, it would be more likely as an accessory to Cox before the fact than as the actual murderer. She might, for example, have got Elton to the place.'

'And your own conclusion?'

'I think she's innocent, but that's only my opinion and we cannot strike her off the list.'

'I agree: we'll leave her on, but mark her "unlikely". Do you agree, Dagg?'

'Yes, I do. And if I may say so, I think it was pretty good getting all that in the time.'

'It wasn't difficult. Now, Rollo: Miss Langley.'

Again Rollo summarized the evidence, continuing: 'Nothing to connect her with it that I can see. We don't know that she had any motive, and there was the maid's evidence that she didn't leave her bedroom during the critical hour. I think, sir, Miss Langley might be eliminated.'

'She's a pretty girl certainly,' French said appraisingly.

'She's not all that pretty,' Rollo laughed. 'Besides, Mrs Elton's not a bad looking woman, if it comes to that.'

'Neither she is, though getting on a bit. Very well: elimination of Miss Langley. What do you say to that, Dagg?'

Dagg signified agreement and they went on to Cox.

'We were talking about Cox before you came in, Mr Dagg. He had a stronger motive than anyone. He went to the scene of the crime secretly and denied it. Presumably he could have got Elton out to the summer-house and murdered him before Mrs Elton appeared, though of course there's no proof that he did. In his favour are the facts that he didn't register any shock when the owl was mentioned, and that it's very doubtful whether he would have had time to do all that was necessary.'

'Would you leave his name on the list?' French asked.

'Yes, sir, I think I should.'

'I'm afraid you're right. Very well. Underwood.'

'Underwood's another possible. He also had a strong motive and was near the place at the time of the crime. It's true again that we can't prove he was there or that he got Elton out or that he knew the garden. On the other hand it doesn't seem likely from his manner that he had handled the owl. All the same, sir, I feel sure that we can't take him off the list.'

''Fraid you're right again. Then Croome.'

'After he met Underwood Croome could have gone to the garden and committed the murder. No doubt he could have got Elton out by some trick. Of course again we've no evidence that he did either. Further, we don't know that he had any motive for the crime, but we think he had a strong one for keeping Elton alive: to preserve his job. The only suspicious thing about Croome is his manner, though that's not very convincing. It might be accounted for by fear of suspicion or by his knowledge of the Mrs Elton-Cox intrigue.'

'Then you would eliminate Croome?'

Rollo hesitated. 'I think so, sir.'

'You're doubtful, and so am I. I think we'll leave the name, but mark it "unlikely". Harte we've just eliminated. Who's left? Mrs Underwood?'

'I thought it might be Mrs Underwood at one time, but I don't think so now. It's true she might have been coming away from committing the murder when she saw Cox, but her motive is scarcely strong enough and she didn't react to the owl test. Besides, for what it's worth, she didn't seem to me that kind of woman.'

'I can't see Mrs Underwood committing a murder and that's a fact,' put in Dagg unexpectedly. 'She's a fine woman and thought a lot of in the town.'

'I entirely agree,' French nodded. 'Although we know that impressions are not evidence, I for one hold that the psychological argument carries weight.'

Rollo looked from one to the other. 'Then I should leave her on the list, but mark her "unlikely"?'

'Right.'

'Then there are a number of others: Moffatt, the head clerk; the three Alinghams, and the two Pegrams; Hawthorne, the chauffeur, and Moggridge, the gardener. All these I suppose are possibles, but we've got nothing against any of them, and on the face of it none of them seem likely.'

'What we want,' said French, 'is to find out what brought Elton to the garden. That would probably give us all we want.'

'No suggestion of that yet, sir?' Dagg asked.

'No. Probably Elton had a note which he destroyed, but of course we can't prove that. We've got to tackle the point, though I'm hanged if I know how. Now let's see: that gives us Jeffrey Elton, Harte and Miss Langley scratched, so to speak; Mrs Elton, Cox and Underwood bunched together, but with Cox leading by a neck, and all the others so far behind as to be practically out of the running.'

'That's about it, sir,' said Rollo.

'Yes, that would seem to be sound,' Dagg agreed. 'You've got a bit of work to do still, Mr French.'

French nodded. 'You've said it, Dagg. But that's enough for the moment. Let's call it a day and talk about something else. Have another drink?'

They sat chatting for some time longer, till Rollo realized that the picture he had hoped to see was over for that night.

14

The Stricken Household

While French and Rollo were pursuing their interminable inquiries, an indefinable but unmistakable change had come over the atmosphere of Chalfont. Not too gay or lighthearted at any time, it had now grown grim, almost malignant. Fear in fact had taken possession of it. Fear was present everywhere. It stalked the corridors and lurked in the corners of the rooms. It coloured the conversation and darkened the outlook. It grew in the hearts of the occupants.

With all of them the fear was the same: fear for their lives or for the life of a dear one; fear of arrest and of what would follow arrest. Fear that each day might be the last on which they would live as normal individuals; that before night they might be in a prison cell, only to come out twice during their lives: once for the hideous ordeal of trial, and then for that end which just did not bear thinking about.

Nothing tangible had occurred to inspire this fear. It centred round Chief Inspector French. But he himself was anything but alarming. He had conveyed no hints that he suspected anyone. He had been invariably polite and agreeably matter-of-fact. He had never suggested that he doubted their statements. Outwardly everything had been reassuring.

It was not, however, what they knew that frightened them, but what they did not know: what French might have discovered but had not spoken of; what he might yet discover if he had not already done so. For the truth was that the conscience of not one of those intimately connected with the dead man was entirely clear. In the heart of each was the remembrance of some fact or facts which, if discovered, would be extraordinarily hard to explain away. It was this inner realization, rather than the external facts, which was making cowards of them all.

'What absolutely appals me,' said Julia to Mollie on that Monday night on which French and Rollo had been prevented by the visit of Dagg from seeking refreshment at the pictures, 'is the police finding out about my meeting Frank in the garden. *No one* knew except us two. How *could* they have learnt it?'

'Guessed it, I expect, and pretended they knew.'

'But how could they have guessed it? I tell you there was *nothing* to suggest it. And then that clerk, Underwood, knowing about Frank. How could that have got out? And Croome probably knows. Who else? Have we been living in a fool's paradise?'

Mollie shrugged. 'Once French knows it, it doesn't matter about anyone else. And he doesn't seem to think anything of it.'

'Ah, but we don't know. Police don't say what they think. And what else have they discovered? We don't know that either.'

'But there's nothing else to be discovered. I mean, so far as you're concerned.'

Julia made a despairing gesture. 'Isn't there? Suppose they

learn that you knew and had got Perkins out of the way so that I could slip up and downstairs? Suppose they learn that I had asked Mrs Underwood not to tell that she met Frank on the drive? That would make things look pretty bad.'

'Not worse than before. Naturally you were trying to hide your meeting. It had nothing to do with—with Richard.'

'Worst of all,' Julia went on, 'what has Frank said to them? Have our stories tallied? Suppose there's a discrepancy? Then they won't believe us, and then—anything might happen!'

'That'll be all right too,' Mollie assured her. 'If Frank denies it, it will be to save your reputation and if he has to admit it, he'll tell the truth: which is what you've done. The accounts will be the same. Mummy dear, you're upset and quite naturally. There's really no need for it.'

'My dear child, what a comfort you are! I am terribly worried about Frank. If only I could see him! But of course I can't. That's what makes is so dreadful.'

There was silence for a moment and then Mollie said slowly, 'It's just occurred to me: couldn't I see him for you? Suppose I were to ring him up and ask him to go into the post office at exactly eleven tomorrow. I would be buying stamps and I would meet him: quite accidentally and quite openly. We would naturally talk for a moment. I could ask him then.'

Julia looked first doubtful, then eager. 'Oh, if you only could! But do you think it would be safe? You'd ring him up from a call box of course?'

'Of course.'

'Do you know, I think you might. What a relief it would be! You'd have to be *terribly* careful. If someone were to overhear you it would be worse than ever.'

'I'll manage it safely, never fear.'

Once again Mollie was lucky in her call: she got through to Frank himself.

'Of course I'll be delighted,' he assured her, and rang off. At eleven next morning as Mollie turned away from the counter with her stamps, Frank Cox walked into the post office. The meeting was obviously unexpected and they could scarcely do other than stop to say good morning. Frank's 'How is Mrs Elton?' could be clearly heard by those standing near, then their voices naturally dropped, as they moved out of the way of those entering.

'Julia's a bit upset,' Mollie said softly, having glanced quickly round. 'She's had to admit about meeting you in the garden and she hopes you've both told the same story.'

'I've had to admit it too,' Frank answered, 'and I've told the exact truth. I expect she's done the same, and if so, there's nothing to worry about.'

'That'll ease her mind.' Then louder and moving towards the door, 'Yes, I think it's stopped raining. Good morning, Mr Cox.'

He smiled in a restrained way. 'Good morning, Miss Langley, and my kind regards to Mrs Elton.' He turned towards the counter while she left the building.

She was delighted at the success of her mission. Julia would be much happier and to give her mother happiness was a great joy to Mollie.

Farther down the High Street she chanced to meet Jeff, who was returning from a call on a brother solicitor.

'Hullo, what brings you here?' he greeted her. 'Eleven o'clock. Time for coffee. Come and have some in Johnson's.'

A few other people were in the restaurant. He chose a table in an alcove which was reasonably private.

'I've just been talking to Frank Cox,' she told him when the waitress had withdrawn. 'Met him in the post office.'

'How did he seem?'

'All right.'

Jeff made as if to speak, then hesitated.

'What is it?' asked Mollie.

'Nothing.'

Mollie was suddenly anxious. 'You were certainly going to say something,' she declared.

Jeff hedged, but she insisted, and at last very unwillingly he answered. 'Well, it's not a thing I should mention of course, but did you happen to notice him at dinner—that evening?'

'In what way?'

'You didn't then. I thought he looked—a bit—er—off colour. Probably not feeling fit.'

She swung round and looked into his eyes. 'What are you hinting at, Jeff? Come on: out with it!'

Jeff looked annoyed. 'I'm not hinting at anything; I mean— Well, hang it all, he did look as if he had just had a—er—pretty bad shock.'

'Then you mean you think—?'

'No, I don't. Hell! This thing's getting on my nerves. No, I don't suspect Cox, if you must have it. All the same, he did look pretty badly upset.'

'We're all upset, if it comes to that.'

'Yes, but that was before—we knew. Oh damn it! You're right. This thing has got under all our skins. Cox is upset, and Julia's upset, and I know Underwood's upset, and from the look of Croome, he is too. Even Harte's upset, though I don't know why he should be.'

'You're not upset.'

'I? I'm scared absolutely stiff.'

'As a matter of fact, I'm a bit scared myself.'

'You don't look it.'

'Neither do you. Anyhow, you haven't anything to be scared about.'

'Oh, haven't I? Hasn't it occurred to you that as far as motive goes I'm first favourite? Everyone else is a mere also ran.'

'Don't be silly. No one would suspect you.'

'You mean my halo is large enough to convince French. What a hope!'

'But seriously, Jeff, you're nuts. What could they have against you?'

'Everything. First I'm—er—his heir. Fifty thousand or more instead of four hundred a year. You'll admit there's something there. Then there's the office. Instead of being treated as a rather leprous kid, I'm boss of the whole show. There's something there too.'

'But you have an alibi; you told me.'

'The most suspicious part of the whole affair. It's a ghastly alibi; just looks as if it was made up.'

'Oh, well, if you're determined to convict yourself, I can't help it.'

'Yes, but I haven't come to the worst point yet. If French gets hold of it I'm done for.'

She looked at him more anxiously. 'I didn't know there was anything else. What is it?'

'Why the thing that gives point to the rest: the reason why I want money and a better position and Chalfont and to be my own master: the fact that I want to marry you of course.'

'Jeff, do be reasonable. We can't think of such a thing now.'

'The police could all right. And I don't see why you couldn't too.'

'Well, I couldn't! Not even think about it, much less discuss it.'

Jeff had put a good face on it, but she realized that beyond his joking manner he was acutely uneasy. When they left the restaurant she felt that she had given him comfort, and she thought how strange it was that both he and her mother, older people with a presumably greater knowledge of the world, should turn to her for help and sympathy. It gave her a warm feeling of satisfaction.

Jeff's references to Frank Cox, however, gave her anything but satisfaction. It was the first time any of them had put into words the dreadful feeling of suspicion which she believed was creeping into all their hearts: it was into hers at all events.

She also had noticed Frank's manner at dinner and had supposed he was ill. Afterwards—when they knew—she could not get his appearance out of her mind. There was his hasty temper. She earnestly longed to believe his story of finding Richard dead, but though she put a brave face on it to her mother, she herself could feel no certainty. Now here was Jeff sharing her doubts. She saw that unless something was quickly discovered, all their relations would be poisoned.

Though Julia and Jeff thus had the relief of discussing their position, four of the other persons who felt in a like case did not do so: three because they had no opportunity, the fourth because he could not bring himself to put his fears into words. Cox's anxiety was greater even than Julia's. He also was profoundly amazed and distressed by French's learning of the meeting in the garden, and he saw more vividly than she did how badly the circumstances would look if set out in court with the skill of a prosecuting counsel. And if he feared for himself, he feared even more for her. If he were arrested, nothing would save her from a charge at least of accessory before the fact, if not of actual conspiracy to commit murder. In both their cases he saw that the motive was obvious and that the garden meeting gave not only a perfect opportunity, but a practical connection with the crime. Grimly he realized that in the past men and women have been convicted on far slighter evidence.

Anxiety was also deep in Harte's mind. Like the others, his conscience was troubling him. He feared the police might get to know his official character, and he knew that if they did, the proverb might well read: Give a man an old lag's name and hang him. He did not see that they could exactly prove motive, but he realized that if it were suggested that Elton had got hold of his secret and threatened to reveal it, it would sound a very plausible motive indeed. And he had no alibi. If Elton had slipped out of the house unseen, so could he; at least so it could be argued. Harte was unable to discuss his fears and the more he brooded over them the sharper they seemed to grow.

If fear reigned in the hearts of Cox and Harte, Croome was beset by absolute panic. Here also his conscience was not clear. He had been interfering in matters which he should have rigorously let alone. What if his employer's wife and her lover were meeting in London? It was nothing to him. Why hadn't he had the sense to shut his eyes and take no action? Fool to think he could turn it to his own advantage If what he had done came out, these cursed police might say that Elton had discovered it and was going to sack him. That would be a motive all right for he would be unlikely to get another job. And he had had ample opportunity: or they would say so. Worse still, he had tried to mislead French on that very point. He had first let him think he had posted that confounded letter of Elton's, believing that this would account for more of his time during the dangerous period. Then French had somehow found out he had not done so. Outwardly he had got out of it all right, though with the police you never knew. They said nothing, but went on quietly snooping, and then suddenly you were for it. Like Cox and Harte, the more Croome reviewed the past, the more precarious his position seemed to grow.

The last member of the quartet was Underwood. He alone of the four could have had the ease of unburdening his mind and the comfort of a sympathetic hearing, if he had turned in his trouble to his wife. But he could not bring himself to do so. He did not wish to worry her, and he did not see that nothing could have worried and hurt her more than his silence.

Underwood was no fool and he very clearly appreciated his position. His motive for murdering Elton was so clear that it cried aloud to heaven, his opportunity was equally obvious, and he had been seen close to the scene of the crime at about the time of its commission. A couple of hours after the affair he had presented himself in an unduly excited frame of mind at the Green Pig, and he had no alibi for the intermediate period.

That evening he had taken too much drink, a thing contrary to his habit and which proved that he was in an abnormal condition. His shell-shock had weakened his self-control. Like Cox, Underwood could well imagine how the case would sound when presented in court by an able counsel, and as he did so, he shivered.

He tried to hide his fear, but from his wife at least he could not do so. Carrie Underwood knew what was in his mind and it terrified her. She saw as clearly as he did the case which might be made against him. And she knew that her action, if discovered, would strengthen that case. Her application to Julia would show how seriously she took their trouble. If Julia reported that to the police—and if she thought Frank Cox was in danger she no doubt would do so—it might prove the last nail in William Underwood's coffin. As in the house of Chalfont, so in the Underwoods' home, fear reigned.

Pegram was another to whom Richard's death came as a severe personal shock. A murder meant a police investigation into the antecedents of every person who might by any stretch of the imagination be guilty. From such an investigation Philip Harte, as an inmate of the house, could not possibly hope to escape. The jealously guarded secret of their relationship would almost certainly become known, and perhaps that discreditable Canadian episode as well. Pegram had a lively appreciation of how unpleasant this would be for him. Apart from the disgrace of having a jail bird nephew and of having employed him in his works, it would be obvious that he had unloaded him on Elton. From every point of view his reputation would suffer.

Even Jenkins was uneasy as a result of the tragedy, and as in all the other cases, it was because of his conscience. It was not his fault that he had learnt of his employer's fondness for Mrs Elton: that had been an accident. But it was no accident that he had spoken of it afterwards. If his talk had led to Elton's death, he would be morally guilty of murder. Apart from this, if his employer were to learn of his indiscretion, the sack was the least he could expect.

Thus it was that a number of those who had been intimately associated with Richard Elton during his life, were profoundly and adversely affected by his death. It was as if his passing had released an evil influence which had entered into the hearts of those who had surrounded him, inducing fear and unrest and distress. His life had not made for the happiness of others, and the fatal tendency seemed to have persisted in increased measure after his death.

That evening during conversation Julia asked Jeff what he was going to do about Underwood, explaining that Mrs Underwood had told her of his trouble. Without suggestion on her part Jeff answered that he was going to reinstate him, though a small deduction would be made from his salary until the debt was paid off. So this at least was satisfactory.

At Jeff's suggestion it was also decided that Philip Harte should be asked to stay on at Chalfont for a few days longer.

'We'll have to pay him in any case,' he pointed out, 'and while he's looking for a job he can dismantle and sell the laboratory apparatus.'

Julia thought it was nice of Jeff to consult her on a matter which was one for himself alone, and readily agreed. Harte also appeared pleased with the arrangement, which indeed he had every reason to be.

On Wednesday the funeral took place. It proved an ordeal, though it was private and none but members of the family and firm were present. On returning to Chalfont the will was read and Julia learnt that though financially she was worse off than she expected, her position remained satisfactory. The bulk of Richard's money went to Jeff, but she was left a thousand a year for life. Mollie, Croome and Hawthorne received lump sums.

Now the days began slowly to creep by, for Julia and indeed for all who felt themselves menaced, heavy with fears and forebodings. She found her ignorance of what was happening almost unsupportable. She knew the police were acting, but whether their inquiries were drawing a net round Frank and perhaps herself, or whether happier times were in store for them, she had no idea. Always she had before her the horror of arrest; always the fear of losing Frank with ruin for herself and Mollie. With the others in their several circumstances it was the same.

The adjourned inquest was drawing nearer. Then at last, they told themselves, they must learn their fate.

15

The Anonymous Letter

Though French had not solved the problem of the next step in his case, he could not feel other than optimistic when next morning he looked out of his hotel window. His room was at the top of the building, and over the adjoining houses there was a view of the valley, brilliant in the bright spring sun. The sky was a clear pale blue, the air was sparklingly fresh and invigorating, and all around there was an indescribable suggestion of new life stirring. On such a morning it was impossible that things should go ill.

Optimism so born is frequently misplaced, but on this occasion French's anticipations were justified. He and Rollo were just finishing breakfast when he was called to the telephone.

'That Joe French?' came in familiar accents. 'Shaw, by all that's wonderful!'

'Shaw it is. How are you, old man?'

'Fine. It's good to hear your voice. What's the best news with you?'

'Something that may interest you. I've got a bit of information and I rang up the Yard about it. They said you were on the job and gave me your Dorkford number.'

'What's it about?'

'That bird Richard Elton. I've been away over the weekend and when I got back this morning there was a note from him waiting for me. Enclosed was an anonymous letter and it looks as if it had led him to his death. That any use to you?'

'Use!' French retorted. 'It's the thing of all others I want. It's what I've been held up for.'

'Then what shall I do? Send it down?'

'No; where are you speaking from?'

'My home.'

'Then could you take it to the Yard? If so, I'll go up and meet you.'

'Can do. Any hour?'

'What about ten this morning?'

'Okay by me.'

French went back to the lounge. 'Hey, you Rollo, our luck's in. That was Shaw and he's got the letter that took Elton to the summer-house.'

Rollo was suitably impressed. 'My word, sir, that's good! Unexpected too. What do we do about it?'

'We saddle the chargers, otherwise start up the sardine tin. We're due at the Yard in an hour.'

Rollo vanished. Three minutes later the car was at the door. 'Who exactly is Shaw?' he asked as they turned out of the High Street.

'What! Haven't you met Shaw?'

'Can't say I have.'

'Private detective. An old Yard man; left and set up on his own. Insurance work mostly. He's a good fellow. You'll like him.'

Rollo nodded.

'I've not worked with him since you came, I think,' French went on. 'The last case we were mixed up in was one you may have heard of: when Forde Manor, near Cobham, was burnt.'

'I read of it.'

'You remember there was truck with pictures. Shaw was in it because of the insurance, I because a josser got biffed over the head. Interesting case on the whole. Shaw's a sound fellow. If he'd stayed with us he'd have been pretty high up by now. But he seems to be doing all right as he is.'

'He's freer working on his own.'

'Yes, if it's a Sherlock Holmes case where he'd only have to make a couple of inquiries, then smoke a pipe of shag on a cushion and go and pick up his man. But if it's an organization job like finding a taximan, he'd first be heartbroken and then sunk. By the way, you needn't run at fifty miles an hour in a controlled area.'

Rollo smilingly reduced speed. 'It was only thirty-three, sir.'

'Three too many, or better say four to be on the safe side.'

Big Ben had scarcely completed his solemn announcement of the hour when 'Thomas G. Shaw, Private Inquiry Agent' was shown into French's room. He was tall and thin and lanky, with a long draggled moustache of the colour of bleached straw. His garments, taken seriatim, were of good quality and neat enough, yet the general effect was a trifle slovenly. He looked dejected, but his expression was kindly and his blue eyes were honest and steadfast.

'Hello, French, old man,' he said in a drawling and singsong, though not unpleasant, voice. 'Some time since we've met. What have you been up to since?'

'From going to and fro in the earth and from walking up

and down in it,' French answered solemnly. 'What have you been doing yourself?'

'Toddling round, same as you. Slaving away for quarter what I'm worth; same as you again.'

French looked at Rollo. 'I told you he knew a thing or two. This young person is Rollo, Shaw: Hendon, you know, and all that. See what we have to put up with these times.'

'You should have followed my example and got out before it happened. Don't mind him, young man. He barks a lot, but he's not really vicious.'

Rob shot a speculative eye at French. 'So I've discovered, sir,' he answered demurely.

'Oh, you have, have you? A gentleman of insight, I perceive. Well, French, you old humbug, you're interested in Old Man Elton?'

'For my sins. He went out to his garden when he was supposed to be dressing for dinner, and someone biffed him one over the head with a stone owl, an alleged ornament in his rock garden. We don't know why he went out, and if you can tell us, I'll withdraw all I ever said about your leaving the Yard.'

'Looks as if I can. Does a Mr Frank Cox come into the picture?'

'Plumb in the very centre. Is the letter his?'

'I don't know. I'd better tell you from the beginning.' He moved uneasily. 'I can't say much for your chairs, French.'

'That's the easy one that you've got,' French retorted indignantly.

'Oh, sorry; I didn't realize. Well, I've been on a case for the Thames and Tyne: another fire, but not as good a one as at Forde Manor. It was at Newcastle and I came up by the night train last night. The letter was waiting for me. Here it is.'

He passed over an envelope, which French first examined, Rollo looking over his shoulder. It was of the square grey type which French had seen on Elton's desk and was addressed to Shaw in Elton's hand. French drew out the contents, handling it carefully by the edges. It consisted of a sheet of Elton's headed paper, enclosing a folded envelope. On the sheet Elton had written:

29th March, 1940

Personal

DEAR SHAW,

I enclose you an anonymous letter I received by the first post this morning. I have no idea who wrote it and am anxious to know.

Will you take on the job on your usual terms?

Yours truly,

R. B. ELTON.

'How did Elton know you? Had you worked for him before?'

'For himself, no; for his firm, many times. I knew him fairly well from a business point of view, though I have never been at his house.'

'What was his reputation? His character, I mean?'

'Straight, I think, but an unpleasant manner. Cold and sardonic and unsympathetic.'

'Easy to live with?'

'I shouldn't think so.'

The enclosed envelope was of rather poor quality white paper and was of the business size and shape. The address, 'R. B. Elton, Esq., Chalfont, Victoria Road, Dorkford, Surrey', was typewritten. The postmark was W.C.2, and the date the 27th March. With even more care French removed the single folded sheet it contained, laying it flat on his desk.

Like the paper on which most anonymous letters are written, it was a sheet from one of those cheap blocks which are sold by the hundred thousand all over the country. It had no watermark or other distinguishing peculiarity. The message, which had neither address, date, nor signature, was printed in large purple type. Obviously it had been done with one of those children's printing sets in which rubber letters are pushed into a slotted holder, inked on a pad, and then pressed by hand on the paper. It read:

Your wife is in love with Frank Cox and they are consid-ering running away together. They are meeting at summer-house in Chalfont garden at ~~7.30~~ 7.15 on Friday evening 29th inst. If you want proof, be there.

The time 7.30 was printed in type and had therefore been the original hour. This had been crossed out and 7.15 substi-tuted in ink.

'That's what we want,' French said with satisfaction. 'If we can learn who sent that, we've got our man.'

'Quite,' said Shaw dryly.

'There are two interesting points about it,' went on French, 'both referring to time. The first is the date on which Elton received the anonymous letter. The postmark shows that it was posted in London W.C.2 on the 27th, that's last Wednesday. Elton must therefore have got it on Thursday. But in his letter to you he says he received it by the first post on Friday. A discrepancy there.'

'He must have made a mistake.'

'A strange mistake under the circumstances. More in it than that, I imagine.'

'I expect there is,' Shaw conceded. 'What's the other point?'

'The alteration of the time of meeting. Evidently an afterthought.'

'Seven-thirty was the time both Cox and Mrs Elton mentioned,' Rollo pointed out.

'Oh?' put in Shaw. 'Then it's a true bill? They did meet?'

'Oh yes, they've both admitted it. Cox says he found the deceased lying dead.'

'He didn't report it?'

'No. His excuse is that he wanted to keep Mrs Elton's name out of it and also that he was afraid of being suspected.'

'Do you accept that?'

'With reservations, yes. There's independent evidence that he would scarcely have had time to commit the murder, but it's not absolutely conclusive.'

Shaw's hand strayed to his jacket pocket and drew out an exceedingly foul pipe, which he proceeded to fill. 'You know, French, I always think that sort of story is probably true. I know if I were in a position like that, I'd clear out and say nothing. Want of faith in the police, I suppose.'

'I'd probably do it myself,' French admitted. 'We'd both be wrong, of course.'

'That's not the point.'

'No; I agree. But it's interesting about the change of tune. Let's hear what Rollo has to say about that. Rollo's supposed to be the cat's pyjamas at the moment, you know. Well, Rollo? We await your demonstration.'

'An embarrassing situation, Mr Shaw,' Rollo grinned. Then growing serious, he turned back towards French. 'It looks to me, sir, as if the murderer had made a mistake and corrected it. He somehow found out that those two were going to meet at seven-thirty and wrote his letter. Then he saw that he couldn't murder Elton because they'd both be there. So he shifted the time fifteen minutes ahead, to let him commit the murder and clear out before they arrived.'

'Then you think Cox is innocent?'

'I think the change of time proves that.'

'Ah,' said French, 'is that, or is it not, a profound observation? What do you say, Shaw?'

'I'm not going to do your thinking for you, if that's what you want,' Shaw retorted. 'As the matter stands, I don't think it is. If Rollo had said that the change of time proved it wasn't a put-up job between Mrs Elton and Cox, then I think it might be. If he speaks of Cox only, I don't think it is, for Cox might have wanted time to finish the husband off before the wife appeared.'

Rollo nodded at Shaw. 'You're right, sir,' my mistake. It only proves they weren't both in it.'

'Yes, I think we may pass it now,' French approved. 'But I don't like the idea of the mistake. This thing has certainly been carefully thought out. A mistake of that magnitude scarcely seems in the picture.'

'What do you suggest then?' asked Shaw.

'Can't think of anything,' French admitted. 'The original letter looks to me as if the murderer wanted a bust-up in the household: then when he'd written his letter he saw a bust-up wouldn't achieve his purpose and that murder would be necessary. Not very convincing, I admit.'

Shaw shook his head. 'Not very.' Slowly he reared his lengthy form from the chair. 'All this to me is an amusing though unprofitable game. Having handed over the letter, I don't seem to have further interest in the matter. If I did find the writer, who would pay me?'

'No one,' French agreed with alacrity. 'But what about the coroner? Won't you report to him?'

'I don't think so. The letter's all that matters and you can tell him how you got it.' He moved towards the door. 'Then if that's all, I'll be getting along.'

'Well, very grateful to you for coming round and all that,' French said, getting up. 'What about a little bill for the time?'

Shaw winked. 'The Thames and Tyne are paying for it,' he explained. 'Today I'm spending my morning writing up my report on the Newcastle fire.'

'So I noticed. That's fine. I'll let you know what happens.'

'An epitome of life, this,' he went on when Shaw had disappeared. 'The one thing we wanted was to know what brought Elton to the summer-house. Now we know, and I'm hanged if I can see that we're any further on.'

'Don't you think we can trace the letter?'

'We'll try all right. Now, Rollo, how would you set about it?'

Rollo hesitated. 'I'm afraid I don't know, sir. I don't see that we've any clue except the W.C.2 on the envelope. And we can't enquire at all the offices in that area. At least, we shouldn't be done for years.'

'There's just a chance that we can do better than that. Slip off down again to Chalfont and go through the deceased's desk and safe and papers, address book, everything you can find. Note all the addresses ending in W.C.2. And if there are any typewritten letters from W.C.2 bring them along. See?'

'Fine, sir; I get your idea. Shall I take the car?'

'Yes, it'll save time.'

When Rollo had gone French took the letter and envelope

216

to be photographed and tested for fingerprints. Then finding that Sir Mortimer Ellison, the Assistant Commissioner, was disengaged, he went in to report progress. Finally he turned to the mass of correspondence which had accumulated during his absence, determined to clear off what he could before his pupil's return. This didn't occur till the late afternoon.

'Sorry for being so long, sir,' Rollo apologized, 'but there was the devil of a lot of stuff to go through.'

'Got any addresses?'

'Seventeen altogether.'

'My word! That's more than I expected. Let's have a look at them.'

He was pleased to find that they were arranged in alphabetical order. This was one of those small matters which counted so heavily in the young man's favour. Many would not have troubled to place items of the kind in a proper sequence, but either from some innate sense of order or in consideration of those who would afterwards handle them, Rollo invariably did so.

French glanced down the list and handed it back. 'Route them into two circuits, will you, and we'll go round them.'

This was again the kind of thing at which Rollo was good. In a very few minutes he had produced two itineraries, one of the addresses in East W.C.2 and the other in West, and both arranged in order of position, so as to avoid unnecessary walking.

Each taking an itinerary, they set off. 'Just one question in each office,' French directed: 'Did they write to Elton on the 27th? Ring up the Yard at every hour and of course directly you get a bite.'

French walked from office to shop and from shop to office, sending in his card, seeing the manager or chief clerk, asking his question, and getting an invariable negative reply. He realized of course that he was working on a slender chance; it did not at all follow that the writer of the letter had had any previous communication with the deceased. But he had no other clue. Neither had any luck that afternoon and about six they met at the Yard.

'I'm going to take the chance of being here to get a night at home,' said French. 'What about meeting at eight-thirty in the morning?'

Rollo was delighted. There was a certain Miss Ruth German who might be induced to go to the pictures. Eagerly he set out to try his luck.

They were early at work on the following morning and on first call to the Yard he obtained some news. Rollo telephoned that he had found the shop. It was in the showroom of a chemical apparatus manufacturer, and Rollo would wait for French at the door.

Fifteen minutes later French was accompanying the young man to the manager's office. Mr Lewisham was a heavy faced man with a heavy manner, who framed his thoughts with a remarkable economy of words.

'What's all this about?' he asked when French had been duly introduced.

'A murder case,' French answered; 'the murder on last Friday evening of Mr Richard Elton near Dorkford. We're checking up on all letters the deceased received recently. Among them was a communication from this office dated 27th ult., that is, on the Wednesday before his death. We'd be grateful if you'll kindly tell us what that communication was. 'If you've found it, why don't you know?'

'We haven't found it. It's disappeared. We only know it was sent from here.'

'Nothing sent from here could have had anything to do with the death.'

'That's the point. I don't question your statement, but you'll understand that we have to satisfy ourselves.'

'Well, I've told you, and that's enough.'

'Unfortunately it's not, sir. Mr Elton was lured to his death by a message received in a typewritten envelope with a W.C.2 postmark dated the 27th ult. You sent him a communication in an envelope of presumably that description. Of course several other persons or firms may have done so too. You will see that we must follow up all such cases, if only to eliminate them from suspicion.'

The manager turned back to his work. 'I'm not standing for these insinuations,' he said unpleasantly. 'You've come here and asked a question. I've answered it. That's all I can do for you. Good morning.'

French rose. 'I'm sorry you take that view, sir, for it'll mean trouble for both of us. I would have given your people little inconvenience; now I shall have to get a search warrant and send a squad of men to go through the entire place. I hope you'll see your way to reconsider the matter.'

Lewisham swung round again. 'Damn it, that's pretty near a threat. What do you want?'

'To know what communication you sent Mr Elton on Wednesday. To get one of your envelopes and a sample from each of your typewriters. If these don't match, nothing more. If they do, all further details about the letter.'

Lewisham scowled, then without replying pressed a bell push.

'Take these gentlemen to your office, Miss Burke,' he said to the young woman who entered, 'and give them the information they require.'

French had the last word. 'Thank you very much for your courtesy, sir,' he said sweetly. 'Good morning.'

Miss Burke proved more compliant. In a few seconds she had answered French's first question. Elton had been known to them, through correspondence only, as the purchaser of certain chemical apparatus. They had recently put on the market a new range of filters, and the envelope in question had contained a personal letter suggesting that in view of his previous purchases, he might be interested in the new product. A descriptive leaflet was enclosed.

'You didn't notice anything like that among the papers, I suppose?' French asked Rollo, as Miss Burke produced a copy of the latter.

Rollo shook his head. French then had envelopes addressed to Elton on each of the three typewriters in the establishment. A momentary inspection showed that that of the anonymous letter had been done on one of the machines.

Then ensued a detailed enquiry. The typist in question, Miss Joyes, said that she had put the letter into the envelope herself. She was absolutely positive that no other document could have been substituted while it was in her custody. The letter, with others, was collected from her desk by the office boy, Robert Smeaton.

Smeaton said he remembered getting Miss Joyes' letters with those from the other typists on that Wednesday evening. As always, he put them into a despatch case and posted them on his way home. He also was satisfied that none of them could have been tampered with before posting.

'It's as I thought,' said French, as he and Rollo walked back to the Yard; 'an inside job. Someone has got at that envelope after it reached Chalfont. That's going to be our next worry.'

'A blessing to have something to get on with.'

'Yes, though it mayn't be as easy as it looks. Well, let's have a bite of lunch and go back to Chalfont.'

French proved a dull companion during the meal and the run to Dorkford. His mind was full of the new development and how he could best use it, and while Rollo was driving, discussion with him was neither wise nor profitable.

If Elton had not made a mistake and enclosed the wrong envelope to Shaw, which was unthinkable, and if this envelope had not been tampered with in Town, which seemed equally out of the question, he was right in his conclusion that the murderer must have obtained it after it had reached Chalfont. About this two questions arose: First, why had he done so? And second, how?

As to the first of these, his motive was not far to seek. Obviously it was to hide his identity. All the members of the household saw the morning letters, as Croome left them in the hall for each to select his own. A business envelope with a typed address would attract no attention, while one addressed in a disguised hand or with rubber type would provoke comment. Further, the plan saved the criminal from writing or typing it himself, both of which are traceable. The obtaining of someone else's envelope was therefore a very skilful and brainy trick.

How he had obtained it was not so obvious. It was unlikely that he had picked it from the waste-paper basket, for French's examination of the basket had told him that the deceased invariably slit his envelopes open with a knife. Presumably then he had steamed it open, changed the letters, and rescaled it while the gum was moist. In this case, as there was no outside indication of what the envelope had contained, he must have picked a letter at random. French saw that he could easily have done so, as if he had chanced on something which demanded an answer, he had only to slip it among Elton's papers, where it would be found after the man's death.

This definitely proved his suspicion that the murderer was either a member of the household or a confederate of a member of the household. Unhappily it did not get him much further.

But another obvious consideration might do so. The manipulator of the envelope had been aware of Cox's meeting with Julia. French *must* find out whether anyone in the household except Julia herself could have known of this.

He turned over the file and reread Julia's and Cox's statements about arranging their meeting. This had taken place in the belvedere on Box Hill, and there it was utterly impossible that they could have been overheard. Neither had mentioned the meeting to *anyone*. Yet the writer of the anonymous letter had known.

French found it all most puzzling. If it were true there was no possible escape from the conclusion that Julia and/or Cox were guilty.

Was it true? First, could they have been overheard in the belvedere? This must be settled before any further progress was possible. He turned to Rollo.

'I say, let's go round and see this blessed belvedere. Do you know the way?'

'No, but I'll ask.'

As Julia had done, they turned off from the main road above the Burford Bridge Hotel, drove up to the deserted restaurant, and there parked the car. The drive was new to French and he was impressed by its beauty, particularly when they reached the extended view from the top. For some time they stood picking out the various localities, then at last they turned to business.

As has been said, the belvedere was built in the classical

style. It was round with twenty Corinthian columns spaced about its circular wall. This wall extended for only about two-thirds of the circumference, the front, save for the columns, being open. Round the inside was a wooden seat. All was on a tiny scale, the internal diameter being only about ten feet.

Some hundred feet behind was a thick belt of trees and shrubs, though the little building stood out clear of this. French, having examined it all carefully, remained immersed in thought.

'Go into the place and keep up a flow of stimulating conversation,' he told Rollo at length, 'as if you were meeting your best girl.'

Rob gave a dramatic and impassioned impersonation, while French walked round listening. As he had imagined, the effect of the little stone box was to amplify the sound inside, but to cut it completely off from anyone without. So far Julia's and Cox's statements were correct. It was utterly impossible that their talk could have been overheard.

French felt more puzzled than ever. With his present information he was loath to arrest the lovers, and yet he did not see what else was possible.

Lost in thought, he returned with Rollo to the hotel.

16

The Hypothetical Niece

French, dismounting from the car, checked Rollo as he was about to drive to the garage.

'I wish you'd run out and ask Harte if he saw that circular about the filters. I've no doubt it reached Chalfont, but I'd rather prove it. I'm going to stay here and check over my notes.'

He went to the lounge, and finding it deserted, threw himself into an armchair. He felt dispirited. The case was not going as he could have wished. He had learnt a lot but in the essential of finding the murderer he was no further on than when he started. Moreover he feared that he was at a dead end. He had obtained all the information which his lines of research were likely to yield. What he wanted was a new approach.

Of course he could not reproach himself with his failure. Everything he had done up to the present had been necessary, and his time had been so fully occupied that he could not have taken on anything more. It was only now that it was possible to look round for fresh clues.

Fresh clues unhappily were not so easy to come by. For

some minutes he racked his brains fruitlessly. Then it occurred to him that he might make something of the rubber type. If he could trace its ownership it surely should be a help. It might even settle the case. If, for example, it had belonged to Julia or Cox, he would probably have to look no further. He wondered whether he could trace it?

On the whole he thought it unlikely that the murderer would use anything which had been for any time in his possession. One cannot always keep one's property secret, and when the letter was described at the inquest, it might have given rise to awkward questions. If this were correct, the outfit must have been purchased for the occasion. Where?

Not surely at a local shop, lest the salesman should come forward with his information. More likely somewhere in Town.

Possibly at a big stores, on the assumption that the larger the turnover, the smaller the attention given to individual transactions.

Though speculation as to place was but little removed from guesswork, in regard to time French felt himself on firmer ground. Cox and Mrs Elton had fixed up their meeting, on the Monday before the tragedy, thus creating the material for the letter: therefore if the outfit were bought, it was between Monday and Friday afternoon. Here at least was something to start on.

It was, French saw, a job for the organization. As he was at a dead end at Dorkford, he decided to return to the Yard and himself conduct the inquiry. Rollo having by this time reported that Harte had not seen the circular, they drove up again.

On arrival French found that the technicians had learned little further from the anonymous letter. It bore only Richard Elton's fingerprints, with one or two of Shaw's at the edge.

225

There was nothing about the paper which would enable it to be traced, though there were sufficient irregularities in the type to identify the printing outfit, could this be found.

Next morning the search began and soon a strong force was inquiring at likely toyshops, taking these in the order suggested by French. After an hour he was called to the telephone.

'I think I've got what you want, sir,' came a deep voice. 'The toy department of Harridge's. Will you come over?'

'I'll go now,' French returned.

The saleswoman said that on the previous Wednesday week—she had looked up the transaction in her docket book and was sure of the date—she had sold two items to a tall, thin customer. He had wanted presents for his little nephew and niece, and had bought a printing outfit and doll. The printing outfit was of a standard make, in which rubber letters were pushed into a holder, inked on a pad and pressed on to the paper.

'I'll take one of the same kind,' said French, putting down the money. 'I wonder,' he went on when he had received his parcel, 'if the man who bought it is among those?' and he handed her photographs of all concerned in the case, as well as a few others to regularize the test.

It was with profound relief that he watched her glance over the cards, look at one intently and then hand it back with the remark that it was a good portrait and. that she would swear to the man anywhere.

The photograph was Croome's.

'Thank you,' said French and he meant it.

'A step forward, Rollo; actually a step forward! Can you believe it?'

Rollo made suitable sounds of wonder and elation.

'Croome's an able man,' went on French, 'but if he can get out of this he's a deal more able than I think him. If we go down at once we'll have time to see him before he gets busy over dinner.'

An hour later the two men were back at Chalfont. Settling themselves in the library, they sent for Croome.

'Sorry for bothering you again,' said French with his disarming smile—he wished to put the man off his guard—'but one or two points have arisen since we had our talk. Just sit down a moment, will you?'

Croome distrustfully obeyed.

'Did you buy a doll for your niece in the toy department of Harridge's last Wednesday week?' French went on casually, but watching the man.

It was obviously a knockout blow. Croome stared, his face grew a mottled grey, and he swallowed once or twice without speaking.

'Well,' said French, leaning back and keeping his eyes fixed on him, 'that's a simple question surely? Why do you find it difficult to answer?'

Still Croome stared in silence.

'And if you did,' French continued even more easily, 'you can doubtless take us to your niece and let us see the doll and get it checked up by the young lady in the toy department?'

French was amazed at the suddenness of the man's collapse. He believed he would now get all he wanted. His manner changed.

'I'm afraid the game's up, Croome. I don't know whether you'd like to make a statement? You needn't unless you want to, but I have to warn you that if you do, what you say will be taken down and may be used in evidence.'

Croome was now ghastly. It was only after some efforts that he was able to speak.

'I see,' he said tremulously, 'you know I was there. So I needn't deny it. I did buy the doll.' He was striving hard for composure. '

'I was aware of it.' French's voice was dry. 'It's perhaps only fair to tell you that I know all about the letter and the rubber printing outfit and so on. Care to tell me about it?'

'My God!' Croome gasped, 'I know what you're suggesting! You think I killed Mr Elton. But I didn't! I didn't! It isn't true. I swear it!'

'I haven't accused you of it. But if after my warning you wish to tell your story, I'll listen to it.' He paused. 'Well, what would you like to do: get it off your chest or wait and consult a solicitor?'

Croome had now gone to pieces altogether. 'Tell you,' he declared earnestly; 'tell you everything. It can't do me any harm, because it's the truth. I've done wrong, I admit that. But I haven't done what you think.'

French forbore to make the obvious reply and presently Croome, with the expression of a man about to make his first dive from a high springboard, began his statement.

'It's true that I did go to Town and buy the doll, but I didn't want it for my niece: I haven't got a niece as a matter of fact.'

'No,' French interrupted; 'you got it to cover the purchase of the type.'

Croome wiped his forehead. 'That's a fact, sir, though how you guessed it, I don't know. You say you know about the letter too: well, I printed it with the type. I printed it and left it for Mr Elton.'

'I know you did. But why?'

The man hesitated. 'Well, if you've read it I needn't try to keep it dark. You know about—Mrs Elton and Mr Cox?'

French thought it was in his favour that he spoke with reluctance.

'Of course.'

'How you got on to it all in the time beats me, but it was a true bill. I got a whisper about it and—'

'From George Jenkins.'

Croome made a helpless gesture. 'Yes, sir, it was Jenkins told me. But I—I checked it up for myself. I—I followed Mrs Elton one day to Town on my motor bike and found they were meeting at the Bellerophon Hotel. That was last Wednesday fortnight. I—'

'Why were you interested?'

Croome seemed to find this an even more difficult question.

'Well, you see,' he stammered, shifting about on his chair, 'I thought—I mean—Well, it was this way. Things hadn't been so easy for me, as you might say, since Mr Elton married: though of course that's a long time now. But I was here with him before Mrs Elton came and I—I had a better time.'

He paused as if expecting French to help him out, but French remained silent.

'I had a freer time and more power and so on before the marriage, you understand,' he went on. 'Of course I did my best for both Mr and Mrs Elton all these years, but when this about Mr Cox happened, I thought it might make a difference. I couldn't help hoping there'd be a blow-up and that Mrs Elton would go and I'd get back my old position. But it didn't seem to be going to happen. I was all right up to then, but after that I don't deny I did wrong. I thought if the trouble didn't happen of itself, I might make it happen.'

'What did you do?'

'I thought if I was to let Mr Elton know what I'd learnt, it might do the trick. If he believed me he'd probably make inquiries and get the truth for himself. But I would have preferred to have given him evidence that he couldn't have doubted. So I watched carefully and I got the evidence.'

'How?'

'Two mornings later, that was last Friday week, Mrs Elton got a letter with a typed envelope and a Dorkford postmark. I watched her open it and I saw from her manner that it was something pretty special. So I naturally suspected that it must be from Mr Cox. Well, she went out during the morning and then I—I—' He stammered, made some ineffective efforts to continue, and came to a halt.

'Go on,' said French irritably. 'Can't you tell your story without balking at every hurdle?'

'I again did what I don't deny I shouldn't have done,' he went on. 'I—I—had copied Mrs Elton's keys and I opened her desk and read the letter.'

French made no comment and Croome continued with more confidence. 'It purported to be from a lady in St John's Wood, and it said that in answer to Mrs Elton's ad. she had a historical picture of King James the First at the site of the belvedere on the Burford Crag on Box Hill. Well, I'd heard from Jenkins that Mr Cox collected such pictures, so I thought he'd had something to do with it, and this seemed confirmed by this London letter having a Dorkford postmark. So I checked the address up in the London Directory and found there wasn't any such place.

'I guessed then that it was a letter from Mr Cox, and I saw what must have been her answer written below in pencil. It was in a simple sort of code and was easy to read. I judged that it meant that they were going to meet at the belvedere at twelve-thirty on the following Monday.'

All this time French was steadily revising his estimate of Croome's brains. Such a man would make a formidable antagonist and it would be necessary to weigh his statement with the greatest care. Again he said nothing and again Croome went on.

'I knew the place well and I soon saw what I could do. I'm a bit of an electrician, wireless and so on, and it happened I had a sensitive microphone and a coil of light cable. I asked leave for that Monday to go to Town to meet a sister, and I went up to the belvedere and fixed the mike under the seat. I made a cut in the grass with a trowel and put in the cable so that nothing would be noticed. Then I hid in the shrubbery and listened.

'I didn't hear every word they said, but I heard most of it. She had seen me in Town and thought I was out for mischief. He wanted to go to Mr Elton and ask for a divorce, but she said Mr Elton would refuse. Then he wanted her to go away with him, but she couldn't make up her mind. At last they fixed up to meet on the following Friday night; that's last Friday. They arranged that he'd come to dinner.'

'Where was the meeting to take place?'

The sweat glistened on Croome's forehead as he answered, 'At seven-thirty at the Chalfont summer-house.'

'Did you mention what you had overheard to anyone?'

'No, sir; to no one.'

'Not to Underwood, for example?'

Croome looked horrified. 'No, sir, certainly not.'

'Very well. Go ahead.'

'I thought at once that if I could get Mr Elton out to the summer-house at seven-thirty it would do all I wanted. But at first I didn't see how I was to tell him without giving myself away. Then I thought of printing a letter with a child's outfit and on Wednesday, my half day, I went up and bought it as you know.'

He paused as if he had reached the end of the story.

'Don't stop,' French told him. 'I want the whole thing in detail just as if I knew nothing. I want to know if you're speaking the truth, and I can only do that by comparing what you say with what I know of the facts.'

French had found that a remark of this kind was valuable. It produced misgiving or relief, according to the suspect's intention. Croome showed unmistakable relief.

'I'm glad you do know so much,' he said, 'for otherwise you mightn't have believed me. I bought a writing pad and with gloves on printed my message to Mr Elton. But I couldn't see how to give it to him. If I'd left it on his desk he'd have made inquiries and sooner or later I'd have been for it. Then I thought of using one of his own envelopes. On Thursday morning I picked out an unimportant looking typewritten one from his letters and steamed it open. I took out the letter and destroyed it—it was only an advertisement—and put in my printed one. Then next post I slipped it back among the letters on his desk. He—'

'Steady a moment,' French interrupted 'Let's get that clear. You say the letter came by the morning post on Thursday. When did you put it back among Elton's mail?'

'That evening, sir, Thursday evening. There are only two posts in the day. I left it on Mr Elton's desk—that desk you're sitting at—with half a dozen others.'

'All right. Carry on.'

Croome looked distressed. 'That's all,' he answered hesitatingly. 'When Mr Elton didn't turn up for dinner on Friday I was anxious, but when Mr Harte told me he was dead I was absolutely terrified. I thought—it was my fault; that if I hadn't sent the letter it wouldn't have happened.'

To this French did not reply. Instead he asked another question. 'Tell me again at what hour you suggested that Mr Elton should go to the summer-house.'

'Half-past seven.'

'You're sure it wasn't a quarter-past?'

Croome started. 'I'm quite sure,' he said after a pause.

'I don't question that you printed in half-past. But are you sure you didn't alter it later with pen and ink?'

The man was evidently completely mystified. 'No, sir; I printed it half-past and left it half-past. I'm absolutely positive.'

'Now think carefully. Could anyone have seen you playing your game with the letter?'

Croome shook his head. 'I'm sure no one could or did.'

'Anything you'd like to ask him, Rollo?'

Rollo's eyes flashed with satisfaction. 'Only one question, sir. I'd like to know whether Croome on Thursday evening put the letter among the others on his way into this room, laying them together on the desk, or whether he brought it in separately, the others being already here?'

It was a good question. French was pleased. He nodded to Croome.

'Separately. I brought the others in when the post came, then went up to my room, got my own, and slipped it in among the others.'

'What time was that?'

'About quarter-past six.'

Rollo sat back and glanced at French. 'That's all, sir, thank you.'

'Just one other question, Croome,' said French. 'When I

233

asked you just now had you put quarter-past seven instead of half-past, the question obviously touched a chord. What do you know about it?'

'I assure you, sir, I don't know anything about it. That's why I—' He stopped, evidently realizing that he had given himself away.

'After that,' French was quick to point out, 'you needn't continue to deny it.' He paused, then went on: 'Let me suggest that you saw Mr Elton going out?'

Croome remained silent, staring before him in dismay.

'I see you did,' French went on; 'and very naturally. You had written your letter and you wanted to see the result. Is that it?'

Croome bent his head. 'Yes, sir; I see I must admit it. I kept a watch on the side door from the cellar and I saw Mr Elton go out and then Mrs Elton. Mrs Elton came back, but he didn't. That was what frightened me so much.'

'Why the hesitation? 'Pon my soul, getting a statement from you is like getting pitch out of a bottle. What time did Mr Elton go out?'

'That was it, sir. That's why your question affected me. It was just before the quarter: immediately I got back to the house.' He paused, then added: 'Perhaps I should say, sir, that it was because of wanting to see how the thing would work out that I gave the letter to Mr Underwood. Otherwise I should never have dreamt of passing on such a commission.'

'Never mind about that. When did Mrs Elton go out?'

'At half-past, sir.'

'When did she return?'

'Ten minutes later; at seven-forty.'

For a moment French remained sunk in thought. 'That'll do, Croome, for the present,' he said. 'I can't say what may

234

be the result of what you've told me; you'll hear that later. You may go now.'

With an expression partly of relief and partly of apprehension Croome murmured 'Thank you, sir,' and disappeared.

'That's a slippery one,' Rollo exclaimed when the door had closed. 'There's not much wrong with him for running a decently planned murder. Brains! That's what he's got.'

'His tale will need a deal of checking.'

'I thought it sounded true, sir. It agrees with everything else we've learnt.'

'Yes, but if he has all those brains you've been raving about, it would.'

'I suppose that's so,' Rollo admitted, somewhat dashed.

'Besides,' French went on, 'if he was guilty, that's exactly the story he'd tell. What else could he say? You see now, Rollo, how cases progress. We get what looks like vital information and it leaves us where we were before. No further on, curse it all. But no; I'm wrong. The statement has some value after all.'

Rollo slowly shook his head.

'It pretty well clears Mrs Elton. If she went out at half-past seven and returned ten minutes later—and it's her own statement too—she could scarcely have committed the murder herself; not with Cox there at all events, while if she had tricked Elton into going out for Cox to murder him she would not have gone out herself.'

'That's certainly true.'

French smiled. 'Incidentally I overdid my rule of imagining possibilities, and I'll tell you as a warning. When Croome said Mrs Elton had gone out at seven-thirty I suspected collaboration on Miss Langley's part; that she had called Ada to her room to leave the coast clear. But of course if Mrs Elton returned at seven-forty instead of seven-forty-five, there could be nothing in that.'

'All the same I wish I had thought of it,' Rollo said ruefully.

'Never mind. As I see it now, one of three things must have happened. Either Croome committed the murder, as he could have done, or he talked to someone else who did. Suppose for instance Croome altered the letter and Underwood did the killing? Or again someone might have noticed him tampering with the letter, opened it, seen his chance and taken it. This last admittedly not very likely.'

'No, I suppose not. Then what do you think we should do?'

'Now, Mr Inspector Rollo, just answer your own question.'

Rollo grinned. 'I think we might assume Croome was speaking the truth and see if it led anywhere. We might try to find out who could have seen him take the letter out of the pile in the hall on Thursday morning or put it back here that evening. I admit I don't know how, for anyone who had been monkeying with it would simply deny it.'

'H'm,' said French; 'we'll have to think about that.' He looked at his watch. 'Getting on to seven. We can't do much for the moment; they'll all be going to dinner. And that reminds me . . .'

His unfinished sentence was greeted by Rollo with approval.

17

The Managing Director

When suitable action had been taken in connection with French's unspecified idea, Rollo retired to his room to write up his notes. Reappearing, he was met with a demand for a summary of his conclusions about Croome.

'I must be sure your stuff is not too ghastly rubbish,' French explained succinctly.

Rollo, delighted, whipped over the pages of his notebook.

'We provisionally accept Croome's statement for the following three reasons: first, his printing of seven-thirty in the letter. This is consistent with his wishing Elton to find Cox with his wife, but not with a desire to murder him.'

He looked up from his manuscript and French nodded.

'Second, it's likely that he should want to recover his privileges by getting Mrs Elton out of the house. It's unlikely that he should wish to murder Elton, as this would not only spoil his scheme, but would probably lead to his own dismissal. He must have known Mrs Elton disliked him.'

'Right. And third?'

'His manner. It completely changed. At former interviews

he appeared to be lying; this time I'm sure he was speaking the truth.'

'It's the voice of Solon! Wasn't Solon the wise man, or was it Socrates? In other words, that seems okay. Then if Croome is innocent, someone else took out the letter and changed seven-thirty to seven-fifteen. Have you anything about that?'

'Only one point I've added since our talk. It's about hours. If Croome's statement is true, the letter must have been taken on Thursday evening between the time Croome left it in the library and Elton's arrival. Normally that couldn't have been long. It couldn't then have been put back till Friday evening, just before the dinner party.'

'How do you make that out?'

'Well, there probably wouldn't have been time to steam open the envelope and get it back again on Thursday evening. But perhaps we could make some inquiries about that. Then it wouldn't have been very safe to replace it on Friday morning, for the letters were left in the hall and Croome and the members of the family were about. So I thought Friday evening seemed indicated, and this would check with Elton's covering letter to Shaw.'

'Not unlikely.'

'Then I wondered if this was the letter Elton had sent Croome out to post.'

'Also possible. I think, Rollo, we'll trot up again to Chalfont and see if we can put the thing a step further.'

'Tonight, sir?'

'You've said it, my son. Thinking of the movies?'

'I'm told it's a poor programme.'

'Lucky for you.'

Croome had not a great deal to add to his earlier statement. Asked for more details about his leaving his letter on Elton's desk on the Thursday evening, he said: 'I had left it in a locked suitcase in my room, for I didn't want to carry it about in case it should be seen. I intended to have it in my pocket when the post came, so as to slip it among Mr Elton's on the way here. But the post happened to be early that evening, so I left the letters in here, went up and got mine, brought it down here and slipped it among the others on the desk.' He added that this had called his attention to the time, which was just six-fifteen. Mr Elton was then in his bedroom and about fifteen minutes later he had heard him coming downstairs and going to the library.

'So that if someone else took it to alter the time, it must have been between six-fifteen and six-thirty. Did you see anyone about during that period?'

This seemed a new idea to Croome and he brightened up considerably.

'No, sir, I saw no one. Of course I shouldn't have: I was in my pantry and the dining-room.'

'What I don't understand,' said French when the man had gone, 'is how the second thief of the letter knew of its existence. There was nothing remarkable looking about the envelope. Why should he have suspected it?'

'A bit of a stumper, right enough. I suppose Elton himself couldn't have altered the time?'

'Why should he?'

Rollo looked a trifle sheepish. 'I don't know, I'm afraid. It just occurred to me.'

'It occurred to me too,' French answered, 'but I couldn't make sense of it. We'd better postpone that and see where these folk were during the critical period. I think we can save time by taking them all together.'

Having sent Croome to prepare the way, they joined the

party in the lounge. French was extremely pacific. He was sorry to trouble them again and at such a time, but he was held up by the answer to one question and he would be grateful if they would give it to him then and there. In brief; he was trying to trace the movements of a certain individual between six-fifteen and six-thirty on Thursday evening—the evening before the tragedy—and to help him he would like to know where everyone was at that time. At this there was some grumbling.

'Hang it all, chief inspector,' Jeff expostulated, 'how can we be expected to answer a question of that sort? Who remembers where they were at given hours of given days. I mean when nothing special has occurred?'

'I realize the difficulty, Mr Elton,' French answered smoothly. 'I hope you'll do your best.'

Presumably they did their best; at least all achieved replies. Harte had been with Richard Elton in the laboratory, Julia and Mollie had been together in the lounge and Jeff had been in his room reading some letters which Croome had just brought up.

'Not very helpful,' Rollo commented when they were back in the library. 'It may be true or again it may not.'

'Mrs Elton and Miss Langley corroborate each other,' French pointed out.

'What do you consider the corroboration worth, sir?'

'Exactly nothing,' French smiled. 'And neither of the others had any at all. Indeed corroboration by a witness who cannot be produced is always slightly suspicious.'

'So that we're no further on?'

'I wonder if it doesn't suggest dual action?'

'Meaning, sir?'

'Two people. What about Jeffrey and Underwood: Jeffrey

making the arrangements, Underwood doing the deed? Or Mrs Elton and Cox? Or any other pair you can think of.'

'There are difficulties.'

'Of course there are difficulties.' French broke off as if an idea had struck him. 'Look here, Rollo,' he added with more interest, 'there is a point in it after all. Let's try and check up on some of those statements. Get Croome to send in that girl—What's her name? Ada Perkins.'

Rollo, obviously curious, did as he was told.

'Sit down, Miss Perkins,' said French when she had arrived. 'I'm trying to trace where Mr Elton was on Thursday evening,' and he repeated his little story.

It happened that she was able to help. Elton had been in his room. She knew because she had gone to the door to do some tidying and could not get in. That was about five minutes past six. He was there, she was sure, for nearly half an hour.

French was delighted. 'It can't be that we're on to a discrepancy at last!' he exclaimed when the girl had gone. 'That checks with what Croome said, but compare it with Harte's statement! If Elton was in his bedroom, he wasn't in the laboratory.' Then he shook his head, though the twinkle remained in his eye. 'I can't believe it. Too good to be true.'

'Glad you feel that way about it too, sir. I was afraid my depression was just inexperience.'

French eyed him suspiciously.

'Shall we have Harte in?' Rollo went on hastily.

'Not yet,' said French. 'We'll find out something about him first. Turn up those letters Elton wrote before he engaged him. Bring them along to the hotel and we'll read them and then knock off.'

Now they had reason to bless the deceased's love of method. In a folder labelled 'Harte' were copies of all the letters which had passed. Throwing himself into an armchair in the deserted lounge, French read them in turn.

The first was from Elton and read:

DEAR PEGRAM,

As you know, I hobby a bit in chemistry, and I want a competent man for a few weeks to assist me, partly to improve my technique, to show me how to use certain apparatus, etc, and partly to carry out the routine part of a few experiments.

Do you know anyone who might suit, or, if not, where should I apply? Also what should I pay?

A suitable man might live in the house.

To this letter Pegram had replied:

DEAR ELTON,

It was rather a coincidence that I should have received your letter today, because it happens that I do know of a man who might suit you: a thing which might not happen again in ten years. He is one of my own staff, a man named Philip Harte, and he has been with me for six years. He is a really excellent chemist. He took his degree at Leeds and has done useful work with me. His bearing and manners are good and I think you could safely take him into your house. I pay him £400.

His failing is that he will not take responsibility and has to be given instructions on every point. This is a serious drawback to me, though possibly it would be an asset to you. I do not want exactly to get rid of him, but if he were to find another job, I should not stand in his way. Do not think, however, that I am trying to unload him on you. I suggest that you see him and then form your own conclusions.

Elton's last letter was that to Harte, laying down the terms of the engagement, which French had already considered.

In the folder was also a small double-leaved memorandum book with carbon sheet. It was about half used and the carbon pages bore copies of instructions to Harte. The last was dated for Thursday 28th March, the day before the murder, and read: 'I have received an invoice for the specimens from Connemara. When this arrives please go on with it before completing the Grampian stuff, as it seems more promising.' The recording of what most people would have given verbally was an extreme example of Elton's meticulous methods.

'Probably the whole thing will prove a blind alley,' French declared. 'All the same I think a visit to Pegram is indicated. Where does he hang out? Sutton? We'll run over in the morning.'

The Chemical Agencies Works were housed in a series of ultra modern buildings with steel and concrete frames and glass walls. Within, the passages were elaborately tiled, with bronze grill work much in evidence. Mr Pegram's office was suggestive of the lantern room of a lighthouse and contained enamelled steel furniture in assorted cubes, set of by chromium fittings and zigzag decorations like lightning flashes of an extreme solidity. Mr Pegram greeted them courteously, though here again French felt, as had Dagg, an undercurrent of anxiety not easily accounted for.

'I know you're a busy man, Mr Pegram.' French began, 'and I'll not take up much of your time. Just a routine interview.' He read Pegram's statement to Dagg, and when Pegram said he had nothing to add to it, he asked a few innocuous questions. Then after ostentatiously examining his notebook,

he went on: 'That's everything, I think, except some information about Mr Harte, also routine. I've seen the letter in which
you recommended him to Mr Elton. Confidentially, sir, what
sort of man is Mr Harte?'

Pegram looked wary. 'I gave my opinion of him in the letter.'

'Ah yes, but it's what you didn't say that makes me ask.
Do you consider him trustworthy, for example? Dependable
and loyal? That sort of thing?'

'I found him all right.'

'Do you know anything of his family?'

Pegram's anxiety seemed to increase. 'Nothing,' he said after
the slightest hesitation, 'except that I understand that his only
living relative is his mother.'

'Oh? Can you give me her address?'

'I'm afraid not.'

French was puzzled. Why should the managing director
object to discuss Harte? He determined to probe further.

'Where was Mr Harte living when he was with you?'

'I'm afraid I don't know that either.'

French stared. 'Oh come now, Mr Pegram,' he protested,
'surely you've a note of the addresses of your staff?'

'What on earth does it matter if I have?' Pegram sounded
suddenly petulant. 'You've asked me questions which might
properly be asked in your investigation and I've answered
them all. I'm not bound to waste my time giving irrelevant
information.'

'You must know better than that, Mr Pegram. The history
of all who might be connected with the murder is important
to me, and I must see Mr Harte's mother. Once again, sir, will
you let me have her address?'

For a moment Pegram did not answer. He seemed to be
thinking deeply. Then he shrugged as if giving up the struggle.

'You seem determined to know, so I'd better tell you. But this is a painful matter. Moreover, it's a secret and it's not my secret. Before speaking of it, I'd like some assurance that it won't become common property.'

'Nothing that you say will be repeated, unless it's found to be connected with the murder.'

'Very well,' Pegram said ungraciously, 'suppose I'll have to take your word for it. Then I may tell you that Philip Harte has been in trouble with the police. His name is really Holford. His father was in insurance and was sent out to run a branch in Montreal. He took his wife and son—Philip is an only child—with him. Philip got a job in a chemical works, but he made a break, started gambling, stole some money and got two years. While he was in prison his father died, and when he was released he and Mrs Holford returned to this country. They changed their name to Harte, and owing to having known Mrs Harte in old times, I gave Harte a job. I didn't like doing it, but I thought I should.'

'Did he give satisfaction?'

'Complete. What I told Mr Elton was true, he did admirable work while with me. More than that; he showed courage and self-sacrifice. We had a small fire some time ago, and at considerable risk to himself he plunged into the burning office and brought out some valuable papers. There's no doubt he has tried to make good and he has succeeded.'

'But you wanted to get rid of him?'

'I didn't say so.'

'You recommended him to Mr Elton. You wouldn't have done so if you had wanted to keep him.'

'Well, chief inspector, do you find that surprising? His Canadian record might have come out at any time and it would have been awkward. The rest of my staff would have resented what I had done. I didn't want to sack him, but I had determined to let him go directly he had the chance of another job. I admit I took advantage of Mr Elton's inquiry. All the same, I honestly believed he would suit Elton.'

'Then there was nothing in that suggestion that he wouldn't take responsibility?'

'Nothing.'

'It's certainly not the impression his personality gives. Can you let me have Mrs Harte's address?'

Pegram seemed annoyed. 'I hope you're not going to worry the poor woman,' he protested. 'She's had enough trouble as it is and she's not strong.'

'I may not have to call on her, but I should like her address in case some question arises.'

'Oh well, have it your own way.' Pegram looked up a book and announced: '12 Bolsover Street, Surbiton.'

'Thank you, sir. Do you happen to know what Mr Elton was investigating?'

'No.'

'You had a case about patent rights in which Mr Elton acted for you?'

'He was our solicitor. He had been since the firm started in a small way near Dorkford.'

'What was the subject of the patent rights dispute?'

'Well, seeing it's so intimately connected with Mr Elton's death, it was the softening of water by a plastic process.'

French smiled and stood up. 'I'm sorry to have been such a nuisance, sir, and grateful for what you have told me,' he said politely. 'I hope you won't be troubled again.'

'Well, Rollo, did we get the truth there?' he went on when five minutes later they were once again in the car.

'I thought so, sir. Pegram's manner seemed pretty convincing.'

'I agree. All the same I think we'll have to find out some more about Harte before we tackle him. Drive over to Surbiton and we'll see his mother.'

Bolsover Street was on the outskirts of the town in what seemed a fairly good locality. The houses were small but comfortable looking, and each stood on its own piece or parcel of land. No.12 showed no signs of poverty. It had been recently painted and the tiny grounds were neatly kept.

The door was opened by a short, stout, aggressive-looking woman, and the moment French glanced at her the motives for Pegram's altruism became crystal clear. They were as like as two peas.

Desiring formal confirmation of the relationship, French introduced himself appropriately.

'I've just been with your brother, Mr Pegram. He told me about Mr Harte's taking the job with the late Mr Elton. Did Mr Harte like the change?'

Mrs Harte's jaw dropped. 'Did Mr Pegram tell you I was his sister?' she asked.

'No, madam, but it's our job to know such matters. Don't be alarmed. We know your real name and of your son's trouble in Montreal, but so long as we're met fairly, we don't repeat what we're told.'

She was obviously disconcerted to find her secret shared. French chatted to her skilfully and soon learnt a good deal about her son. It appeared that rifle shooting was his chief interest and he played tennis and badminton and a good deal of bridge.

Armed with these particulars, French drove to police headquarters and asked that inquiries be made about Harte, particularly as to whether he was in difficulties of any kind. The superintendent was an old acquaintance and promised to forward any information he obtained to Dorkford.

Rollo seemed pleased at their progress. Now that he knew French better, he would talk while driving.

'I wonder if we're on to it at last?' he exclaimed. 'Do you think so, sir?'

'I'm a little doubtful,' French answered.

'I've felt all through that Harte was a wrong 'un because he always seemed to be hiding something.'

'As a matter of fact so have I, but we know now what it was. Besides, if he has since made good—?'

'We find an old lag who has been got rid of by his employer and his uncle at that,' Rollo persisted. 'And this same man has presumably lied as to where Elton was at a critical moment. I don't know, sir; I should have said it was promising.'

'You may be right. Has it occurred to you that Pegram might well have been mixed up in the thing?'

'You mean in the murder? I hadn't thought of that.'

'I told you to practise surmise. What about this: pure guess-work of course? Pegram has a law case about methods of softening water by means of plastics. Elton acts for him in that case. Immediately afterwards Elton starts chemical research. Pegram knows or guesses, perhaps from some remark Elton has dropped, what he is investigating. After a period of experimenting Elton asks for a qualified assistant. Pegram suspects that he wouldn't go to this expense unless he was on to something worthwhile. Pegram thinks the discovery might be valuable to him. He puts it up to his nephew, whose moral code he thinks is pliable. Harte goes to Chalfont as a spy to learn the secret. Elton discovers what's in the wind and threatens proceedings. Pegram and Harte agree to his liquidation.'

'I'll say, sir, that's ingenious.'

'Damned with faint praise, eh? Well, I don't say it's the truth, but I do say we must consider Pegram's moves in the affair.'

'Do you think that would be a sufficient motive for murder?'

'I think so. It might be a very nasty business for Pegram. You see, the whole thing would come out: not only that he was trying to steal from his friend, but that his nephew was a jailbird. At best it would be an unsavoury scandal; at worst he might lose his job and get a stretch in jail.'

Rollo seemed impressed.

'Two minor points support the idea,' French went on. 'First, Pegram's manner. He was upset about something. Perhaps it was merely that he didn't want his nephew's record to become known; perhaps it wasn't. The second: if Elton was suspicious of the pair, it would account for his trick with the Cairo letter.'

'If Harte was trying to make good,' Rollo put in thoughtfully, 'Pegram might have used his knowledge of the Montreal affair to force his hand.'

French smiled. 'Was he trying to make good? However that's the style. Keep on thinking out possibilities. If we get enough of them they must include the truth. Go on now to the actual murder. Can you work in anything about that?'

Rollo registered an expression of thought, then shook his head.

'Not so good,' French criticized. 'Then look here, Pegram's and Harte's rooms were both to the right of the housemaid's pantry. With a little care, therefore, one could have joined the other. Pegram, we'll say, had a rope ladder in his suitcase. With this Harte got down from the window, committed the murder, and climbed up again. Next morning Pegram took the ladder home and destroyed it.'

'Surely, sir,' Rollo protested, 'there are a lot of items there which they couldn't have foretold? It all depended on the room Pegram was given, for one thing.'

'Quite; I'm just putting up possibilities. There's something in your objection, though not a great deal. Harte might easily have found out where Pegram was to sleep.'

'How can we get to know?'

'Ah, now you're on to it. That's our perennial job, young man, trying to answer that question. It's not always possible and it's never easy. What would you suggest?'

'I'm afraid I don't know, sir. Perhaps try to find out if either of them bought a ladder.' He paused, then brightened up and went on more eagerly. 'What about this? Suppose it was Harte alone? Suppose Elton had found out he was a convict and was going to sack him? Wouldn't that be a motive? It would have meant ruin, for he'd never have got another job.'

French nodded approvingly. 'Quite good. It's ingenious. But it conflicts with two pieces of evidence. The first is that Elton would never have written his note to him about the Connemara specimens if he had thought that work was going to be interrupted—on the day before the crime, mind you. The second is Ada's evidence that he didn't leave his room at the time of the crime.'

'The first point is certainly pretty strong, but I don't think there's much in the second. He might have got Pegram to help him through the window, as you suggested. I was wrong that it must be Harte alone. If Elton had discovered about Montreal, it would be nearly as bad for Pegram.'

French laughed. 'I see you've made up your mind that Harte must hang. Well, I'm with you to the extent that we look into things with these ideas in our minds. When we get to Chalfont we'll begin with Harte's room.'

18

The Dawning Light

They reached Chalfont shortly after lunch and went to the library.

'Better let Croome think we'll be here all afternoon,' French suggested. 'We want to keep our suspicions dark.'

They rang for Croome and asked him if a telephone message had come through, saying they would wait where they were in case it did. Judicious inquiries revealed that their luck was in, for Harte had gone into Dorkford. A reconnaissance in force showed that the coast was clear and they slipped upstairs unseen, locking the door of Harte's room behind them. French's professional conscience gave him some slight twinges about searching a man's room without his knowledge, but he found himself able to bear these without serious inconvenience.

The room, like all those at Chalfont, was large and square. It had two windows facing east along the valley. It was comfortably arranged as a bed-sitting room, with curiously heavy oak furniture. Before the fireplace was a pair of massive easy chairs, in an alcove was the bed, supported on huge square legs, while the small table at its head looked as if it could have carried its pile of books, had these been made of solid lead.

Rollo turned to one of the windows and flung it open. 'There, sir,' he pointed. 'What about that?'

Beneath was a narrow flat roof, stretching for some thirty feet along the side of the house. In the centre it covered the porch at the eastern end of the lower corridor, immediately beneath them a connecting cloakroom, and at the other end the paper store off the library. As Rollo pointed out, from the window to the roof and from the roof to the ground were both easy drops.

'Yes,' French agreed. 'Easy enough to get out of that window, but not so easy to get in again. How could that have been done?'

'Let's just measure it,' Rollo suggested, sidetracking the question.

The two steps, from window sill to roof and from coping wall of roof to ground, proved almost equal, both about 8 ft. 0 ins. This was at the north end of the little building, where, owing to the slope of the ground, the gravel path rose highest.

'Eight feet,' said Rollo thoughtfully. 'He couldn't have got in without help. What about a rope ladder that he could have rolled round him and walked away with afterwards?'

'With that,' said French, 'he couldn't have got up unless he had left it hooked to the window. Same way to get back on the roof he would have to leave a second ladder hooked to the coping.'

'Suppose he had two? They were short and needn't have been bulky.'

French shook his head. 'Here are the objections to a ladder which you should have put up when I suggested it during our drive. First, to get a suitable ladder would take time. If we're correct in our theories, it was only on Thursday evening, twenty-four hours before the crime, that it was decided on. So unless Harte went to Town on Friday, and we know he didn't, he could scarcely have got one. The second is, how could he have disposed of it? He would know that Elton would be missed almost immediately and that the house would soon be full of police. He would never have risked leaving it in his room. From Ada Perkins' evidence we know that he didn't get rid of it before dinner. When could he have done so?'

'Before going to the lab to look for Elton?'

French frowned, though with a twinkle in his eye. 'Now, Rollo, I'm afraid you're guessing, an outrageous thing for an Inspector of the Yard. That he left the dining-room was the merest accident. He couldn't possibly have foretold that Mrs Elton would ask him to search. It was much more likely that Jeffrey and Croome would have handled it.'

Rollo admitted this with apparent regret. 'Suppose, sir,' he went on, again brightening up, 'Pegram was in it with Harte as you suggested? Suppose Pegram came to this room instead of Harte going to Pegram's? Then no ladder would have been wanted. Pegram could have leant out of the window and pulled Harte up. And the same applies from the ground to the roof.'

'Is that right?' French considered. 'If Pegram had followed Harte down on the roof, wouldn't he have wanted a ladder to get back here, so as to pull Harte after him?'

'I don't think so. If Pegram went down on the roof, he could have pulled Harte up from the ground. Then he could have given Harte a leg up to the window, and Harte could have pulled him up after him.'

'It's possible, I suppose,' French admitted, 'though I'm not so sure with a man of Pegram's age. However, once again we'll keep it in view. Now we're here let's see if there's anything which might have made a ladder.'

Their search was rapid, but revealed nothing which could have been so used. The nearest approach to ropes were the cord of Harte's dressing-gown and a pair of light two-feet-six luggage straps in a handle. There was nothing remotely resembling a wooden ladder.

'Very well,' said French, 'that's that. We'll go down to the library and tell Croome to send in Harte as soon as he turns up.'

For once French set the stage for a coming interview. He turned the witness's chair so that a full light would shine on Harte's face while Rollo was ostentatious with his notebook.

When a little later Harte entered, he looked more nervous then ever. French's manner did nothing to reassure him. In spite of his cheery good humour, French could on occasion lie menacing enough. To those who knew him the rarity of this greatly increased its effect.

'It's in connection with the whereabouts of the late Mr Elton between six-fifteen and six-thirty on Thursday evening week,' he began sternly. 'The matter turns out to be more serious than was at first supposed. You told us that he was with you in the laboratory, but now I learn that he was in his bedroom. How do you account for the discrepancy?'

Harte was obviously taken aback. His face paled and his hands clenched nervously together. But he controlled himself and answered normally enough.

'I'm really extraordinarily sorry,' he declared, and it seemed to French with sincerity. 'If you are correct, I must have made a mistake. Mr Elton was with me in the lab at the hour you mentioned on at least two evenings in that week. I thought it was Monday and Thursday, but it may have been Monday and Wednesday. I answered you to the best of my knowledge and belief, but you must recognize that there was nothing to fix the date on my mind. If I have made a mistake, again I am sorry.'

French could make nothing of it. He did his best, but Harte was unable to prove, or he to disprove, the new statement. French felt he was getting nowhere and presently he decided to bluff.

'It's only fair to tell you, Mr Harte, that one thing makes me very suspicious of you, and that is your manner. As you can imagine, we chief inspectors have had a good deal of experience, and your manner tells me that you are hiding something. Of course I can't prove that, but if you can dispel my suspicion, it might be as much to your advantage as to mine.'

To this Harte answered nothing, though he looked acutely uneasy. Then he made a gesture of despair and a little thrill of excitement ran through French's nerves. Obviously something more was coming. Harte moved uneasily and made two or three false starts before unburdening his conscience.

'You've put me in a hole, chief inspector,' he said at last. 'I admit that when you asked me for my history, through fear I didn't tell you all of it. Now I think that not to do so might be more damaging to me still. I've been in quod, in Montreal. Two years for stealing. I had hoped to live it down and that it would be forgotten, but since this happened I have been worrying my life out that you'd discover it and suspect me of the other job.'

'I knew all about it,' French answered easily, while Harte stared open-mouthed. 'But we don't suspect people because of what they may have done in early life, only because of their current actions.'

'My God!' Harte exclaimed weakly, 'if I'd only known that! I should have trusted you and told you. Well, that's a relief!' His manner changed suddenly. He grew comparatively cheerful, as if the weight of his secret had been overwhelming.

'Hell, sir,' Rollo observed when the chemist had gone, 'things don't get much simpler! There's another promising line gone west. At least I suppose it has?'

'We suspected Harte only because of his manner,' French returned. 'Now we find his manner is accounted for. It means we've nothing against him. On the other hand, everything seems to confirm the view that he wanted to hold his job, which involved keeping Elton alive.'

'That's what I think too. Is this the way all cases develop?'

'Pretty much. You'll find, Mr Inspector Rollo, that if you're going to succeed at this game, you'll need all the wits you've got—probably more.'

Rollo grinned, being unable to think of a retort at once sufficiently telling and courteous.

The remark recurred to French with unpleasant force when after dinner that evening he sat down to consider the effect of his new conclusion about Harte. To solve this case it looked as if he also would require all the wits he had—or more.

Though absolute proof had not been reached in any single instance, the following had now been provisionally cleared: Julia Elton, Mollie Langley, Pegram and Philip Harte, Frank Cox, Croome, Mrs Underwood and Jeffrey Elton, while against none of the others who figured in the case, the Alinghams, Moffatt, Hawthorne and Moggridge, were there any grounds of suspicion at all. This left Underwood as the most likely remaining suspect.

French looked up Rollo's notes. Underwood had motive

and opportunity and was near the site of the crime at the time of its commission. Admittedly he had not reacted to the test of the owl, but this might have been due to self-control.

Was it not possible, French wondered, to come to some conclusion about the man? He racked his brains over the problem, but did not see what more he could do than he had already done. The direct attempt to check the statements of suspects he had left to Dagg and his men, as owing to their local knowledge they could handle the work better than a stranger. In the case of Jeffrey Elton this had produced proof that he had taken his car out of the park at the hour he stated. Were Underwood's movements so much less likely to have been observed?

He was about to telephone to Dagg to discuss the point when an idea flashed into his mind.

'Hang it all!' he said to Rob, 'we've been a nice pair of fatheads! There's a possible line about Underwood we've missed. Nothing conclusive probably, but a chance. Ring up the station and say we're going round.'

'I noted,' he continued a little later to the station sergeant, 'that the letter box in Victoria Road is timed to be cleared at seven-fifteen in the evening. I want to know when it was done on the day of the murder. Can we get anyone at this hour to tell us?'

'I think so, sir. The head postman lives not five minutes away and he might know. I'll send round to find him.'

'I'll go myself if you tell me the address.'

As luck would have it, the man was at home.

'The Victoria Road box?' he repeated after French. 'That would be John Straker.' He glanced at the clock on the chimney-piece. 'He's probably still at the post office. I'll go round with you, if you like.'

For the second time their luck held. Straker was going off duty as they arrived.

'I remember the evening of the murder well,' he said, 'just because of the murder. I remember thinking that it must have occurred about the time I was in the neighbourhood. The box is supposed to be cleared at seven-fifteen and that night I was there three minutes early and had to wait.'

'Did you see anyone while you were there?'

'Yes, sir.' I met Joe Anderson, that's a gardener who lives near, and we stopped for a word. While we were talking I saw Mr Underwood. He posted a letter. I don't think he saw us. We were at the other side of the road.'

'Oh,' said French, concealing his interest. 'Can you tell me just what time he posted the letter?'

'Yes, it was immediately after I stopped to speak to Anderson. Say twelve minutes past seven.'

'From what direction did Mr Underwood come and where did he go?'

'He came from Chalfont way and turned up the footpath towards the hill.'

French was impressed with this evidence. It corroborated Underwood's statement on every point. It did more. As he discussed it with Rollo a little later it seemed to both of them that it finally eliminated the clerk.

'It certainly works in,' Rollo declared, turning over the pages of his notebook. 'Croome said he left the house between five and ten minutes after seven; suppose it was seven minutes past. If so, he would have met Underwood about eight minutes past. They would have talked for a couple of minutes, say, till ten minutes past. From the place they met to the letter box is about two minutes' walk: twelve minutes past exactly.'

'So that Underwood couldn't have murdered Elton before posting the letter?'

'Absolutely impossible.'

'And after it?'

'If he had hurried back to Chalfont he might possibly have done it. But he turned up the path, just as he said he did. And as you know, there's no short way across from that path to Chalfont. I think Underwood's out of it, sir.'

To French it seemed so too. Not absolutely proven, admittedly, but so likely as not to matter. Quite definitely it would be impossible to get a conviction against the man.

'Very well,' he admitted. 'Underwood eliminated. Add all that to your notes.'

A step further, even if a negative one! All the same, the removal of Underwood's name from the list did not make the problem any easier. For an hour and more French lingered over the names of Croome and Cox, only to reach the conclusion as to their innocence previously accepted. He was at least satisfied that a conviction against either was as much out of the question as in the case of Underwood.

At last his thoughts strayed back to Jeffrey Elton. He could not forget the vast difference there was between Jeffrey and all the others in the case, in that Jeffrey was the only one with a really adequate motive. He turned over the pages of the file and reread the relevant paragraphs.

1. Jeffrey Elton had no private means, his salary was small, and he could not live as he was accustomed to otherwise than at Chalfont.
2. He wanted to marry Mollie Langley, but had not enough money to do so.

3. He was Richard's principal heir, and if Richard were dead would be wealthy.
4. Richard treated him as an office-boy and he had neither scope nor authority. This humiliated him before the staff. If Richard died he would be head of the business.
5. His manner was uneasy, as if he were keeping something back.

It was difficult to dismiss these points. Of course there was the alibi. But French well knew that an alibi is a double-edged weapon. If it were watertight it was a proof of innocence, but if faked it was equally a proof of guilt. The question therefore arose once again: Could the alibi be broken down?

French had already concluded that it could not. But no human being was infallible. Even a chief inspector of Scotland Yard can make mistakes. It might be well to reconsider the details.

The whole affair hinged on Richard Elton's decision at the interview he and Jeffrey had had on that fatal Friday afternoon. Until Richard had given his views, Jeffrey could not have written his letter to Julian Greer. Until that letter was written and the mistake discovered, Jeffrey could not have composed his amending note. These operations filled every moment of the available time. No, to French it all seemed absolutely watertight.

And yet one point gave him rather furiously to think. If Jeffrey had known Richard's decision beforehand, he could have faked the letters. Granted that information, he could have worked out the mistakes and deliberately introduced it. He could also have prepared the amending note in advance, thus leaving free the half-hour from seven to seven-thirty.

French felt a rising excitement as he pursued this line of thought. Could Jeffrey have foreseen Richard's decision?

Obviously this depended on the question at issue. If it were one to which there was only one correct answer, he might have guessed. How could French settle this point?

A chat with Greer seemed indicated. French rang up the famous K.C. and made an appointment for the next morning.

This gave the chance of another night at home, and in spite of the unpleasant drive in the blackout, both he and Rollo were glad to take advantage of it.

Julian Greer was not at all the typical successful barrister of fiction, aggressive, hectoring, and with a powerful frame and large, strongly marked features. He was slight and had a quiet rather dreamy manner. His triumphs came to him through sheer intellectual power, and by the spell of his persuasive tongue he could almost make a jury believe that his gown was white as freshly fallen snow. He was no respecter of persons and now greeted French and Rollo very much as he would, had a pair of high court judges favoured him with a call.

'It's a nice point,' he said when French had explained his business. He seemed a little troubled. 'I may say that I've met Jeffrey Elton on many occasions and I do not at all consider him the type of person to do such a thing.'

'You understand, sir, that I'm making no accusation: only trying to establish the facts.'

'Of course I understand it, Mr French, and I realize that you are perfectly correct to do so and perfectly justified in coming to me about it. Now you want to know whether Jeffrey could have foreseen the decision Richard Elton was likely to reach?'

'That's it, sir.'

'Well, there's no doubt whatever as to the answer. He could not. There were three possible alternatives, and neither Jeffrey nor anyone else could have spotted the winner.'

French felt bitterly disappointed. Here was another new line proving a dead end. If Jeffrey could not have foreseen Richard's decision, he could not have foreseen the letters he would have to write and his alibi stood.

French got up and began to express his thanks for the interview.

He thought Greer looked at him curiously. 'Of course,' the barrister went on, 'it's only fair to say that those three decisions must necessarily have been clear cut. Also that there were no other possibilities.'

French stared. Then like a flash he grasped the hint.

'Don't look at me as if I were putting up theories,' went on Greer before he could speak. 'I'm suggesting nothing whatever. You understand that, don't you?' He was now smiling broadly.

'Of course, sir, perfectly,' French returned quickly, 'but I—I'm extremely grateful to you all the same.'

So that was it! What easier than to prepare three letters, each embodying a different decision and each containing a suitable error, together with three amending notes correcting the errors? With these ready beforehand the relevant letter could be quickly given to the typist and the corresponding amending note posted without returning to the office, thus giving time for the murder.

Yes, at last it was working in! French felt as if he had obtained a glimpse of the truth and that the end of his case was appearing over the horizon.

Returning to the Yard, he continued his appraisement of the situation. Before he could reach a definite conclusion as to Jeffrey's guilt, two other points had to be determined.

The first was about the anonymous letter. Could Jeffrey have secretly obtained it, altered it and passed it on to Richard?

Again French turned over the file. On the Thursday evening between six and six-thirty Jeffrey had stated that he was in his room. But was he? Might not he have gone down to the library? As far as the evidence went, he certainly could. Why he had selected Croome's masterpiece was a mystery, but as this was equally inexplicable in the case of every suspect, it did not specially affect Jeffrey's case.

Could Jeffrey have returned it? Certainly not on Friday evening. He was definitely at the office too late to have left it in the library before Richard's entry. But he could have taken a risk and done it on Friday morning. And there was no evidence that he had not. There was no proof that the letter Richard had sent Croome to post had been to Shaw. Richard might well have considered the matter during the day, and himself posted Shaw's letter on his way home. As Rollo had suggested, Croome's errand might merely have been given him to enable Elton to leave the house unobserved. There was nothing here inconsistent with Jeffrey's guilt.

The second point was even more critical. Supposing Jeffrey had prepared the necessary letters to Greer, would he have had time to commit the murder?

Here the facts were not in dispute. According to his own statement Jeffrey left the office at a couple of minutes before seven and took his car out of the park at a minute or two past half-past seven, and both these times had been accurately established by independent testimony. Could Jeffrey then, without his car, have gone between these hours from the office to the summer-house, committed the murder, and returned to the park? Further, could he have arranged matters at the office to give him this time?

Incidentally French noticed that the scheme exactly suited the altered hour in the anonymous letter. Seven-fifteen was in the middle of the free time. Though this might have been accidental, it certainly bore a suggestion of design.

French glanced at Rollo, who was again writing laboriously.

'I say, just stop those notes for a moment, will you?' He explained what was in his mind, continuing: 'I want you to go to Elton's office and walk as fast as you can to the Chalfont summer-house and back to the car park. You may even trot. See how long it takes.'

It was not till late in the afternoon that Rollo returned. The double journey had taken thirty-five minutes. It would therefore have been utterly impossible for Jeffrey to have done it and committed the murder in the time. That was, if he had walked.

But Rollo had done better than his instructions. 'I've got it, I think, sir, all the same,' he exclaimed. 'A push-bike. You know, there's been one beside the stairs in the office all the time we've been there. It belongs to that office-boy who's ill. I borrowed one from the sergeant and tried again. Allowing for the blackout I estimated it would take twenty-one minutes. That would leave thirteen for the murder; ample time.'

'Not bad, young Rollo. Even if it comes to nothing, that's the way to go about it.'

'It won't come to nothing,' Rollo returned with unction. 'It's Jeffrey Elton as sure as we're alive.'

French shook his head. 'Don't be too sure, he cautioned. 'You've only proved that he could have done it, not that he did it. As it is, we haven't a hope of a conviction.'

'No one else has such a motive.'

'No good, not enough. We must have something actually connecting him with the thing. If someone could prove that his shoes were spotted with mud as only a bicycle throws it up, it might do. Or of course if we had found his fingerprints on the bike. You see what I'm getting at? Something that would apply to him and to no one else.'

Rollo was disappointed. There was a pause, then he said tentatively: 'I've an idea, sir: probably nothing in it, but what do you think? Suppose we were to prepare an anonymous letter saylng a member of the staff was seen taking that bike out of the office at seven on Friday evening, and suppose we showed it to Jeffrey and watched his reaction?'

French was not particularly impressed with the plan, but he did not want to damp the young man's ardour.

'Well, let's see what hand you make of the letter,' he compromised.

For a time Rollo wrote with even more concentrated effort, then he pulled a sheet off the conventional anonymous letter pad, tore it carefully in half, and handed the upper portion to French. In accordance with precedent it was roughly printed in capitals. It read:

MR FRENCH,

I hear you are supposed to be investigating the Elton case and are not making much of it. Well, Elton was not much loss but I don't like to see anyone getting away with murder.

Do you know that a push bike was taken out of the office about seven that evening by a certain person? He was seen by yours truly. I can prove it if you undertake I won't be—

It was at this point that the sheet was torn in half.

'Why didn't you finish it?' French enquired.

'I couldn't,' Rollo grinned. 'May we try it, sir?'

'Right. We'll go down tomorrow.'

The next day was Sunday and Jeffrey was at home. They saw him in the library.

'We have a communication here, Mr Elton,' Rollo said, keeping to the somewhat tortuous path of literal truth, 'on which we should like your comments.'

Jeffrey, apparently sensing inimical influences, contented himself with a short nod. Rollo handed over the document.

Jeff's face as he read it registered a complicated succession of emotions. First there was bewilderment, which grew more acute as he proceeded. This was followed by a look of lively satisfaction.

'Why, that's good,' he exclaimed. 'It looks like a line on the guilty man.' Then his face clouded. 'But how could anyone have got into the office? Have you seen the writer? Who does he say it was?'

Glancing up, he met the fixed stare of both police officers. Neither answered. Suddenly all appearance of satisfaction was struck from Jeff's face and a growing horror appeared instead.

'What do you mean by all this?' he asked hoarsely. 'You don't suppose—that I took it?'

'We make no accusations whatever,' French said, feeling rather uncomfortable, 'but we must consider possibilities. In connection with your statement you realize of course that the letters do not constitute an alibi? It would only have been necessary for you to have previously prepared letters to meet the three possible decisions at which the late Mr Elton might have arrived. The relevant letters could then have been used whatever that decision. This would have left the half-hour from seven to seven-thirty clear. You must have seen all this for yourself?'

Jeff, now pale and haggard, nodded without speaking.

'I wondered if you had anything further to say on the matter, which might help me to a decision?'

Jeff shook his head. Then slowly he recovered his poise.

'You gave me a bad fright, chief inspector,' he said presently, 'but now I see that this letter writer has done me a good turn. He says he saw the man who took the push bike. Very well, since it wasn't me, it lets me out. What's better still, it puts someone else in. Yes, this is good news. You haven't told me if you've seen the writer?'

'We're attending to that, sir,' French said, getting up. 'In the meantime we're glad to have had your reactions.'

Jeff replied a little indignantly, as if he suspected that he had been the victim of a trap, but French suavely bowed him out.

'Well,' he said slowly, 'your scheme's been a success.'

Rollo looked startled.

'Yes,' French went on, 'a complete success. That man's innocent. He couldn't have acted like that otherwise. Nor indeed if he knew who was guilty, Rollo, we may look elsewhere.'

It was with a sense of frustration and disappointment that French turned back to his problem. He had done a great deal towards its solution. He had proved that various persons could have murdered Elton, but the scrap of additional knowledge needed to decide which had done so, still eluded him. Well, he had been up against it before and he had usually pulled through. There was nothing for it but to try again.

With determination expressed in every line of his figure, he stalked resolutely to an easy chair and once again opened the file.

19

The Fibrous Strand

For some time silence reigned in the library and then French raised his head.

'Suppose,' he said slowly, 'you steamed an envelope open and resealed it and then steamed it open again, would you be able to seal it for the second time with the original gum?'

Rollo looked interested. 'Why not, sir?'

'I don't know. I have an idea the gum would evaporate or get too thin or lose its power or something.'

'We can try.'

Among other miscellaneous objects in the paper store was an electric kettle. This was soon steaming and Rollo operated on half a dozen envelopes.

The result was suggestive. After the second steaming a large proportion of the gum seemed to have vanished. The flaps did stick, though insecurely.

'Promising enough,' declared French, 'when you add the fact that the man who put in the letter couldn't take any risks. What's the betting that he used fresh gum?'

'If he had, do you think it could be traced?'

'If they were different gums micro-analysis might give it. It's worth trying.'

'There are bottles of gum all over the place,' Rollo went on. 'I noticed one in the lab and Jeffrey's room and Croome's pantry as well as here. There may be others.'

'We'll get samples.'

With this new aim they made a tour of the house, obtaining in all samples of four gums. Two, from the library and Croome's pantry, were from similar bottles of Stikard, otherwise all were of different makes.

While Rollo was conducting his search in the laboratory, French strolled idly round. He was impressed by the amount of apparatus which stood on the various benches. It was built up into sets as if a number of similar experiments were in progress.

'A lot of stuff the old man had,' he commented. 'Must have cost him a tidy penny.'

'That's so, sir,' Rollo agreed politely. 'There's only one bottle here; a paste called Holteit. I've got some samples.'

A couple of hours later they were talking to Carr, one of the analytical chemists who worked for the Yard. 'Here,' French explained, handing over the papers smeared with the Chalfont exhibits, 'are samples of gums labelled A, B, C and D. On the flap of this,' he put down a fresh envelope he had taken from Messrs Cato & Lewisham's stock, 'is still another labelled E. I want to know which gum was used to seal this envelope which I've marked X,' and he gave him that of the anonymous letter. 'Think you can tell me?'

'You're not asking much,' grumbled the chemist. 'If you had brought me half a pint of each I might have done it, but how do you think I'm going to get enough off those wretched scraps of paper?'

'I know that not one in a hundred could do it,' French declared brazenly. 'That's why I brought it to you.'

'Do you think if I told an august chief inspector of the Yard he was a slimy hypocrite I'd be sacked?' grinned the chemist. 'All right, leave your miserable specks and I'll do what I can.'

'When shall I come back?'

'I'll ring you up.'

Had it not been that French found plenty of routine work to occupy him, he would have been an impatient man before the summons came. But at last he and Rollo were once again in the laboratory.

'I may tell you I've done a man's job,' the chemist greeted them. 'By micro-chemical analysis I've been able to answer your questions. Very creditable, I think.'

'I said only you could do it.'

'Quite right, but it's been a problem. However, a reputation's a thing that must be kept up. This envelope X,' and he took up that of the anonymous letter, 'has been sealed twice; the microscope shows that, and besides it bears traces of a gum and a paste. Beneath are traces of Gum E and it is clear therefore that it came from the source of this exactly similar one which you have marked E. But superimposed are stronger traces of C, the paste, and I therefore assume that the envelope was steamed open and resealed with C. Does that give you what you want?'

French was staring thoughtfully into vacancy. But he quickly pulled himself together, and after joking adequately with the chemist, who seemed to expect it, he returned with Rollo to his room.

Rollo was obviously puzzled. 'A bit surprising, that. Resealed with the paste from the lab! The murderer was pretty cute to think of using the lab paste instead of his own.

'But did he?' said French dryly.

It was now Rollo's turn to stare.

'It makes one think,' French went on, 'particularly when this is added to what we saw in the lab. Tell me, did you see anything there that surprised you?'

Rollo shook his head.

'Oh yes, you did, but you haven't thought about it. I can't blame you, for I didn't think of it myself till we were in the car. Then I began to wonder. What Carr has told us has made me wonder more.'

'What's the point, sir?' Rollo exclaimed.

'You saw all that apparatus on the benches? Why was it there?'

'I suppose it was being got ready for the sale.'

French made a gesture. 'But that's just what it wasn't. Each of those sets of apparatus meant an experiment in progress. The flasks and so on were full.'

'You mean that Harte was still working?'

'Exactly. Why?'

'I'm afraid,' Rollo admitted, 'I don't see the point. What is it, sir?'

'Harte's statement was that he was preparing for the sale. Actually he's still experimenting. Doesn't that suggest that he's been keeping something secret?'

Rollo looked unimpressed. 'I suppose it does, now one comes to think of it. But still I don't see—'

'The thing of all others we want in this case is someone keeping something secret. Admittedly it's only a hunch, but have we dismissed Harte too quickly?'

'You mean as the murderer?'

'Why not?'

'Well, we thought he was all right. You now suggest Elton had twigged he was a convict?'

'Not necessarily. The suggestion is rather that it was connected with the experiments.'

Rollo hesitated. 'We considered that chemical business before, if you remember, sir, but dismissed it because of Professor Kennedy's report.'

'Kennedy may be right—or he may have been misled. I don't say we're on to anything, but we've got to be sure. Look here, Rollo, we'll try a trick after your own heart. Here's a sheet of Cato and Lewisham's paper and an envelope to match. Type a note to Harte asking him to call on them tomorrow at eleven-thirty. Say they've heard that Mr Elton's stock is to be sold and that they would be glad to buy certain apparatus and perhaps Harte would consider acting as their agent. Post it so that he'll get it in the morning.'

Rollo set to work with alacrity. While he was struggling with his forgery, French rang up Kennedy.

'There has been an unexpected development down at Chalfont,' he told him, 'and we may have to revise some of our opinions about the chemical experiments. Could you come down with us tomorrow morning? We shall be leaving at nine.'

The professor agreed and French rang off, delighted to have at least the evening of his Sunday.

'I'm glad you fixed up a fine day,' said Kennedy when they picked him up at his house in Chelsea next morning. 'What's all the fuss about? Is your friend after a new high explosive or something deadlier than mustard gas?'

'I'm in hopes, professor,' French answered a trifle dryly, 'that that's what you're going to tell me. I may explain that we're again wondering whether Harte may not have murdered Mr Elton, and we hope that a further investigation of his work in the laboratory may give us certainty.'

Kennedy was shocked. 'Bless my soul, chief inspector, you're not serious? And you want me to help you to convict him? Not a very nice job, you know.'

'If you think about the late Mr Elton rather than Mr Harte it won't seem so bad,' French suggested. 'In any case it's only on chemical matters that we wish to trouble you.'

'Tactfully put, I'll admit. Mind my own business and I needn't worry. You're quite correct and I'll help you all I can.'

On reaching Chalfont they learnt from Croome that Harte had just left for Town. They went at once to the laboratory, which French opened with Richard's keys. The professor was surprised at its size and enthusiastic as to its fittings.

'I've seldom seen a better private laboratory,' he declared, as standing inside the door, he ran his eyes over the benches and apparatus. 'Elton must have been much less of an amateur than I supposed.'

'Harte of course was a professional,' French pointed out. 'A good deal of this may be due to him.'

'True. All the same it's unexpected. Well, to business! What exactly do you want me to do, now that you've got me here?'

'Just to tell me what Harte was really doing.'

'H'm. Mayn't be so easy as you seem to think. But I can tell you straight off one thing he was not doing.'

'And that, sir?'

'Dismantling the apparatus for sale. Why, the place is in perfect running order and all those,' he pointed to the sets of apparatus, 'are serial experiments of some sort.'

'That's it then,' French returned. 'Can you tell me of what sort?'

Kennedy nodded and settled down to a protracted examination. Time passed and still the investigation went on, French growing more and more impatient every moment. He was sure that when Harte reached Messrs Cato & Lewisham's and learnt that he had not been sent for, he would guess the trick which had been played on him and hurry back to see what had provoked it. French was anxious to have his information before he arrived.

At last Kennedy turned away from the bench. 'I feel very badly about all this,' he said, 'but that's your responsibility, not mine. However, now that I'm in for a penny, I may as well be in for a pound. Could you find Harte's notes? There must be notes of such experiments as these.'

'Probably in this desk. I have the keys.'

When French tried, he found that he had spoken too soon. One of the larger drawers remained fast in spite of all his efforts.

'That's strange,' he said, turning and twisting with his keys. 'I went though all these drawers when I was making my first investigation.' Then with a grunt of satisfaction he realized what had happened. 'I think it shows we're on to something. He's changed the lock. Get a bar of some kind, Rollo. I'll take out the drawer below it and then you can force it.'

It took only a few seconds to smash the new lock. Within lay the records Kennedy had demanded. He took them out, sat down at the desk, and began to read with care.

Once again time for French hung heavily. Then he glanced up, saw Kennedy's face, and a little thrill of excitement passed along his nerves. The professor's expression was changing from interest to surprise, from surprise to astonishment, and from astonishment to blank incredulous amazement.

'He's done it!' he announced in strangled tones. 'I don't know how, but he's evidently done it! It's utterly incredible!'

'You mean he's found a cheap catalytic agent instead of the emeralds?'

'Yes, that of course, but something vastly more! Something we hadn't thought of before! Something really big! Why,' Kennedy's voice rose in his excitement, 'he's found a way—a cheap and simple way—of turning salt water into fresh!'

French and Rollo expressed their surprise and admiration.

'Good Lord, yes!' went on Kennedy. 'It'll be one of the greatest discoveries of the century! What lives it'll save at sea! The horror of thirst gone! What money and space will be saved when boilers can be supplied from overboard! It's almost unthinkable!'

Though profoundly impressed by all this, French could not forget his own problem. 'Do you say you don't know how he's done it?' he enquired anxiously.

'In general terms it's perfectly clear. The two resins in the presence of the hornblende catalytic agent go on eliminating the salts till none are left. But in detail Harte has been too clever for us. One step in the process, the essential step, has been omitted. There'll be other notes somewhere. You must find them.'

'You're interested in the scientific discovery,' French said a little grimly, 'but I'm interested in my case. And I think this gives me what I wanted to get a conviction. Tell me, is there evidence there of how long it is since he made the discovery?'

'Not exactly, but judging by the amount of work which has been done as a result of it, a considerable time. Ah,' he glanced shrewdly at French, 'I see what you mean. Yes, he must have discovered it before Elton died. That it?'

'That's it, sir,' French answered solemnly.

Rollo looked eagerly from one to the other of his companions. 'I don't think I quite got your meaning, sir?' he said hesitatingly, as if before Kennedy French might not vouchsafe explanations.

But French made no mystery of his ideas. 'Rollo's learning the job, professor,' he explained, 'so we discuss everything without reserve. You, I know, will treat the matter as confidential. Well, Rollo, use your wits. Look here, I'll give you a hint. Harte was putting in a daily report of his experiments.'

Rollo continued staring in a lost way. 'You mean his reports were inventions?'

'Not exactly; they were probably true enough. But he was, so to speak, leading a double life. His reports told Elton that he had made no progress with the problem, while actually he was carrying on a second set of experiments which had given him a process worth millions. That right, professor?'

'That's right as I see it.'

'Very well,' continued French, 'why should he do this? Surely only to steal the process?'

'But if he discovered it?' Rollo demurred. 'I mean, wasn't it his in a sense?'

'Of course it was not. If Elton paid him a salary, anything he found out was Elton's. Besides, the point was specially if covered in the agreement.'

'Yes, I see that,' admitted Rollo. 'But if he had secretly discovered the thing, why couldn't he simply have said nothing about it and left Elton?'

'Because he couldn't have used it. Directly it became known, Elton would have been down on him like a ton of bricks. No, there was only one way he could have made anything out of it, and that was the way he took—to ensure that Elton would not interfere. He was pretty certain that no one else would do so, because from the secrecy Elton observed, he would conclude that no one else knew what was at issue. There's motive enough there for a dozen murders.'

'Yes,' Professor Kennedy put in, 'that's certainly true. A fortune and fame were at stake, and if he could get Richard Elton out of the way, they were his.'

French turned to the door. 'I think that's all we want here. I must search in Harte's room for the notes of those other experiments.'

'Any objection to my coming along?' asked Kennedy. 'I've got interested in the abominable business.'

'I hope you will, sir. If we find the notes your help would be invaluable.'

There were few places in Harte's bedroom in which papers could be hidden. Rollo was set to searching these while French explained to Kennedy the other unsolved problem in the affair: how, if Harte had left the room by the window, he could have climbed in again.

'You say he had to get up a height of eight feet?' responded Kennedy. 'He would want very little help for that. What height could he have swung himself up by his arms?'

'Five feet? Five feet six? I say, Rollo, go and get a box or something a couple of feet or more high and put it below the window here and see if you can get in?'

Rollo glanced round the room. 'Nice little table that,' he observed, eyeing the oak one at the head of the bed. 'I suppose I daren't use it?'

'No, don't be lazy. Get a box.'

Rollo having disappeared, French's eyes swung back speculatively to the table. He had observed before now how strongly it was made. Still more speculatively he laid the rule which he always carried against it.

'Ah,' said Kennedy, 'that's a suggestive move. What height do you make it?'

'Two feet six,' French answered in a non-committal voice.

'Two feet six from eight feet leaves five feet six,' Kennedy went on thoughtfully. 'An interesting coincidence.'

French did not reply. He was moving the books on to the bed. Then he carried the table to the window. Both men stooped and examined its top.

'He would surely have used a rug or a paper?' Kennedy suggested.

'I don't think so,' returned French. 'It might have slipped off when he was pulling it up.'

'Ah, yes; I hadn't thought of that. Just what's your idea, Mr French?'

French eyed the table, the roof, and the path below. 'He'd want a rope or something six or seven feet long, tied to the table,' he said slowly. 'As I see it, he would lower the table from here to the roof, drop down, lower the table to the ground and go on his errand. Then coming back he would stand on the table, and with the rope in his hand swarm up on to the roof, pull the table up after him, move it under the window, swarm in, and again pull up the table. How would that do?'

Kennedy's long thin finger advanced. 'What about that?' he pointed.

On the polished top of the table were a series of five concentric scratches.

'I noticed them,' said French. 'They certainly suggest a gritty shoe.'

For a moment there was silence, then French picked up the table and with a swift movement turned it upside down. He began to examine the bottoms of the legs.

'Ah yes, that's an idea. Better put it on the bed. Steady on, the lens will do it. Let me.' Kennedy peered closely with a high magnification lens. 'Just hand me my bag, will you?'

From the case he took a small forceps and began working at one of the feet. Presently he removed a tiny object.

'Bit of gravel,' he declared with satisfaction. 'If it's the same as that on the path, you'll find it a help. Congratulations! I often wondered how you fellows got your evidence. I must admit I'm impressed.'

'You came at a lucky moment, sir, and incidentally you've done a fair share yourself. Now I wonder if I'm not on to the next step? I remember noticing two things when I searched this room.'

He opened a drawer and took from it a couple of luggage straps in a handle. Pulling off the handle, he buckled them together and measured them.

'Two two-foot-six straps less the overlap of the buckles makes four feet nine altogether,' he remarked. 'That would be long enough and strong enough to lift by, if we had some way of attaching it to the table. And what about this?' He pulled the cord from Harte's dressing-gown, which was hanging on the back of the door.

Kennedy nodded emphatically. 'Passed under the legs at opposite corners and knotted to make a loop, it should do the trick.'

French watched with eagerness while Kennedy bent with his lens over the upper edges of the legs. Presently he gave another grunt of satisfaction.

'If I'm not careful I'll begin to think this is my case, not yours,' he said. 'The forceps, please.'

From a scarcely visible splinter he drew a tiny fragment of some fibre-like substance. 'I think it's the same as the cord,' he announced, 'but the microscope will quickly tell us. If this clicks, I think you'll have proved your case.'

French's appreciative remarks were interrupted by a sound

of heavy breathing at the window and with a sudden jump Rollo appeared. Without much difficulty he swarmed over the sill into the room, then hanging out again, he drew in a rope at the end of which dangled a small packing-case.

'Good man,' said French. 'I told you once you had a great mind and now it's proved. See what we've been thinking of while you were away.'

Quickly he put the table right up, tied the cord to the legs, attached the straps and placed the whole affair beside Rollo's box. As pieces of apparatus they were identical.

'Motive,' said French slowly, checking the points off on his fingers. 'Opportunity. And if that soil and stuff that you found, professor, checks up, a definite connection with the crime. Yes, I think we're getting on.'

Professor Kennedy nodded. 'I said you had proved your case.'

'To my own satisfaction perhaps,' French admitted, 'but I'm afraid we couldn't go into court without something more. However, I've got an idea about that.' He stood gazing slowly about the room, then seemed suddenly to come to a decision. 'Yes, that'll do. Let's leave everything as we found it and then clear out. Don't make any noise going back to the library. I don't think we were seen coming up and I don't think anyone knows we were here. Then we'll ring for Croome, say we've finished for the day, and go to the hotel. Over a spot of lunch we can fix up our programme for getting evidence for court.'

Five minutes later they turned out of the Chalfont drive.

20

The Tipsy Policeman

On this same afternoon Julia Elton sat alone in the Chalfont lounge, staring before her into vacancy and wishing that Mollie would return from Dorkford, where an hour before she had gone to shop.

For Julia time had never dragged so appallingly as during these tragic days. While on the surface life seemed to flow on as usual, she was aware that behind the scenes dark and terrifying forces were in operation. Of these she knew nothing except that they were inimical: they threatened her entire happiness, perhaps even her life. The police came and went; they asked questions, they disappeared, they came back and asked them again, they had conferences in the library, but what they were really doing and what they thought about things were to her shrouded in complete mystery. This ignorance of what was going on about her she found almost insupportably irksome, so much so that she began to look forward to what she had at first dreaded, the adjourned inquest, in the hope that whatever she learnt, her suspense would at least be ended.

The one thing which might have relieved her was the one thing she was denied: to talk things over with Frank Cox. No matter how black the outlook seemed, she felt that to share her fears with him would be to rob them of half their terror. Mollie was the only person to whom she could turn for sympathy, but even to Mollie she did not care to talk, partly because of the danger of being overheard, and partly because it was not fair to add her own worries to those of the girl. Alone she fought her fear and like everyone else tried to act normally, but in spite of their efforts the atmosphere remained strained and tense.

Julia did not see it, but on this same afternoon the silver lining of this overwhelming cloud had already appeared above the horizon. The first hint of it came that evening in a very unexpected way.

They were having coffee in the lounge after dinner, she and Mollie, Jeff and Harte—for somewhat to her surprise Harte had not yet left—when they heard a ring at the front door. This was followed by voices in the hall, one raised excitably, the other, Croome's, in a protesting murmur. A moment later the lounge door was flung open and Rollo entered.

Julia stared at him with amazement which quickly turned to disgust. He was wearing an overcoat and carried his hat in his hand, and both bore traces of mud. His face was flushed, his hair ruffled and his tie crooked. He stood gazing stupidly from one to the other, while a smell of whisky became perceptible and gradually increased in strength.

'Evening,' he muttered thickly, swaying perilously. 'Sorry t'intrude 'n' all that. Had a fall. Motor bike, y'know. Chap picked me up. Gave me a drink.' He stopped, transfixed a chair with his eye, with an air of purposeful intensity made for it, grasped it firmly and lowered himself into it. 'Bike side-slipped,' he went on, apparently surprised at having reached his objective. 'Might've been worse.' He sat blinking amiably at nothing in particular.

Jeff rose, also with an air of purposeful intensity. 'Were you hurt?' he asked.

Rollo blinked at him. 'Hurt?' He felt his arm delicately. 'Shoulder a bit. Nothing t' speak of. Came off—quite a crack.'

'Look here,' Jeff went on, 'you're shaken from the fall. You'd better go to bed. I'll run you down to the hotel.'

Rollo raised his good arm in a gesture of protest. 'Thanks. Ver' good 'f you 'n' all that. But mus' wait for the chief. Coming up here.'

'Mr French? Coming here tonight?'

Rollo nodded several times. 'Yes. Spot of bush'ness. I was to meet him.'

'You're not in a state to do business,' Jeff said more sharply. 'Let me drive you to the hotel and I'll explain to Mr French when he comes.'

But Rollo would have none of this. He argued that he had been told to wait for his chief and that to do anything but wait for him was quite outside his powers. Jeff hesitated.

'Give him some black coffee,' he said at last, turning to Julia.

The cups were small, but with some trouble Jeff persuaded him to drink three. To some extent they pulled him together. Indeed he now looked ashamed of himself and essayed an apology. 'Chap picked me up,' he explained. 'Had a flask and gave me a drink. 'Fraid I took too much. Not accustomed to it, you know.'

'That's all right,' Jeff answered shortly. 'But you can't stay here like this. You must lie down somewhere. Will Mr French be long? What does he want coming up at this hour?' There was petulance, Julia thought, as well as irritation in his tone.

'Got the whole thing taped,' Rollo answered with a self-satisfied smirk. 'Fix up everything tonight.'

Each of his four hearers stiffened to attention.

'What's that?' Jeff asked and his tone had grown very sharp. 'Do you mean that he's going to finish up the case tonight? That he knows—who did it?'

Rollo shook his head. 'He doesn't know—yet. But he knows how to find out. We'll learn the truth tonight—all of us.'

Jeff had grown suddenly serious. Julia glanced at him in surprise. This was a new Jeff. Never before had she seen such iron determination in his voice and manner.

'How's he going to do that?' he asked with what she felt was misleading nonchalance.

Rollo with some apparent difficulty achieved a wink. 'Ah,' he said, 'that's it, isn't it?'

Jeff thought for a moment. Then he laughed, though there was no laughter in his eyes. 'Ah,' he said, 'trying to do the big man, are you? You don't really know anything about it.'

Rollo's smile was wiped off his face as a sponge removes whitewash from a window. 'What do you mean?' he asked roughly. 'Of course I know all about it.'

'Not you,' declared Jeff contemptuously. 'I don't believe a word of it. French wouldn't trust a child like you with his secrets.'

Julia was fascinated in spite of herself. This was a duel and she waited almost breathlessly for Rollo's reaction. The whisky had broken down his self-control and he let himself go.

'Call me a liar, would you?' he snarled angrily. 'I'll let you know about that! Liar yourself!'

Jeff let him storm on. Then he cut in. 'Ah yes, any windbag can rant like that. It's all you can do, for it's all you know.'

Rollo was almost beside himself. 'If it's all I know, what about this?' he shouted. 'The murderer was in this house that night. He was seen climbing into an upstairs window. He got on a table and pulled the table up after him. Mr French just learnt that this afternoon and he's coming up tonight to look at all the upstairs tables. The one that has grit in its feet from the gravel will be the one that was used. That'll give him the bedroom, and the bedroom'll give him the man who used it. So now, Mr Cocksure, what do you say to that?'

The atmosphere had become electric. Julia felt a thrill of excitement as if something irrevocable was about to happen. Harte made a quick movement.

'Oh, get him to bed out of this,' he said to Jeff. 'We can't keep a drunk man shouting here before Mrs Elton.'

Rollo with some difficulty pulled himself to his feet and advanced threateningly towards Harte.

'Say I'm drunk, do you?' he shouted. 'I'll teach you to—'

But Jeff also had risen. Firmly he took the excited man by the arm.

'Come to the car,' he said sharply. 'You want to lie down and then you'll be all right.'

For a moment it seemed as if Rollo would strike him, then suddenly the fight went out of him and he allowed Jeff to lead him from the room.

'Can I lend a hand?' Harte exclaimed, following. The door closed behind them.

'Well,' said Mollie, after a moment of pregnant silence, 'if that doesn't beat the band! Rollo drunk! And I thought that young man was a model of all the proprieties. All the same, there's something more in it than meets the eye.'

Julia gasped as if the tension had gone out of the atmosphere. 'Oh, isn't it all *ghastly*! Just the last straw! I do think we might have been spared this.'

'There's more in it than you think.'

'I should have thought it simple enough.'

'It's anything but. Didn't you notice when Jeff took his arm?'

Julia looked at her. 'Notice what?'

'Jeff seized him by his bruised arm. If what he said was true, it would have hurt like hell. But he didn't seem to notice it.'

'Too drunk.'

'Was he? I'm not so sure. Did you notice anything about his cheeks?'

'Only that they were flushed, as one would expect.'

'To me they looked suspiciously like make-up.'

'Gracious, child, what are you suggesting?'

'I don't know, but the whole thing struck me as jolly queer. It looked as if—'

Her remarks were interrupted by a sudden noise, apparently from upstairs. There was a shout, rapid steps and then the dull, heavy sound of a fall. The two women stared at one another. Julia wrung her hands.

'Oh my God! What's happening now? What is it? Mollie? Haven't we had enough?'

Mollie was already in the hall and after a moment Julia joined her. The silence upstairs was now complete, but below the door from the servants' quarters opened and Croome appeared, his dark face yellow and stamped with an expression of absolute terror.

'What is it, Croome?'

As Julia spoke Jeff ran downstairs. He also was looking

white and shaken. He motioned them back into the lounge and shut the door behind them.

'It's Harte,' he said in a low voice. 'I'm afraid it'll be a shock to you, Julia. He's—dead.'

A little later French came in.

'I'm terribly sorry for all this,' he said. 'It was unavoidable, but I think what has happened is best for you. Philip Harte was guilty of the murder of Mr Elton and he committed suicide when he discovered that we knew.'

Julia stammered some reply. She could scarcely retain her composure, so profound was first the shock and then the sense of relief which swept over her. Here was something unexpected: no fresh disaster, but the end of this hideous period of suspicion and horror, the end of fear! More! It was not only the end of the nightmare, it was the beginning of hope; the opening of a new life of sanity and peace. The shadow was lifted. She was free. And Frank was free. There was nothing now to prevent their happiness. Marvellous! As she looked, at Jeff and Mollie, she saw her own feelings reflected in their faces.

It was from Rollo that they afterwards learnt the details. He came in somewhat sheepishly to apologize for the part he had had to play. French had determined to see whether Harte could not be induced to incriminate himself, so as to ensure that the public prosecutor would approve their case. Rollo had therefore put up his intoxication act, as they all agreed, highly realistically.

'Except for your bruised arm,' put in Mollie. 'You forgot to wince when Jeff grabbed it.'

Rollo seemed to take this reflection on his histrionic abilities so seriously to heart that Mollie, taking pity on him, assured him that in spite of it she had been completely deceived. At this he once more beamed.

While Rollo had been baiting the trap in the lounge, French and Dagg and Kennedy had hidden themselves upstairs in the room next to Harte's. Rollo, having allowed Jeff to shepherd him out of the lounge, was able before Harte appeared to put Jeff wise to the situation. 'Get rid of Harte,' he whispered urgently, 'and take me out to the car.' The scheme worked better than they had hoped. Jeff and Rollo out of the way, Harte hurried upstairs and into his room. French, on quietly opening the door, found him with the table upside-down under the light-pendant, feverishly examining its feet.

French had won the fight, yet he lost an important round. Harte had an unlit cigarette in his mouth, and he pulled at it as he straightened himself up, staring at his unwelcome visitors. His face slowly became drained of colour and for a while he stood motionless, surveying the scene. Then with an obvious effort he pulled himself together.

'Quite a party, isn't it?' he said, but his voice was hoarse and strained. 'What do you think you're playing at? Eh?' he went on in a harder tone, 'what's the game? What—?'

He was interrupted as French, with a lightning bound for so elderly a man, leaped forward and snatched the cigarette from his lips. Harte gulped, then laughed harshly.

'Ha, ha! Very smart! Very clever. But just not quite clever enough! You thought you'd got me and you thought you'd got my secret! And you've missed both! You've been fooled: Mr Meddler French and Dog Rollo. Fooled!'

He staggered and French and Dagg seized him.

'Emetic, quick!' French cried urgently to Kennedy.

'No good,' Harte said, now speaking with obvious difficulty. 'I've lost, but you—haven't won. The cigarette has been ready for this. When the letter—turned out a forgery—I suspected and when I—heard that playacting fool below I—knew.' His head dropped forward.

French seldom swore, but as they lifted Harte on to the bed he gave vent to a succession of blistering oaths. 'Prussic acid,' he said as he smelt the pallid lips. 'We can't do anything.'

The main question settled, a short further investigation together with a little justifiable conjecture, enabled French to clear up the few points which still remained doubtful.

Harte being anything but a fool, he must quickly have suspected from the general circumstances of his engagement by Richard as well as from Richard's manner, that there was more in the business than met the eye. Though Richard had apparently spoken to him only of softening water, Harte had evidently seen that if the process could be made a commercial success, the sea water problem would also be solved. Probably indeed it was in this, and not merely in softening, that Richard himself was interested.

Harte must then have made sufficient progress in his experiments to believe that he was likely to find what he was looking for. Were he to succeed, the process would bring in a fortune. Would Richard share it with him? Whether he had sounded Richard on the point, or whether his knowledge of Richard's disposition told him that this would be a wasted effort, French could not of course ascertain, but obviously Harte had believed he would get nothing. He would then necessarily have been faced with a powerful temptation. Should he inform Richard or should he keep his knowledge to himself? Clearly he had fallen to this. He had devised the double series of experiments and the reporting of one of them. Then eventually came the success of the secret set and the prospect of fame and wealth. Then came also the realization that as long as Richard lived neither would be his. On this it was surely not too much to assume that the idea of murder had germinated in his mind. French visualized him as determined to get rid of Richard and Richard's ownership, though not in the least seeing how to do it.

So far French felt himself on firm ground. His next step was admittedly a guess. Fortunately the point was unessential and its actual details did not particularly matter. On Thursday evening shortly after six he pictured Harte entering the library and seeing Richard's letters on the desk. He was accustomed to dealing with chemical letters and would almost certainly glance at their addresses. Then French visualized him going for some purpose into the paper store and through the partially open door watching Croome enter and place the anonymous letter among the others. French saw that if so much were granted, the rest followed automatically. Under the circumstances Croome could not have kept something stealthy out of his manner. This would have aroused Harte's curiosity. He would have gone to see what Croome bad been doing and would have found the extra letter. He almost certainly detested Croome, who had been supercilious to him, and doubtless he had taken the letter with the idea of opening it and perhaps getting his own back on Croome. Whether this was the actual motive did not of course matter: the point was that he got the letter.

Harte could seldom have experienced a greater surprise than when he read it. It could only have been a moment before he saw that here, as it were a gift from the gods, was the solution of his problem. Croome was obviously playing some game of his own—Harte might have suspected blackmail or he might have guessed the man's true motive—and a police investigation into the murder would therefore lead, not to himself, but to Croome. Could he utilize the situation for his own ends?

How he had done it French already knew. For the essential portions of the case there was ample proof. In addition to a powerful motive and adequate opportunity, Harte's guilt was shown—apart altogether from his suicide—by his falling into French's trap and examining the feet of the table, as well as by his preparation for suicide should he be discovered. Indeed the mere existence of the capsule of prussic acid in the cigarette, had he been unable to use it, would have gone a long way towards hanging him. The method of the crime was established by the identification of the grit in the table leg with the gravel of the path, by the piece of fibre with the cord of the dressing-gown, by the use of the laboratory paste on the envelope, by the fact that the change of time in the anonymous letter was found to have been done with a pen and ink similar to Harte's, and by his exclamations just previous to his death. Finally, on the sleeve of an old brown jacket were found three drops of blood of the same group as Richard's.

At the adjourned inquest French's evidence produced a verdict which delighted everyone at Chalfont. After a suitable interval Jeffrey and Mollie were married, and some months later Frank Cox and Julia followed their example. Underwood's little irregularity was overlooked and he was reinstated in his job, and Carrie Underwood frequently came to discuss gardening with Julia. Frank Cox's cottage, which they hoped, if they got through the War alive, would be enlarged by the addition of a new wing.

The one fact which caused disappointment to all concerned was that Harte had shrewdly retained one essential feature of his discovery in his mind, as no note of it was ever found. The new process was therefore lost, together with the fortune it would have brought.

As for French, though he had lost his man, he had won his

case. Later he received Sir Mortimer Ellison's rather whimsical congratulations and was glad to be able to report that Rollo had made good on his first major job and that his appointment as inspector should be confirmed.

As he sat down once again in his room in New Scotland Yard, French thought with longing of the Green Sand hills of Surrey. Then with a short sigh he drew over to him the file of a case of burglary in Lambeth.

By the same author

Inspector French's Greatest Case

At the offices of the Hatton Garden diamond merchant *Duke & Peabody*, the body of old Mr Gething is discovered beside a now-empty safe. With multiple suspects, the robbery and murder is clearly the work of a master criminal, and requires a master detective to solve it. Meticulous as ever, Inspector Joseph French of Scotland Yard embarks on an investigation that takes him from the streets of London to Holland, France and Spain, and finally to a ship bound for South America . . .

'Because he is so austerely realistic, Freeman Wills Croft is deservedly a first favourite with all who want a real puzzle.'
TIMES LITERARY SUPPLEMENT

By the same author

Inspector French and the Cheyne Mystery

When young Maxwell Cheyne discovers that a series of mishaps are the result of unwelcome attention from a dangerous gang of criminals, he teams up with a young woman who is determined to help him outwit them. But when she disappears, he finally decides to go to Scotland Yard for help. Concerned by the developing situation, Inspector Joseph French takes charge of the investigation and applies his trademark methods to track down the kidnappers and thwart their intentions . . .

'Freeman Wills Crofts is among the few muscular writers of detective fiction. He has never let me down.'

By the same author

Inspector French and the Starvel Hollow Tragedy

A chance invitation from friends saves Ruth Averill's life on the night her uncle's old house in Starvel Hollow is consumed by fire, killing him and incinerating the fortune he kept in cash. Dismissed at the inquest as a tragic accident, the case is closed—until Scotland Yard is alerted to the circulation of bank-notes supposedly destroyed in the inferno. Inspector Joseph French suspects that dark deeds were done in the Hollow that night and begins to uncover a brutal crime involving arson, murder and body snatching . . .

'Freeman Wills Crofts is the only author who gives us intricate crime in fiction as it might really be, and not as the irreflective would like it to be.'　　　　OBSERVER

By the same author

Inspector French
and the Sea Mystery

Off the coast of Burry Port in south Wales, two fishermen discover a shipping crate and manage to haul it ashore. Inside is the decomposing body of a brutally murdered man. With nothing to indicate who he is or where it came from, the local police decide to call in Scotland Yard. Fortunately Inspector Joseph French does not believe in insoluble cases—there are always clues to be found if you know what to look for. Testing his theories with his accustomed thoroughness, French's ingenuity sets him off on another investigation . . .

'Inspector French is as near the real thing as any sleuth in fiction.'   SUNDAY TIMES

By the same author

Inspector French: Found Floating

The Carrington family, victims of a strange poisoning, take an Olympic cruise from Glasgow to help them recover. At Creuta one member goes ashore and does not return. Their body is next day found floating in the Straits of Gibraltar. Joining the ship at Marseilles, can Inspector French solve the mystery before they reach Athens?

Introduced by Tony Medawar, this classic Inspector French novel includes unique interludes by Superintendent Walter Hambrook of Scotland Yard, who provides a real-life detective commentary on the case as the mystery unfolds.

'I doubt whether Inspector French has had a more difficult problem to solve than that of the body 'Found Floating' in the Mediterranean.' SUNDAY TIMES

By the same author

Inspector French:
The End of Andrew Harrison

Becoming the social secretary for millionaire financier
Andrew Harrison sounded like the dream job: just writing
a few letters and making amiable conversation, with luxurious accommodation thrown in. But Markham Crewe had
not reckoned on the unpopularity of his employer, especially
within his own household, where animosity bordered on
sheer hatred. When Harrison is found dead on his Henley
houseboat, Crewe is not the only one to doubt the verdict
of suicide. Inspector French is another…

'A really satisfying puzzle … With every fresh detective story
Crofts displays new fields of specialised knowledge.'
                                                DAILY MAIL